# I DIED

# AT

# FALLOW

# HALL

# I DIED AT FALLOW HALL

### BONNIE BURKE-PATEL

Bedford Square
Publishers

First published in the UK in 2024 by Bedford Square Publishers Ltd,
London, UK

bedfordsquarepublishers.co.uk
@bedsqpublishers

ISBN
978-1-83501-079-2 (Hardback)
978-1-83501-080-8 (Trade Paperback)
978-1-83501-081-5 (eBook)

2 4 6 8 10 9 7 5 3 1

Typeset in 13.25 on 16.2pt Garamond MT Pro
by Avocet Typeset, Bideford, Devon, EX39 2BP
Printed and bound in Great Britain by
CPI Group (UK) Ltd, Croydon CR0 4YY

MIX
Paper | Supporting
responsible forestry
FSC
www.fsc.org    FSC® C171272

*For Kawan and Som, always.*

'Such is the beauty of the garden that it is our desire that it be maintained perpetually and with great care. We therefore enact a lasting covenant on the walled garden; cottage garden; and surrounding acreage, that the resident gardener may live in the cottage without rent, providing he maintains these gardens to the satisfaction of His Lordship.'

*Deeds, Fallow Hall, 1784*

Upper Magna in autumn is a world purified by fire. The leaves are a blaze of forest and crimson, and sweep across the landscape, reaching up into the sky from skeleton fingers, carpeting the paths underfoot. Against the burning, dropping leaves, the air is fresh and cold. Behind such clarity, there is the faintness of woodsmoke and sweet rot. Everything is clean, stark, beautiful not in its beginning but its end.

From Fallow Cottage, the land rolls outwards, a carpet that at first looks endless. The garden used to extend beyond the horizon too, before parcels of land were sold to the neighbouring farmer. At the doorstep of the cottage is the kitchen garden, thick with the harvest season, behind its walls, the orchard, the rose arbour, and from there, the mad tumble of the wildflower meadow. In the hollow, below everything else, is the stream, a hem of woodland, and rising up again on the opposite hill, Fallow Hall watches everything.

From the cottage, Anna Deerin looks out on the garden like a first love, pulls down the sleeves of her jumper, and puts her tools in the wheelbarrow. Her elbow aches as she lifts it and steers it towards the farthest corner of the kitchen garden. This work has echoed in strange ways across her body – strains in muscles she never used in her past life; the rust and microbes in the soil sometimes staining patches on her hands, and when, come the evening, she strips her sweaty clothes off and into the machine, her body is oddly patched; milk-pale from sternum to ankle, but golden and freckled on the back of her neck, and her arms and hands, like she is wearing long gloves to a ball.

Today Anna wants to start clearing the last vegetable beds. Where the rest of the kitchen garden is overflowing with its fruits, these are barren. They are the last of what she had been greeted by eighteen months earlier, the whole of Fallow Cottage a wasteland. Weeds strangling anything foolish enough to raise its head, the tumbledown sheds home only to rain-bloated cardboard, when anything metal – tools, gates, chairs – had instead been dragged out to die in the open, to oxidise and rust. It will take seasons and years to raise Fallow fully, but with these beds cleared, the last of the dead flesh will at least be scraped from the bone, and everything will be new growth.

'Afternoon, Mrs Polready!' Anna smiles and waves.

'I'm sure these bouquets get more beautiful every week.' Mrs Polready drifts over, holding her daughter's hand. The posies are arranged in jam jars, and the larger arrangements in buckets, and they adorn the end of the trestle table.

'August and September are good for the quantity of wildflowers, but I actually think October produces the best colours.' Anna runs a hand over the variegated coppers and pinks. The Polready girl is wearing pink, as always. 'Would you like one in your hair, Imogen?' Anna asks, and glances at her mother to receive a nod of permission.

Deftly, Anna picks a cosmos out of one of the jars and shucks a frond off with her nail, then leans over to gently weave it into the little girl's plait. She tweaks and adjusts it.

'Thank you.' Imogen blushes. 'You smell nice.'

'Thank you, Imogen. That cosmos looks at home in your beautiful hair.'

The little girl glows. Her mother buys a bunch of snapdragons and some apples, and Anna waves again as they thread their way to the next stall. Imogen's head is still twisted back to look at her.

The wind picks up across the green, and Anna buttons up her coat.

'Ms Deerin, it's always lovely to see you here! A new face is a good face.' Paul Wolsey makes a beeline for the stall, Barbour flapping in the breeze. Anna has been at the farmers' market every Saturday for nearly a year now.

'The community has been so welcoming, Mr Wolsey. I've landed on my feet,' she says. 'How is your wife feeling now?'

'So much better, thank you.' Mr Wolsey moves his eyes back to the apples and late berries. 'It's good of you to remember her.'

'Please send my regards – I've been thinking of her.'

Joanne Wolsey is abject, wilted, as quickly forgotten by her husband as an umbrella, and Anna knows he will say nothing to her. She sells him a jam tart and before he leaves, he glances again at her mouth and breasts. Sam Deneuve, the local GP, buys a madeira cake, and Anna slips Jake Mason a brownie and winks at his smiling mum. Happiness costs so little for children. She fills the reverend's Bag for Life with fruit and vegetables, and stacks a dozen eggs in the empty carton he brings, and he asks her to keep the change. 'Wonderful to be able to shop local.'

Anna greets the villagers she knows, and asks the names of those she doesn't. She put make-up on this morning, and has to be careful not to rub her face and smear it.

There is a sort of rhythm to Upper Magna's Saturdays, she finds, lulls and swells in custom, each villager bobbing on the crest of their own routine. She has come to anticipate when they will visit, has on her tongue the rapport that has developed between them. *I held a lemon cake back for you. Did you get the*

*wi-fi working in the end? Your car? Is your grandson, granddaughter,*
*wife, boyfriend, uncle, cat doing well?*

Alex Johnson usually has his pottery stall next to hers, but
he's doing a county show this weekend, and a lady selling
handmade cards is there instead. Anna waves across to her.
Standing still all day, Anna wishes it were warmer, or that she
could be wearing jeans under her coat instead of a skirt. But
this is the Anna that the village admires.

She sits down in her canvas chair and skims her fingertips
over the tufts of clover and trefoil that the parish council has
tried to eradicate, but that pitch through heedless, powerful.

She watches the teenage couples, keen to be seen together
by their peers, and the way they curl and stroke their fingers
round each other's palms as they wander hand in hand, proudly
implying a greater intimacy in private than they can show in
public. They take videos to post on social media, harnessing
the beauty of the place that is also their prison. A few families
come by Anna's stall and she makes sure she acknowledges the
women first, because to acknowledge their husbands before
them is how gossip starts and business ends.

Already it is past two o'clock. Anna is impatient to pack up.
She has sold almost everything, and she wants to get back to
the garden. The dark creeps up early now, and she needs to
put the chickens back in the coop before the foxes come out
looking, and there are apples to pick before they fall, and the
weeding is never finished.

Anna tries not to fidget and instead watches the thinning
crowd. Men are making their way to the pub to watch the
match on Sky Sports, and women in expensive leggings call to
their children to get a move on. On the far side of the stalls,
Anna notices a tall man she does not recognise. He stands out,
the only Asian in this crowd of white faces. Like everyone else,
he is dressed in an outdoor jacket and walking boots, yet the

rest of Upper Magna is looking at him too. She can see the stallholders' heads turn slightly as their eyes eat him up. He drinks the coffee he has bought and pretends not to notice their noticing. He gets his phone out of his pocket, sees there is no signal, and tucks it back. His clothes are a touch newer than the rest of the villagers'.

The newcomer drifts past the butter-yellow cottages of Cotswolds stone that box in the back of the village green; ignores the butcher and pie stalls; pretends to be interested in Ella Purley's candles when she calls him with her pitch: *You must have a girlfriend who'll be impressed with a candlelit dinner?* Ella does not vary her line, even for those villagers quietly acknowledged to be gay. The man politely extricates himself and moves on. As he nears Anna's stall, the copper on duty greets him.

Anna arranges her small smile. 'The rain's due soon.'

'That'll make for a change then.' It has been drizzling all week. The man has a slight London accent, which she thinks he is conscious of. 'What are these?'

'Physalis – cape gooseberries. Try one.' She peels away the papery outer shell and hands him the fruit. 'They can be used in sweet or savoury dishes—'

'Hitesh,' he tells her, and appears bemused by the taste in his mouth.

'It's a bit acquired,' she laughs and hands him an apple instead.

'Well, I know what this one is, at least.'

'More than Eve, then.' Anna picks up her book as Hitesh browses the stall; people do not like to feel they are being watched. She examines his profile and the working of his jaw. The rain starts as foretold, a gentle patter to remind humans of their place. Anna pulls her hood up.

'Ms Deerin – how are you faring in this dreary weather?'

Anna stands as her landlord approaches. 'I quite like it, Lord Blackwaite.' In the periphery, Hitesh does a double take. 'A little rain never hurt anyone.'

'Good for the garden, I expect. It's looking lovely from the Hall, by the way. Stunning, with the leaves changing.'

'Thank you – although I'm not sure I can take credit for the seasons. What can I do for you?'

'I need your assistance, Ms Deerin – we're having a winter gala this year, the first in decades, and I'm looking for someone to do the flowers.' He spreads his arms. 'And who better than you?'

From the corner of her eye, Anna sees the newcomer wave a parting hand. Anna's own drifts upwards in return, but now Lord Blackwaite is deep in explanation, and he requires all of her attention.

Anna.

A palindrome; a name that ought to make her feel special.

But as a child, she had hated it, and the way it made her feel invisible, occluded. As she grew, she found that in the act of speaking, writing, her name began – only to turn back and erase itself and her, a betrayal.

Then she reached womanhood, and that name became what Anna needed to know. To be a good woman. Pleasing, mouldable, doe-eyed and a good fuck, intelligent yet free of *opinion*. She realised that to be these things and no things, or to appear to be so, was not unlike her name, which started and erased itself.

Anna. Flat-chested, sweet-freckled, dark-haired. Quite plain or intensely appealing. If no one looks closely, she can give no offence.

Now she has the garden at Upper Magna, and no one is looking. She is alone for nearly a mile in each direction.

Anna drops to her hands and knees and begins picking out detritus from the final vegetable patch and casting it into a bucket. Pebbles, weeds, screws, bottle tops. She works quickly because the rain is due again, and if the soil gets wet it will be harder to clear.

There is a garden again now. The first true garden at Fallow Cottage since before the Second World War. God-like, she has raised it from nothing. It is only seeds and earth really, but it feels miraculous. She brushes away the scrub and tangle and thinks of how she will lay out the rows for kale and marrows. This new life has lost none of its novelty; she still feels a pang each time a seed throws out a green shoot and begins to grow.

It is unmediated.

The art critic John Berger said that all those paintings of women looking at themselves in a glass – the Rokeby Venus and her sisters – the male painters, the male patrons put a mirror in women's hands and called them *vain*. Anna knows the truth of this, that women are always to watch themselves – to know precisely how they look as they cross the room. They are to watch their own lives and to perform their womanhood. But if they are caught taking a glimpse in the mirror they have been given? That is vanity.

Perhaps, Anna often wonders, perhaps I only listened to Berger because he was a man.

Still, she wants to put her fingers under the edges and peel it back – this dual vision she has been taught since birth, this watching of herself.

She looks harder.

Anna.

Finally, the earth is cleared and it is time to break and turn the vegetable bed. Anna scratches past the topsoil to feel underneath, and like much of Fallow's earth, it is dense and clayish. The pickaxe weighs almost as much as she does, but she can still heft it and bring it down, and it is the best way to break the clods.

The clouds shift and the first drops of rain begin to spit and patter. There's no harm in that, Anna thinks, the ground is breaking well. She stops to clear away some rotted wood. The earth underneath looks good quality – richer than anticipated – and after a few minutes she drops the pickaxe back into the wheelbarrow and takes up the gardening fork.

Then the rain begins in earnest. Suddenly it is clattering from the sky. It lands so hard that the loose soil froths and spatters, and the broad leaves of the other beds are bowed down. As soon as it starts, Anna is soaked, so she may as well finish what she is doing. You can only get wet once – that's the refrain here in Upper Magna.

With her boot, Anna presses the fork down into the earth and can feel the snap and crack of buried twigs giving way. The new earth comes to the surface, dark and flecked with something white. Anna digs again, and more of the white speckle comes up. Again, and this time a larger fragment turns to the surface. She sticks the fork in the ground and pushes the wet hair from her face with a forearm.

It is bone, smooth under the gardener's dirty fingers, apart from the splintered end. She holds it up to the sky to be cleaned off. The sun is still bright behind the clouds and she can see there is no marrow left inside. It is greying where the calcium has leached out – returning what was borrowed. She turns it this way and that. In the summer, she had brought up the skeleton of a fox, or maybe a small dog in the rose bed; it is surprisingly hard to tell when the soft tissue goes. Likewise, she cannot tell from the piece in her hand what is buried, but Anna needs to take it all up or it will be hard to plant the bed. If she takes away the top layer of earth, the rain might wash the rest away from the bones. She can come back later and pick out what is left, perhaps bury it again in the meadow.

The ground boils under the force of the rain and Anna works quickly now, shovelling mud to one side. Veins of chalky white appear and disappear from view. It is hard to establish the length of what is buried. A few ridges are briefly visible and she guesses these are the ribs. If she finds the head she might know if she is dealing with something small, or if she has to take up a whole horse. The rain has got inside her boots and soaked her socks, and as she crouches down it seeps between her toes. She uses her hands to clear where the skull might be.

More by touch than sight, Anna finds a socket. Her fingers slip off bone-smoothness and into nothing. She snatches her hand back. Probing gently, she works her way to the next cavity; the eyes are close set, a predator rather than a prey animal. Slower now and panting, Anna scores a sopping trench with her hands and works inwards.

The rain is freezing and collects anywhere it can: in the wells of her ears, the backs of her knees. The soil is in her nail beds and mouth and it tastes of iron and minerals and damp. The crown of the skull comes into view, first from the earth. Then the brow. Anna wipes it clean, then her own cheeks, where the rain begins to dilute tears.

It is so much smoother than she would have expected. So much more and less than itself.

She wipes the caul of mud from the noseless face, as a midwife once wiped away the newborn membrane, because of course, once, this was a person.

*February 1967*
February is a miserable month. A low and creeping month that dampens any good spirits with its chill and mists. It is not as though the Hall feels jolly in December, but at least I

can drag in holly boughs and take nips of brandy while I feed the Christmas cake, and if you belt out carols in the kitchen, they bounce back like you've been joined by a choir. But in February there's nothing to sing and it's all grey chops and boiled potatoes again.

I can hear Mother clumping round upstairs, no doubt straightening out the sloppy corners on the beds I made. I've never done them quite right, or at least not deliberately. Mother's fastidiousness is a hangover from when she was housekeeper here, from the days before she married Father and became mistress of Fallow. God knows how she was a housekeeper when she walks like an elephant. Perhaps that's why Father married her, so she would sit down and stop stomping. It did not work.

The entrance hall needs vacuuming, but I am quite comfortable in the parlour with an Iris Murdoch novel and some tea, and it's hard to see the urgency. The dirt is harming no one, and once I vacuum, it is only a matter of time before there's more. Running a household is only so much treading water.

I read another chapter of *that Irish authoress*, as Father calls her. But he will also call me idle if he finds me here, and more than that, I do not want Mother to see the vacuuming is not done and do it herself.

I will be a good daughter and do it. I will. Up now, lazybones.

I emerge into the dark of the corridor, and breathe in childhood and present. It is term-time and Sprat is up at Oxford and the house is full of those uncanny echoes it throws about when it is only Father, Mother and me. It ought not to since there are carpets – it's indecent.

'Have you done the vacuuming yet?' Mother's voice rings down the wide sweep of the stairs as I emerge into the entrance hall.

'Don't bellow, it's unladylike,' I yell back. 'I'm about to do it now.'

I hear her laughing, then there is the sound of the study door opening and both Mother and I make ourselves scarce.

The utility room's flagged floor is so cold I can feel it through my shoes. I am half tempted to put on my pea coat while I vacuum, and dither about whether to fetch it or not. And that's when I spot them, under the twin-tub – two little brown-black pellets. For God's sake.

'Mother, they're back!' I yell up the great staircase. 'The bloody rats are back!'

Anna cradles the head for a while. It sits in her lap and looks up at her. The rain hammers down. Eventually, Anna rests the skull back in the earth and finds a tarpaulin.

Hitesh Mistry is at the spare desk they have taken out of storage. The station's windows are coated in reflective film, and it lends a further pall of grey to the weather. The window looks out onto the car park, then a country lane. The Cirencester DCI had told Hitesh that Upper Magna was the biggest village in the rural catchment – a good place to get acquainted with the countryside. Hitesh thinks he has seen more populated corner shops.

The rain is biblical, full of blind force. It is collecting in depressions in the tarmac and creates the illusion of deep pools, waiting to swallow the next person who steps down from a Land Rover to report a break-in; domestic violence; drug dealing.

Hitesh rubs his face and looks back down at the report. He had not known that theft of farm vehicles was such a problem; even less, that he would care. But the farmer – a broad, weathered man – had struggled to hold back tears when he explained his tractor had been stolen during the night, only a month after the combine harvester had been stripped for parts.

'I don't know if the farm can keep going,' he had said, and they had looked away from each other as his voice cracked.

Hitesh does not understand why anyone farms. Between the thefts, bad harvests, floods and precarious market conditions, the margins are wafer thin. What hard, thankless work to choose. Perhaps, he thinks, perhaps these people would argue that farming is not a choice at all. Perhaps he is too much of a townie to understand.

'You don't take sugar, do you, boss?' The young constable puts a mug down on a pile of folders.

'Oh cheers, yeah.'

Hitesh's new colleagues do not quite know what to make of him, but they are trying.

'Do you think these vehicles are being nicked to order? Or are they taking them and trying their luck selling to other farmers?' Hitesh asks.

'Farmers all know each other, don't they? Seems a bit risky.'

'Taking them out of area?'

'Yeah, could be. Get them over to Herefordshire or down Hampshire, no one's going to ask where they're from.' PC Barnard nods and goes back to his arrest paperwork.

Hitesh leans back in his chair. The ceiling is made of ancient plasterboard squares. Plenty are missing or broken and like the puddles outside, give the impression of vast dark spaces behind them. The station is a neon-lit strip holding its own place in nothing and nowhere.

Hitesh puts out alerts on the missing tractor and logs the new report with previous thefts. There isn't much hope of recovering any of them without a tip-off; it's the same as with bikes and mopeds in the capital. Across the hills, how one human violates another remains the same. The victims are made to feel like Icarus for the hubris of having owned anything, are shown their vulnerability, then cast into the sea.

Hitesh lets the mug burn his fingertips. He reads his many emails. Each time he clears one, another appears. A phone is going in the background but the sound is so ubiquitous in stations that he has learned to ignore any but his own. The rain keeps beating down. Something in how unrelenting, how indiscriminate it is, is compelling. Hitesh watches for several minutes as it soaks everything under the sky with the same unvarying force.

'There's a call-out, boss,' PC Barnard shouts over. 'We need to go.'

'So there's a Fallow Hall and a Fallow Cottage?' Hitesh asks PC Barnard.

'Yeah, and the cottage is in the Hall's grounds. You'll see.'

The constable is hunched eagerly over the steering wheel. Hitesh feels that he should manage the young man's expectations. 'If it's properly old land like you're saying, then there'll have been lawful burials there over the years. The body could be Tudor or Victorian. I've had to call archaeologists a few times.'

'Of course, yeah.'

They continue to navigate lanes that are one car wide and full of potholes. Twice, the constable brakes sharply to avoid a rabbit, then a fox. Hitesh has had to crawl round the roads since moving but Barnard is local and takes them at a clip. There is nothing Hitesh savours about attending a body, but he still feels the buzz it is almost impossible to eradicate. It will always be there, in anticipating the unknown, and in the power that is part of duty.

They bounce over a track formed of ruts and tree roots and canopied overhead by oak boughs, then the men park behind a single-storey stone cottage. Hitesh pulls his hood up and follows Barnard around the front onto a vast plot. Fruit and vegetables and flowers that Hitesh could not name flourish and crawl across beds and trenches until they finally hit the limit of the garden wall. He cannot remember the last time he saw so much life in one place. At the far end of the garden is a slight figure under an umbrella. Her face is tilted downwards towards the ground so that she looks like a mourner at the graveside. As they get closer, he notices the young woman is soaked through, except for the late addition of a jumper. She turns her face towards them, and though now she is blotchy and free of make-up, Hitesh feels the pitch-drop of his stomach. 'From the market?'

Anna Deerin nods. 'From the market.'

'This is PC Barnard.' Hitesh motions towards his colleague.

There is a tarp on the ground, already sagging under the weight of the rainwater.

'I damaged the body,' Anna says, 'with the gardening fork, when I was digging. I think that's why the ribs are splintered.'

Hitesh kneels down and lifts the sheet. It is a churned mess, but he can see where bone erupts here and there from the soil. 'I understand this will have been upsetting, but we're hopeful of an innocent explanation.'

Anna answers quietly, 'There's a small hole in the back of the skull and a large one at the front. I didn't dig near the head, I used my hands.'

She holds Hitesh's gaze and after a moment, he nods.

Anna is covered in mud to her elbows. It is still on her face and in her hair. They have asked her not to wash it off until samples have been taken, so she sits on the sofa in the dingy living room, arms awkwardly held out from her sides. The two policemen are back in the garden now, waiting for whoever it is that comes to examine a body.

Since Anna cannot touch anything, she has not offered to make tea. Her wet clothes have long since drawn the heat from her body and she is shivering. She stands to warm up, moving in cramped laps around the living room.

Fallow Cottage is nothing without its gardens. The bungalow itself is unremarkable: dark and unattractive, recently modernised with faulty central heating and an electric shower. When Anna took it up, she went to Ikea and bought a single bed and the cheapest sofa. The space is so spartan it is laughable. Only the bookshelf and the larder are full.

Anna watches through the window as a van arrives. There is an endless conversation between the men who get out and the ones already here. Finally, between signalling and shouting and instructions lost in the thunderous downpour, they begin to establish a cordon. They are trying to be careful, she can see, but their boots still catch the borders of vegetable patches and crush the upturned supplicant faces of the cyclamen.

Anna runs her tongue along the back of her teeth. It throbs in her mind, the blunt-toothed grin; above it, there is a hole in the forehead. No flesh left to know who it might have been — not age nor gender nor race. That hole is where a lover's kiss ought to be, or an acne scar, or any of the things that belong on a living face. But she can hear someone coming into the cottage and she has to box it all up, pack it away into a corner of her mind for later. *But I will not forget you.*

Hitesh comes into the living room and apologises for the wait. 'These things take forever. Can't afford to lose any evidence.'

'Does it look like a bullet hole?'

'On first appearance.' He rests against the windowsill.

Outside, the rain is still pouring down, and Anna can see a tent being erected over the body. Everything is drowning.

'Are you cold?' Hitesh asks, suddenly noticing.

'Just damp. I'm okay.'

It is an obvious lie, but he does not try to tell her so.

'So,' he says, and opens a battered reporter's notebook, 'when did you move to Upper Magna – you're not local either, right?'

'May before last. I took up the tenancy on the cottage and gardens.'

'Where were you before that?'

'London, working in a department store.'

'Really?' Hitesh looks up from his notes. She can see him examining her, trying to piece her together from her face and clothes. 'Why the move here? A quiet life, getting back to the land – that sort of thing?'

Usually she just says yes. 'Well I didn't have any real problems, so I had to seek out hardship.'

'I didn't mean it like that—'

'It's okay, you can think it.'

And then Anna grins and it takes them both by surprise. Hitesh laughs. 'All right then.'

'Upper Magna's a strange place if you're from the city.'

'So I'm learning.' Hitesh composes himself. 'Why did you go up to Fallow Hall to call us – no signal down here?'

'I don't have a phone,' she says, 'or a car. I had to walk up and call from Lord Blackwaite's landline.' The walk had taken a long time. The meadow and the stream, the woodlands that guard the house. Anna had caught her shins on brambles and fallen on the steep, wet path. When the technician takes swabs, he will find her blood too.

Hitesh frowns. 'Everyone has a phone.'

'I don't have one.'

'How do you manage all the way out here? Why not have a mobile?'

She shrugs. 'It's expensive. The conditions of the tenancy mean I live here rent-free, but I only make what I earn from the market. I have a handcart to get things down there, and a laptop to order supplies.'

'That sounds difficult.'

'It works well enough, as systems go.'

Hitesh scrutinises her and she remains blank. 'And the remains – do you have any idea who it might be?'

'None,' Anna says.

Hitesh exhales and straightens up. 'I'm sorry, it must have been a shock to find that.'

She shrugs. 'I'm not the one who was shot.'

'I'll send someone in to take samples, then you can wash.' Hitesh nods and pockets his notebook.

Anna is left alone again. Her eyes are beginning to ache from the effort of not crying but she has no idea how long it will be before the police leave. All she has now is a brief moment. She listens hard. In the eaves of the cottage the magpies are cackling and their burrs bounce one to another. Outside, the rain has stopped and above the sound of the police is sweeter birdsong. Anna examines the mud drying onto her jeans and the condensation on the windowpanes. She lets the external world fill her up and crowd out everything else until the threat of tears recedes and she steps behind the boundaries of herself again. There, she is safe.

The technician comes in and murmurs soothingly as he asks Anna to turn her hands this way and that. She looks appropriately stunned and meets his eyes often enough that his professional regret slides into something that is real. Afterwards, she lays out a tray of tea and a cake she made for market and takes it to the back of the forensics van where white-suited men are milling round like patient ghosts.

'For when you get a few minutes' break.' Anna smiles sadly.

'Thank you, ma'am. We don't get tea very often on this job.'

Anna stays to chat with them a while, about the weather and their families, then she goes inside and stands under the weak stream of the shower and slowly gets clean. She puts on a fresh dress and waits as a WPC performs a search of her few belongings. 'Sorry, my love, it's routine.' Anna answers more questions, directs people to the bathroom, makes more tea. In the garden, there are the remains of a life, and her own is being walked across by strangers, but the dam will hold until she goes to bed that night, when a lone officer will be left watching over the white tent, and she can cry without anyone seeing.

'What is this place called, Hitesh?'

'Upper Magna – I told you, Dad.'

'And it's near to Bicester?'

'Cirencester. Did the cleaning lady come round yesterday?'

'You shouldn't have rented your flat out. What if you want to come back?'

'I'll be fine. Did the cleaning lady come and do the house for you?'

'Yes, yes, she came. Have you shaved yet? You look like a Muslim with that beard.'

'God's sake, Darsh.'

'What would your mother think?'

*Click.*

The rain stops as suddenly as it started and leaves behind the smell of greenery, tarmac and the world washed clean. Hitesh climbs the hill to Fallow Hall and breathes it in, letting it clear his lungs.

It is a cruel punchline to have moved from London to nowhere's lesser-known cousin and, within a fortnight, to have found a body. He had moved so that something, anything, would change, and now he's back doing the same thing he did for the last ten years. Yet Hitesh feels the lightness that is pressing against his breastbone and does not want to ask why. Ducks pass overhead, fat with conversation, and he cranes his neck to watch them fly into the distance.

Bones and fruit and tarpaulin and rain. Upper Magna is a strange place, it is true. He feels it, in the autumn sun low in the sky, in the burnishing light that flicks off puddles and scars in the road. All around, the russet leaves are caught in the act of turning, and for an instant, Hitesh feels himself blurring at the edges, his outline bleeding into it. Surely there could be no harm in it if he shut his eyes and let the land claim him. He keeps walking.

Fallow Hall comes into view, roof first, as Hitesh reaches the hilltop. He climbs the steps into the portico and looks for a doorbell or a buzzer but cannot find one. There is a brass door knocker, and reluctantly, he uses it, then stands back and examines the dove-grey stone. He thinks the house is Georgian but could not say why with any specificity. When he was a boy, his mother watched *Pride and Prejudice*, and dragged him and his father round the nearest stately home, which was not dissimilar to this one. Then again, Fallow Hall is as much a film set as a real place, Hitesh thinks, in as far as it bears on most people's lives.

No one comes to answer the door. Hitesh tries the knocker again, then descends the portico steps and peers through one of the sash windows that line the ground floor. Inside is a room full of ceramics and mahogany furniture. Nothing stirs. He tries the next window, and the next. He is two thirds of the way down the east wing when he spots Lord Blackwaite in his study. He is at a bureau, hand on his chin as he reads something in front of him. Hitesh pauses to watch a minute. Lord Blackwaite fulfils all Hitesh's expectations of an aristocrat – tall and broad, unbent by age; he is a man who inhabits himself fully, and without reservation. Before he came to Upper Magna, Hitesh would have assumed this stereotype was as false as others, yet for Lord Blackwaite at least, it is true.

Hitesh raises his hand and knocks on the window and Lord Blackwaite starts. The younger man lifts his warrant card to the glass to reassure him.

*February 1967*

'Well what do *you* want to do with them, then?'

'I don't know, Mother, but if we put that down, the dog will snuff it, because he eats literally everything.'

'What about if we put it right back under the washing machine where he can't get his nose in?'

'Is it worth the risk? What are we going to tell Father if we kill the dog trying to get the rats?' I raise my eyebrows.

Mother looks down at the box of rat poison in her washerwoman's hands. 'We could get a cat?'

We look at each other, and burst out laughing.

'We kicked the dog, who killed the cat, who ate the rat, who stole the cheese,' I sing, and when we finally get our giggles under control, 'It's no good, we're going to have to catch them.'

Mother sighs. 'I'll find the traps. I think I put them in one of the outbuildings.' She scratches her nose in the sort of way she chastises me for doing. 'This is the sort of problem your brother is good at solving.'

'It is.' We stare helplessly at the treacherous twin-tub that has given the rats safe harbour. 'We could wait for the end of term and hope they don't breed before then?' I am only half joking.

Mother sighs again and checks her old-fashioned pin curls in the small mirror above the drying racks. 'When I was housekeeper, Bennett the groundsman had a meat tenderiser he kept specially.'

I am appalled, and then confused. 'But how did he catch them?'

Mother cocks her head. 'He was very patient. Sat on a stool next to wherever they were coming out, sometimes for an hour or two. Then when their heads popped up, he had excellent reflexes.'

'Oh good Lord.'

Mother spreads her hands, as though to criticise my modern sense of squeamishness. We stare at the washing machine again for a long time.

'Mother, are you asking me to find you a meat tenderiser?'

'Good afternoon.' Lord Blackwaite steps back from the front door.

'I'm sorry if I surprised you.'

The older man waves a hand. 'I ought to get a proper bell installed. You're the police, then. I presume you need to speak to me about this afternoon?'

'I do.'

Lord Blackwaite nods gravely. 'Come in.'

He ushers Hitesh into a grand entrance hall that smells of dust and wood polish, and Hitesh must restrain himself from peering further into the house.

'I'm sorry not to offer you refreshments but I'm afraid Pauline doesn't work on Tuesdays and she's the only staff here off season,' his host explains.

'It's fine. This won't take long.'

'Please, this way.' Silently, they walk the length of the wing and enter a private library, where Lord Blackwaite motions Hitesh to an armchair. From his seat, Hitesh examines the bookcases that run floor to ceiling and the whole length of the room. They are full of clothbound editions and estate records, heavy with the weight of history. On the console table is a globe that he expects still marks Prussia.

Lord Blackwaite does not take the seat opposite the policeman but moves around restlessly, sweeping ash back into the fireplace grate, adjusting ornaments on the mantelpiece.

When he does not settle, Hitesh prompts him: 'I understand Anna Deerin came up here after she discovered human remains in the cottage gardens.'

The older man's nostrils flare, perhaps in shock or irritation, but when he speaks, his voice is even and patrician. 'That's right. Shocking, quite shocking. Have you seen a lot of… this?'

'A lot of bodies, yes.' Hitesh is frank.

'How long have you been with the police?'

'For a decade, in London until now.'

'And where are you from originally?'

'London.' The air feels dense. It is cool, but sweat prickles up under Hitesh's collar and he wishes he could open a window. 'I understand that the cottage gardens used to be a part of Fallow Hall?'

'Yes, in a manner of speaking. It's still part of the estate, you understand. But legally, it's under a covenant and so it's given over to a gardener, rent-free. I haven't dealt with it directly for quite some time,' Lord Blackwaite clarifies, 'but I can tell you that nothing in living memory – and I am seventy-three now – would explain what Ms Deerin found.'

'Upper Magna is a small community. It must be quite a shock.'

Lord Blackwaite stops, as though hearing his name called by someone out of sight, then he seems to make a decision, and folds himself down onto the opposing armchair. 'That's one of the reasons it's so hard to comprehend, Inspector. No one is a stranger here.'

'Perhaps you can fill me in about the Hall? I'm still not sure I understand the setup.'

'I appreciate it is opaque from the outside. Perhaps it's not... intuitive. Very well. The Hall operates as an independent business from the cottage. Up here, we're open for visiting for six months of the year, and we also host weddings and events year-round. We recently became a trust, in fact, to give us a new lease of life.'

Hitesh glances at the small green fire exit sign above the door, and tries to imagine what it would be like to have strangers trekking across his home, day in, day out. It makes him uncomfortable. But then, he has seen hundreds of homes as a police officer, and none of them like this.

'I imagine the upkeep of this place is costly,' he probes.

'Historic buildings are a law unto themselves. But we are quite well situated, as things stand.' Lord Blackwaite is sharp, repudiating what has not been said.

Hitesh remains impassive. 'Has Fallow Hall been in your family long?'

'Since it was built – 1780. Of course, the land itself is much older. Upper Magna can be found in the Domesday Book, in fact. But my family came into possession of the estate and built the Hall in the eighteenth century.'

'That's a long heritage.'

'It certainly is. It's a privilege and a responsibility.'

The two of them regard one another. For a moment, Hitesh can hear the blackbirds outside the window.

'And Ms Deerin walked up to use the phone around noon, after finding the remains?' Hitesh asks.

'That's right. I feel quite sorry for the poor girl.' Lord Blackwaite softens. 'She's a capable young woman actually, highly capable, but it would be a shock for anyone.'

'How did Ms Deerin come to be at the garden? She said

she hadn't been here long. Who was the gardener before her?'

'We were lucky enough to recruit Ms Deerin about a year and a half ago, as you say. I was a little sceptical to begin with. She's young and had never managed a garden before. In fact, I don't believe she's ever lived in the country before. But she was the only applicant and she has done a tremendous job with it. Before she arrived it had been vacant for a long time.'

'How long?'

'A very long time. One way or another I don't believe there has been a cottage gardener since the last one was killed in the Second World War.'

'Why not?'

Lord Blackwaite seems momentarily at a loss. 'I believe there was a local labour shortage after the war, and once the line was broken it was never really picked up again. It doesn't earn any money for the estate so my father didn't prioritise it. Particularly not once it had become overgrown. I had quite forgotten about the covenant until we became a trust and all the deeds were reviewed.'

'So the site has been untended – abandoned – for decades?'

'In that sense, it is an ideal place for hiding a body, if that's what you mean – I'm afraid so,' Lord Blackwaite agrees. 'I don't know what else to tell you, Detective.'

Hitesh stands and offers his hand. Lord Blackwaite's grasp is firm and surprisingly hot. 'I appreciate it's been a long day, but I'll need to send a technician up to take a DNA swab.'

Lord Blackwaite lets go of his hand. 'I'm sorry – I don't understand?'

'It'll help us rule out any familial relationship with the remains.'

'I would certainly know if a family member was buried in the cottage gardens.'

'The Hall has been in your family so long that the skeleton may be historic. I appreciate it's—'

'Inspector, I understand that you are only doing your job, but my family have always been buried in Upper Magna's parish church. The whole village used to be within the bounds of the estate and St Mary's was the family chapel. There are no other family remains here.'

'I understand this might be upsetting. But we can't assume that that has always been the case.'

'I'm sorry, this is an intrusive – and, I believe, unnecessary – request—'

'It isn't a request.'

Lord Blackwaite's face sets into a mask.

From the walls of the library, portraits of bygone Blackwaites look down at them. Hitesh is alien to the place, and the place to him.

From: Richard Deerin
Subject: Birthday!
Morning Annapops
How's the garden doing? Hoping we can come and see it soon?
Will you be back for mum bday? Xx

To Darshan's horror, Hitesh's mother had taught her son how to prepare his own meals. The piercing whistle-shot of the pressure cooker is always a reminder of those arguments.

'That's not a boys' job, Manju.'

'And who'll cook for him at university? Or if I get hit by a bus? Or if you finally chew my brain too far and I marry a rich man instead?'

Hitesh takes the pressure cooker off the gas ring and tempers the mustard seeds, asafoetida and cumin that spice the dal.

His mother had always served it with a pile of white rice but he grudgingly tosses a handful of spinach leaves on his plate instead and sits at the kitchen table to eat without tasting.

The sky had been so open above the bones, which at least had been too large for a child. Hitesh is more accustomed to fleshed bodies on pavements and under bus shelters, in flats and storage lockers, in places where depravity seems less at odds with its environment. He thinks of Anna Deerin and Lord Blackwaite; whatever comes of it, their lives will always be divisible into the periods before and after today.

Hitesh consumes the dal mechanically and lets his eyes rest on a spider that has made its home above the fridge. The detective's new house is fine. It is a pretty Victorian cottage, and central in the village, as far as you can be in the centre of a puddle. He has to duck his head climbing the stairs, but he has been here a fortnight and muscle memory has begun to take root. He finishes his food and begins the washing-up before realising the old tea towel is in the wash and the others are still packed. Everything in his life has been in a box for eighteen months; first packed when he gave up his flat to move back in with Darshan and Manju and never unpacked; then moved out to Upper Magna where they sit in the second bedroom. Hitesh wonders whether he ought finally to take out his belongings. At the very least he needs more tea towels.

Hitesh climbs the stairs, head ducked, and goes into the spare room. The last tenant left a standard lamp, which he switches on now, causing the dozen or so boxes to cast their graveyard shadows. Outside, the foxes bark and scream at each other. With a sigh, Hitesh opens the first box, full of books. The second and third are the same. He has no shelves, and piles these to the side. The fourth is boxing gloves and a skipping rope. Hitesh cannot imagine there is a local club to join, and closes it again. In the fifth are photographs and oddments, and at the bottom, a red cardigan. He sits back on the floor. He had forgotten, even though he had chosen it and placed it there.

Hitesh picks the cardigan up and buries his face in it. It smells like his childhood, washing powder and cardamom and the sweet, musty perfume his mother had worn all her life. He had taken it from her drawers as he helped Darshan pack her things away. He had wanted to take one she hadn't had in hospital because everything Manju had worn there had filled up with the awful stench of reheated food and cleaning fluid and the loss that was coming.

The smell makes Hitesh warm and safe and sick and alone. She is teasing and chiding and reminding him that sometimes, occasionally, his father is right. He is six and upset that a friend has laughed at him. Nine, and grazed from falling off a skateboard. Fifteen, twenty-five and heartbroken, thirty-four and celebrating his last birthday with her. He is always pulled close in the crook of her arm, and never again.

It cracks Hitesh, as fresh as the first day. He cries silently. Lets it fill his lungs and chokes with it. Feels it wrack and burn in his chest, and tear the muscles between his ribs. After a while, he wipes his eyes and folds the laundry drying on the radiator.

Anna looks respectable, obedient. A nice young woman. Why would she not do all those things that boys are never taught to do? To put away things that are left out. To decorate the house at Christmas. To notice when things need repairing or replacing. To put bleach in the toilet. To make sure there is food in the cupboards.

To put the kettle on.

To undertake the hundred small tasks a day that are nothing in themselves, but the accretion of which takes time that men do not surrender, yet never acknowledge the surrender of by women.

Anna is twenty-seven and now wears the beloved face to market, and smiles and makes the people of Magna feel nice about themselves. Then she comes home to her garden, and has only herself to please.

She looks at the ceiling in the half-light of the arthritic dawn. In her lower body she feels a familiar ache and knows if she moves she will feel wetness too. She does not want to move yet. She thinks of her dreams, which had been haunted by a figure always on the edges of her vision. Anna had swung her head this way and that to get a better view of them, but they were always just out of reach. She had known who it was anyway, since when she had turned to look, she had caught flashes of milky-white joint, and spread all round her were flecks of soil.

Anna sits up. From the side of the bed she can see to the back of the kitchen garden where the white tent bulges and ripples in the breeze. She stares at it for a while; inside it could be anything – a swing, an abattoir, a chapel. But she knows that it is a person and that probably they did not want to die. Anna can feel the blood pooling and goes to the bathroom.

The clots are bright in the toilet bowl and Anna leans forward to reach for a pad from the cupboard under the basin. Today they will come back to finish exhuming the body. She wonders if they work like archaeologists with brushes and string, or whether everything is plastic and steel like on television. She washes her hands and looks at her face in the mirror; it's a little drawn, maybe, but otherwise unaltered.

It is time to get dressed and let the chickens out, but first Anna turns up the hob and puts the kettle on for the PC she can see through the kitchen window. She carries a pot of strong coffee and a jug of milk out on a tray and knocks gently on the car window to wake him.

'Sorry, ma'am, nodded off for a moment there.'

She passes the tray through and tells him he is welcome to use the bathroom if he needs it.

The officers have told Anna she can go about her business as long as she avoids the tent and the area they have pegged off round it. She needs to pick a crop of fruit in the orchard before it falls and goes bad, so she lets the chickens out, calls them each by name, picks them up to check for mites, strokes their combs, then goes to get the handcart and baskets. It is fresh this morning, dry apart from the dew gathered on the ground. There is a brisk wind sweeping down the hill and Anna ties her hair out of her face and pulls a hat on.

Apples and pears are ripe when they come away with a simple upward lift; if they have to be tugged, they are not ready yet. These almost drop into Anna's hands as she reaches for them, and are so plentiful that it is difficult to make progress. Whenever she thinks she has taken all one tree has to offer, another plump fruit appears by her ear, demanding to be picked. Soon the strain begins to settle across her shoulders and her shins ache against the ladder, but it is not in her nature to pay it any attention. She works in silence, filling basket after basket.

Eventually Anna sits on the top rung to rest and eat from her harvest. The pears are soft and drip juice down her fingers and chin. Anything she cannot sell now she will turn into preserves and mincemeat to sell at Christmas, or store in the cold-shed. It is a living that must be eked out, and there is only ever a hundred in the bank. But before, it had not mattered because Anna had Fallow, and if months were lean she had no one else to feed and no one to see it.

Over the top of the orchard wall, the tent plastic is still snapping in the wind. Anna wants to lean over and ask them who they are.

*What were you to Fallow? What was Fallow to you?*

The plastic snaps its non-answers into the wind.

Perhaps the garden will feel peaceful once the bones are gone. It ought to, without a corpse; certainly without the police. But Anna knows that the bones were at Fallow long before she was, and lay in the sediment while she brought the garden back to life. She had not known they were there, but they had been, and when they are gone the garden will be altered, and all else with it.

*Snap, snap.*

Anna stands and begins to work again, until every basket is full.

Lord Blackwaite comes by the garden at two, an hour or so after the police have finally packed up and left. Anna sees the outline of his flat cap and jacket as he makes his way down the hillside from the Hall; he disappears for a minute into the dip at the bottom, then emerges over the crest of the wildflower meadow where she is working. As he approaches, she drops her gloves into the pile of goosegrass she has weeded, and tries to remove the last clinging burrs from her fleece.

'Good afternoon, Lord Blackwaite.'

'How fitting to find you here, Ms Deerin. I wanted to ask if you'd had any more thoughts about flowers for the gala. But more importantly – have you recovered from your awful discovery yesterday?'

'I'm all right now, thank you.' She doesn't meet his gaze. 'In a way, I know so little about her, it's hard to comprehend. It doesn't seem very real.'

'Her? A woman, then?'

'So I gathered from the technicians.' They had paid Anna no mind as she had brought out tea, chatting to her and each other. They seemed not to regard Anna as a suspect, only as a naive civilian to be shielded from the more brutal aspects of their work. 'They'll know more soon. Whether they'll update me, I don't know.'

Lord Blackwaite nods grimly, and the wind sweeps down the hillside and rattles the dried seed pods. A few short weeks ago, the meadow had heaved with flowers of every shape and hue. Their names had been beautiful in Anna's mouth: love-in-a-mist, heath speedwell, corncockle, wood avens. A few flowers still sway with the breeze now, but they are outnumbered by those that have dropped off, and peer up from the ground, as though at Judas.

'Well, quite dreadful. I hope the matter is swiftly put to rest, truly. An awful thing.' Lord Blackwaite clears his throat. 'The winter gala – it will be the first in decades. It will celebrate the first year of the new trust, put Fallow back on the map, bring it onto the radar of new people and so forth. That's the plan.'

'It's a beautiful house – it should find recognition.'

'Quite so.' Lord Blackwaite appraises her. 'Not that many people understand what Fallow needs, or at least, they don't place the right value on it. A place like this doesn't survive by itself. It stands or falls with those who care for it.'

Anna nods. 'Nothing much survives on good intentions.'

'Fallow requires few romantic ideas and plenty of commitment to dry detail, I'm afraid. I worked for many years to build it up from hardship.'

She wonders what he is looking for. 'I hope it always has such a committed guardian, Lord Blackwaite. I certainly intend to care for the cottage gardens as best I can.'

Her landlord smiles approvingly. 'I know you will. Now, the gala: I'm trying to evoke the heritage of Fallow Hall – in a way, we want to put its beauty and history on show as the best argument for why people ought to support it. Local notables will be attending, of course, but also people from London, society and business people and such.'

Anna has noted the slightly threadbare state of the armchairs in Lord Blackwaite's study. London means money.

'It'll be December, so there won't be a lot of choice.' She thinks back. 'Last year there was plenty of hellebore about that time, and witch hazel. Lots of holly and dark foliage, juniper for texture.'

'Excellent, Ms Deerin. Having flowers from the estate is another way of representing ourselves. It will be too cold to host any of the event outdoors; it would be wonderful to bring some of it in.'

'Then I'll come up during the week, ask Pauline to show me the rooms where it will be held. Get a feel for what's needed.'

Lord Blackwaite stays a while to talk. He has come to know every inch of the estate during his years, and asks her about drainage and whether the cottage will be warm enough during the frosts. They talk about this and that. They talk about things that are not skeletons. Anna listens to his sonorous voice and all its finely shaped vowels and consonants. There is no laziness; each phonetic unit is pronounced in full. It is the peculiar, unmistakable accent of the upper class, not affiliated so much to region as to pedigree. Anna remembers last December, when she had been invited to a drinks reception at the Hall. The star on top of the Christmas tree was made of blown glass, and had flicked broken light across the faces of titles and personages, and she had wondered that a world like this still existed.

'You will take care now, Ms Deerin? We might be a long way out in the countryside, but Magna is a community. It's here for you, if you need it.'

'Thank you, Lord Blackwaite. Really, I do feel very welcome here.' Anna smiles and can feel that the wind has turned her nose and cheeks red.

Her landlord nods approvingly and returns the way he came. Despite the wind, the day is clear and the low sun's Midas touch stains the treetops and the grass gold. Anna's wrist still aches from her fall yesterday, when she climbed the same route to use the Hall's phone. She crouches and goes back to pulling up the parasitic growth.

From: Anna Deerin
Subject: Re: Birthday!
Hi Dad,
Are you and Mum all right? Sorry for the radio silence, it's been busy during harvest. All good here. Lots of customers at the stall. I'll see if I can get back for Mum's birthday weekend. Did you get that appointment for your knee?
A xxxx

Manjula Mistry's death certificate had borne only her name and a brief note about the bowel cancer that killed her. There had been nothing about her patience, her humour, her killing wit. Nothing about the months of tongue-tied adoration when her son moved home, when they had gone for walks in the park and pretended it might be okay, and the penny-edged peace that had held between Hitesh and his father for her sake. The certificate hadn't even listed the agony, the indignities of her illness, and all its endless rounds of treatment to postpone what they knew was coming. That piece of paper was a brutal thing.

On Hitesh's screen are the first details of the Fallow body. A woman in her twenties or thirties. Body interred in the last thirty to seventy years. Gunshot to head. Angle of entry wound and depth of grave indicative of homicide. Textile evidence too degraded to yield result. Further tests commissioned.

Even Manju had been given her name.

Hitesh leans back in his chair and rubs his face again. She was killed in living memory, then. He calls to PC Barnard, who approaches eager as a puppy, and Hitesh can't help but like him.

'Details are in. Women are almost always killed by intimate partners or family, so there's every chance that if she's local, her killer is local too. Perhaps even alive still.'

Hitesh expected Barnard to be excited by this, was prepared to remind him of a life that had been lost. But instead Barnard scratches the stubble on his head, the same colour as the wheat stubble in the fields, and looks uncomfortable. 'Y'know, it could've been my sister. Or any of the women I've dated. Horrible, really.'

'Yeah.'

The station's electric lights buzz and flicker. In the car park, civilian staff are just arriving on shift.

Barnard clears his throat. 'So what do we do?'

'Upper Magna and the surrounding area are pretty small, so if she wasn't just passing through, her disappearance is going to have been noticed by someone. We'll check records and local news archives. Who else has a long memory round here?'

*March 1967*
Easter bloody Sunday.

Father kicks us out to go to church at midday and I just have to pray the lamb won't burn while we're gone. He doesn't come with us, of course. But he has no sense of smell and he will not notice if the lamb joint has caught until smoke starts pouring into his study. Preparing for the worst, I have bought some ham from the butcher as well.

Mother looks bright. She jiggles her handbag up her wrist, then slips her arm through mine. She's wearing the lilac gloves she reserves for churchgoing, neat as a pin. She married Father long enough ago now that the Magna-ites have stopped feeling she has risen above her station and regard her as truly their better.

Mr Ferris waves from the path that runs from the other side of the hill and will join ours in a V-shape before long. 'Good morning to you all,' he calls.

'Good morning, Mr Ferris. Happy Easter to you,' Mother greets him.

Sprat is back until Trinity term starts and he walks beside us, swinging his arms loosely, because if anyone is without a care in the world, it is him. Even the rats only took him half an hour to deal with. 'Beautiful morning, isn't it, Mr Ferris?'

'Quite beautiful!'

I resist the urge to roll my eyes. It *is* a beautiful morning, though. The daffodils are thick on the ground and the air is so clear it can be drunk. It is nearly like freedom.

We enter the church and shuffle into the family pew at the front, where the freesias that adorn the lectern lean over to brush the handrail. Mrs Williams makes a beeline for Mother, and I turn to Sprat so I don't have to pretend to be interested in her small talk.

'You've lost weight,' I tell him.

'The food in college isn't as nice as yours.'

'My food isn't nice.'

'Then imagine college's.'

We giggle, sandy heads brushing against one another in conspiracy. It's not as though I don't love my home. It's not as though I don't love my family.

'How is His Lordship?' I can hear Mrs Williams asking Mother. She still asks every time she sees us. Her own mother used to work at the Hall, I believe.

Mother tells me Father was quite the socialite before the war, before his face was a mess of scars. I was too young to remember his face as it was. I only know this one, which is unsmiling. All a child wants is to please her father, and I don't know how and never have.

'What are the women like at Oxford? In my mind, they're practically aliens. Ninety per cent forehead and ten per cent glasses.'

Sprat stifles another giggle. 'Well, not far off on some counts. But there are some stunners too, the brains and the beauty.'

'Come on then. Tell me what you won't tell Mother—'

But then the organ pipes up and we have to stop talking.

There is the Easter liturgy and the sermon, the hymns and the comforting drone of the psalms. The vicar's voice is clear but it gets cramped in by the tiny dampness of the church. He is quite a handsome man, really. Dark curly hair, and his chest is broad under the vestments.

Stop it. I might not believe in God any more, but it isn't right to have these thoughts in church. Surely there are some things that ought to be respected.

But I'm well into my twenties now and really, I would like to have sex. A kiss. Anything. At this point, the vicar would do.

Fallow is such a damned chastity belt.

The sofa upholstery is too malnourished to fully pad the angles of the cheap pine frame, whatever the position of the sitter; Anna migrated to the floor to read in the evenings long ago. Now, she sits cross-legged on a cushion and flicks to the index of a gardening book, then turns to the relevant page. It does not answer her question. She reaches for the next book in the stack, which she has collected like paper treasure from Magna's charity shops. This one cannot answer her either. Apparently onions bolt because they have free will, and nothing will stop them. She sets the gardening books aside and reaches into the pile she brought home at the weekend, all old exhibition catalogues and novels.

Anna straightens her legs and flexes her ankles; she rests the book of engravings open on her lap. It is a subject she knows nothing about. That is why she bought it. Drinking in all she never had the time for before. She turns the pages slowly, running her eyes over the fine lines and the faces, the gothic details, and the symbols she doesn't entirely understand. Then she pauses – this plate is labelled 'Albrecht Dürer, *Knight, Death and the Devil* (1513)'. At first she sees the buildings massed on the hill, gazing down on the valley below. Then her eyes drop to the resolute knight, who stares forward, intent on his mission. Behind him is a hog-faced Devil. To his side, Death is king in his crown, clutching an hourglass, waiting. Death is all wrong, Anna thinks. He is too fleshy. Eyeballs, and fingernails, and hair on his skull. His face is intent and expressive as he leans in to speak to the knight.

Anna sees the blank skull in her hands. Her Fallow sister, as she has come to think of her, this woman who had lain close by all the while as Anna had toiled, and sown, and reaped. The sister's face had had no expression, no meaning. Death had been a robber, not a king. She closes the book.

It is bridge morning. At first, Hitesh thinks this is a stroke of good luck, but he studies the hand-drawn board outside the church and realises they run two mornings a week and also on a Thursday evening, so perhaps this is how the parishioners generate the output of gossip that PC Barnard claims. 'You can't get better than retirees for knowing everyone's business.'

Hitesh hesitates on the path. He has no familiarity with churches, beyond a few friends' weddings. This one looks picturesque, all mossy with age and English mizzle. The tombstones lean drunkenly and the spire pierces the slate sky. It looks timeless, organic rather than something built by human hands – something that was once new. Hitesh walks around to the back, where a prefab hall has been plonked next to the medieval structure. He opens the door into the lobby and is relieved to see a noticeboard cluttered with leaflets and, through the safety-glass doors, an expanse of grubby linoleum floor and stackable chairs – just like every community centre and temple hall he has ever been in, down to the limey smell of the floor cleaner.

'What's he hoping to do after that?'

'Law, I think. At Warwick or Durham, maybe. I must check with Liz, I can never remember.'

A kettle is whistling somewhere beyond the kitchen hatch and two dozen retirees are chattering. The noise is prodigious and for a minute, no one notices Hitesh enter. He scans the room to see if there is an obvious organiser, and at the far end sees a grey-haired man in a dog collar.

The reverend is deep in conversation with one of the tables, so Hitesh crosses the hall to introduce himself, and as he does, their eyes begin to pick up. By the time he is halfway across the room, they have given up the pretence of talking and playing bridge and openly stare at him.

'Are you from the police?' asks a woman in a gilet.

'Uh, yes.'

A hubbub spreads outwards, a ripple of excitement that threatens to crest into open questions. The vicar takes pity on him and crosses to shake Hitesh's hand. 'We've all heard about the body at the cottage.'

'That was fast.'

'If three people in Upper Magna know a secret, you can guarantee it's not a secret any longer. Reverend James Watts,' he adds, introducing himself.

Turned half to address Watts and half to address everyone

else, Hitesh finds himself thrust into his appeal. 'DI Mistry – I'm with Cirencester CID, working out of Magna station. Yes, we have found a body. The next step is to confirm her identity. We're hoping that somebody is able to provide information about who this woman was.'

'A woman, was it?' One of the bridge players nods knowingly.

'Can't you just do a DNA test?' comes a voice from the back.

Not really knowing who to reply to, Hitesh addresses the room at large. 'That's not really how it works. We need a comparison sample. And to be completely honest, this body was buried somewhere in the latter half of the twentieth century. Forensics priority is going to be given to live cases where people might still be at risk. We aren't going to get most of our results back for a couple of weeks. What would really help now is a lead as to her identity. Anyone who went missing, or somebody behaving strangely in the period between, say, 1960 and 2000.'

'That's a big chunk of time,' says his gilet friend.

'It is,' Hitesh agrees. 'I understand people may not want to discuss sensitive issues in front of everyone, but perhaps I can leave some contact details—'

'That Annie girl in the eighties, she cleaned for us – remember she had that sad face all the time?' A gentleman dressed in various shades of brown turns to his partner. 'Do you remember? She was definitely doing drugs.'

Behind them, the reverend dips his head into his hand, then surfaces again. 'Perhaps DI Mistry can use the vestibule? Anyone who would like a discreet word can excuse themselves to talk to him in the course of the morning?'

'That would be ideal,' Hitesh agrees.

'You'll get a fair number just wanting to chat or gossip, I'm afraid, but they do want to help – they're good people really.

Upper Magna is a good community.' Reverend Watts settles Hitesh in the vestibule with a cup of milky tea. The plastic seat creaks and wobbles under the policeman, as though it has not been designed to be sat on by an adult male.

'It's all right, we get it a lot as coppers too.'

'Well, we're the safety net these days, aren't we? Mental health, loneliness – drugs coming in from the city now, too.'

Reverend Watts has a crumpled face, and the soft wattle folds of his neck rest on his collar. Perhaps this is what a life of care looks like, Hitesh thinks, and glances at Watts' bare ring finger.

He smiles. 'You're right. I hope you've been spat on fewer times than I have though.'

The reverend laughs, then waxes serious. 'If it's of any interest, I do remember a young woman, actually, about the time you mentioned.' Hitesh gestures to the seat opposite, which creaks dangerously as Watts sits. 'In the late seventies, I think it was. I was only about twenty-five and quite green. She was a single mother, you see. Celia… something – Foster, perhaps? Anyway, it wasn't easy back then. Things were thawing but there was still a lot of hostility towards single mums. There's an element of stigma even now. Anyway, Celia moved to the area, came to church a few times and told me she was having trouble getting anyone to rent a cottage to her.'

'What happened?'

'Nothing much. I asked around, trying to find her somewhere. But then she stopped coming to church and dropped out of contact. I put it down to a slightly chaotic life, assumed she had moved away.'

'And what makes you think she might be connected to the body we found at Fallow?'

'Nothing really, beyond the gender and time frame.'

Hitesh thinks there is another impulse somewhere under

this, and waits. The vicar shifts slightly and opens his hands. 'Perhaps I'm just feeling guilty. I see a lot of people in need but they either pass away or I see them round about the village. Not to say that I can help them all – but I tend to find out what happens, one way or another. With Celia, I didn't. For a long time now I've thought that I should have tried harder to find out what happened to her. I may have been guilty of the assumptions of the time.'

Hitesh finds Watts' humility disarming; he does not defend himself as he explains.

'I understand, but with the number of people who cross your path, you'll never get to hear everything, certainly not everyone's endings, happy or otherwise.'

'It's difficult – a lack of closure.' Reverend Watts lets out a short laugh and looks away.

Hitesh jots down a note. 'Even if it's Celia, unless you killed her, it's not on you.'

Reverend Watts turns back, grateful. 'Well, I hope you're right. I'll let you get on now. Watch out for Mr Grant, he's prone to start on politics.'

'Was she, um, itinerant? You know, a working girl?'

'Not that we're aware of. Is there anyone in particular you were thinking of?'

'Oh, God no. I just thought, you know, it's often these women who get bumped off. People don't miss them.'

The man in front of Hitesh looks mortified at the idea he would be connected with such an individual. Not when he used to run the family wine business.

'Do you have any information about who she might be?' Hitesh asks.

'No, no. I expect things will start coming to light soon. People will get talking. Well, best of luck.'

Seemingly without any embarrassment at having come to pry, Mr Imber puts his hands on his cord trousers and stands up with a grunt. The door back into the church hall has barely swung shut behind him before a neat head is stuck round it.

'DI Mistry?'

'Yes?'

'Gloria Finchley – and this is my husband, Geoff. We're on the fundraising committee of St Mary's,' she says, as they shuffle into the vestibule. They are wearing sensible shoes, and Hitesh suspects they are members of the National Trust.

'We don't want to raise your hopes, we've just got a few small things that have occurred to us,' Gloria says as they seat themselves.

Hitesh's expression of easy attention is one he has honed for years, and Gloria starts unfolding the conversation the couple shared over toast that morning. 'We've been at Upper Magna forty years now, ever since we got married, so we've seen a fair number of people come and go. One girl in particular jumped to our minds immediately, didn't she, Geoff? Maria Martins – she used to live at the end of our street.'

'Went off the rails,' Geoff pipes up.

'Geoff, it's not the Dark Ages,' Gloria chides. 'She had mental health problems – drugs too, in the mix, I think.'

Geoff rolls his eyes but takes up his wife's thread: 'Anyway, her parents eventually booted her out after one episode too many. It was quite the scandal, at the time. Not the sort of thing that happens round here.'

'She went to the same school as the other local girls, yet the poor thing turned out so differently,' Gloria sighs. 'Anyway, we didn't hear a thing about her afterwards, and her parents acted as if she had never been born. They both died of cancer a few years apart – oh, in the nineties, it must have been. I'm not suggesting in the *slightest* that they would have killed her, of course – just that they lost track of her a bit. She might have been vulnerable to someone undesirable passing through.'

Gloria and Geoff look at Hitesh expectantly, and he writes down Maria's name. 'Thank you, I'll certainly look into that.'

'You know, it's a long shot, but she did have awful problems.' Gloria looks troubled and strokes her scarf. 'You can't help but think of your own children, can you?'

'It's good of you to think of Maria,' Hitesh reassures them.

They get up to leave. 'Do you know Madj at the Bombay Spice?' Geoff asks, suddenly. 'We get takeaway from there most Thursdays.'

'Uh, no. I'm new to the area.'

Geoff hums thoughtfully. 'Good luck with it all, then.'

Alone again, Hitesh creaks back in the chair and looks at his notebook. Half a dozen people have come to talk to him. They have been friendly, fascinated, horrified. They have all been white, middle-class, happy to talk to the police, whose presence is to them a complete novelty. Through the safety glass, Hitesh can see them helping to clear away the tables and chairs as bridge morning comes to a close. A handful are visibly different – less well off, physically unwell, some perhaps struggling with their mental health. It strikes Hitesh that these are the individuals he expects at community events, and that it was the ex-professionals and retired antique dealers he was surprised to meet. 'Upper Magna is a strange place,' Anna Deerin had said.

Hitesh's notes are full of vulnerable women. Single mothers, addicts, waifs and strays. It is true that those on the margins are always more at risk of violence. No one thinks the woman found at Fallow Cottage was like them. She was a victim, but somehow an expected one, after a life that differed sharply from their own. They don't blame her, per se, but somehow her death was a sad consequence of her life. In the gossip they gave

him, none of the village bridge players described the horror
that Hitesh knows goes on in nice houses too. After more than
a decade's policing, he knows that women aren't safe anywhere
there are men.

Anna's back is aching so she kneels on the border of the bed
and leans over to pull carrots from the ground. They are
lumpy, pungent, some a little lewd. They do not look like the
vegetables sold in the supermarket. She tosses each of them
into a crate by her side, content that Magna-ites know better
than to prize regularity.

Last year, Anna barely planted the kitchen garden, and
its offerings were meagre. She still had proper savings then,
she had planned for it. This autumn, she cannot harvest fast
enough. Even under her inexperienced hand, the earth is
producing more than one person can collect. She understands
now why farms of any size have to hire labourers. She scrapes
her living, but is never hungry.

Amid all this bounty, one corner of the kitchen garden is
barren. She cannot help looking at it as she works. The cleared
bed is a startling void amid the greenery, like a tumour has
been excised and the wound left to close itself. Anna supposes
no one mourned the woman there. When what had been done
was done, she had been left to rot down with the leaf mould.
People cling to the idea they will be remembered, grieved for.
Memory is their insurance in the face of death; perhaps for a
generation, longer if they are Great Men. But not this woman.

The blackbirds call between the trees beyond the wall of the
kitchen garden, and Anna finds herself hoping that whoever
killed the Fallow sister remembers her often. If one person
is left with her name and her face, it ought to be them. She
ought to root in their mind and refuse to be dug out. She ought
to chase them while they play with their grandchildren. Anna

hopes that her killer is terrified now she has been unearthed; she hopes that any peace they had is buried in a shallow grave.

She puts the carrots in the cold-shed and walks up to the Hall.

'How are you, Dad?'

'The house is cold.'

'Is the boiler working? Can you see the pilot light if you look at it?'

'Of course the boiler is working, I'm not a bloody idiot. It's a cold autumn.'

'Fine. How are you doing?'

'You already asked that, Hitesh.'

'Fine, Darsh. Did the solicitor call you? He wants us to sign some more papers.'

'Yes, he called. He wants us to come in person instead of posting them, so he can charge us more money. Bloody thief.'

'He probably is overcharging, but neither of us know how to get probate otherwise, so I'm not prepared to argue with him.'

'It's our hard-earned money. I don't want to throw it away on that man. He's taking advantage of knowing the system.'

'Dad! That is precisely what legal advice is for! Of course he's charging us – he's not going to work for free. We can either do what he says or you can work out the probate application yourself.'

'Fine, if you don't want to be an executor, I'll do it alone.'

'That's not what I said, Darsh.'

*Click*

Anna approaches the Hall through the woods at the back, but as she reaches the crest of the hill, she can see over the shoulder of the west wing, into the formal lawns that skirt the front of the house and compose the view that has welcomed visitors for centuries. Keith McCarthy, the groundskeeper, trundles his way between the beds, pausing to yank up weeds. Anna waves to him but he seems not to notice.

At the back door, Pauline welcomes her. 'What drama, Anna. Come in, come in.' Anna steps into the utility room that serves as the housekeeper's domain and is engulfed by the warmth that persists above the flagstones. An electric kettle is coming to a boil on the worktop. 'You're just in time for a cuppa. Tea?'

'Thanks,' Anna accepts gratefully. 'You've felt it up here too, then?'

The housekeeper is spry in spite of her age and assembles a plate of biscuits and two cups of weak tea. 'Well, you know, finding a body does tend to put a bit of a spanner in the works. I think His Lordship has found it all a bit stressful.'

'That's understandable,' Anna chuckles.

Pauline perches lightly on her stool and Anna pulls another across the flags to sit with her, between the chugging of the washing machine and the hum of the tumble-dryer.

'You don't ever seem to tire, Pauline.'

'That's the sherry, dear – keeps things going nicely.'

Pauline nips up to make herself a note of something, then returns to her seat. 'Anyway, to what do I owe the pleasure?'

'The gala. Lord Blackwaite has asked me to provide the flowers from the garden.' Anna sips her tea.

Pauline nods knowingly. 'He did mention. Quite right. You'll want to see where they'll all be going?'

'Please.'

Pauline pops the rest of her custard cream in her mouth and beckons Anna to follow her. The two women leave the fug of the utility room, step briefly into an old servants' corridor, then into the house proper.

'What's the gossip then, my love?' Pauline asks, as they pass cabinets laden with silver plates, and wallpaper that lifts and whispers with the draught.

Anna sighs. 'Only that there is no gossip. No one seems to know a thing about who she is. Which doesn't seem fair, particularly when you've been killed.'

Pauline bobbles her head. 'Well, don't take it to heart, if you can help it. Plenty of reasons to be miserable without adding a girl you never knew.'

'That's downbeat of you, Pauline,' Anna chides.

The older woman chuckles. 'A necessary tough shell, after so many years running this place.'

They step into the dining room, where a table longer than Anna's whole cottage stretches out and still does not reach the far end. Anna looks closer and can see the chafes and scratches of knives and forks that even Pauline's polishing cannot eradicate. She turns her face upwards, to where the chandelier glints down knowingly. She exhales.

Keith McCarthy is clipping a hedge outside the sash window. Anna does not know how, but even alone, he is laconic. She raises her hand to wave again, and this time he is forced to acknowledge she is there, on the other side of the glass. He raises a hand and turns back to what he's doing.

Anna studies the housekeeper from the corner of her eye. Nausea peaks and troughs in her stomach. 'You saw a lot here, over the years?'

'This and that, I suppose. It's always been my job to manage the cleaners in peak season, when it can't just be me running around with a duster. Women taking on seasonal cleaning jobs? Find me a single one who didn't have a sad story I could let myself get swallowed by if I wasn't careful.'

Anna drifts a hand over the dining table. 'Did any of them ever disappear?'

Pauline gives her a sharp look, then her eyebrows drop and she softens. 'After a while, you harden yourself, so you don't sink with the ship. I'd never remember all their names, my love, let alone whether they bothered to come back.'

'Of course.' Anna weaves her fingers together.

Pauline senses the innocence she has punctured. 'Now who's downbeat? You've got too much youth and beauty to be wasting it.' She squeezes Anna's arm. 'So, this is where Lord Blackwaite is going to have the guests dining for the gala. What are you thinking?'

Anna dreams again. Breadcrumbed earth trails the cottage floor and she follows it outside. The sky is orange and underneath it is a woman. She waves to Anna and Anna waves back. The woman raises her hand and knocks on the air, and Anna can hear it all the way across the garden. The woman opens her mouth but all that comes out is a scraping, scuttering noise.

Anna sits up in bed. Around her the bedroom is dark and cold. After a minute, she lies back down and pulls the covers up. This quality of darkness would have been unfathomable before she moved to Fallow; however long she stares at it, her eyes do not adjust. There is no light to adjust to.

Outside, the foxes are crying again, and the wind forces its way through the gaps in the single-glazed windows, whistling and howling. Anna closes her eyes. She can feel the warm muddle of sleep and turns deeper into the covers to wait for it.

There is a knock on the front door. Anna sits upright. For a moment, she is unsure what to do, and reaches out to illuminate the bedside clock, but the dark has made things strange and her hand falls into empty space.

There is another sharp, clear knock.

Anna fumbles round for her discarded fleece and puts it on as she leaves the bedroom, feeling her way across the bungalow to the hall.

'Hello? Who's there?'

There is no answer. The wind hisses through the doorframe, and Anna fumbles for the hall light switch. With the light on, she can see the gooseflesh on her forearms.

'Hello?'

Anna listens but there is no reply. She waits as long as she can bear to. Then she crouches and pushes open the letterbox, peering as far as she can into the black, but no one is there. She sits back on her haunches and waits.

The silence that follows is so long that Anna wonders if the knocking was some freak event – the wind carrying along apples, or some other improbable cause. Somewhere in her thoughts, she recognises that these are the moments between not knowing and knowing. She crosses to the back door and picks up a weeding tool from the basket. She thinks about turning the rest of the lights on but it will only make her more visible and the dark outside more opaque.

'Who is it?' she shouts once more. 'I'm going to call the police.'

There is still no reply. Anna can see the woman in her dream waving from her flower-patch grave; another instinct seizes her and she scribbles a note on a discarded envelope.

*3 a.m. 10 October. Someone outside. Anna Deerin.*

Anna places this note inside a kitchen cupboard where it might be found.

There is a scraping sound.

It stops suddenly, then begins again.

It has a metallic edge, something being dragged across the surface of the cottage outside, skittering and jumping over the uneven stones. Anna is rooted in the kitchen and turns her head to follow the noise as it moves across the building, back and forth.

Then the door again. Not knocking this time but banging, one blow after another. Someone is striking the wood over and over, so violently that the door shakes in its frame. The force of the blows sends plates toppling from the sideboard, shattering on the flagstones. A shard strikes Anna's shin and she runs – flies to the bedroom and with only the faint glow of the hall light, looks for a nook, a space, a haven, anywhere she might be small enough and quiet enough that she will not be hurt.

Anna's room is almost bare, but in the corner is the airing cupboard. She pulls it open and stuffs the towels and linen under the bed. She catches her knees and hands on every corner in the near-darkness but eats the sounds she wants to make. Then she folds and twists herself to fit into the space at the bottom of the cupboard, between the pipes and wooden boards, and bites down on the pain as she catches the beds of her nails between the door and the frame as it swings shut.

As suddenly as it started, the banging stops. Then the crashing of glass.

The silence is stretched thin and ringing. Anna can taste the sweat that is at the edges of her mouth and plasters down her hair. She thinks she has wet herself before the iron scent reminds her of her period. Everything is shaking; her breath, her fingers, her legs, shoulders.

Anna is waiting.

Anna is waiting.


At five in the morning, Hitesh gives up on sleep and goes for a run. The weather is damp and chilly, and his time is far from his best as he picks through the dark and across drifts of slippery leaves. He returns home and showers, makes coffee and notes the new greys that stand out against his black hair as though they belong to someone else entirely. He drives to work.

The reflective film on the station windows washes out the pink dawn and Hitesh lets himself be numbed by the droning of the office radiators. His eyes are dry from tiredness. Everything down to his bones is tired.

At his desk, with another coffee, Hitesh wakes up. Further details about the Fallow woman have arrived from the coroner: she is Caucasian with British dental work, but they will not know if she is local until they receive a mineral analysis; her pelvic bones suggest she has never given birth. The head wound implies a rifle or long-barrel gun. When she was a child, she had broken her left arm, a typical injury from a fall; it had healed well.

It is the last detail that causes Hitesh to flinch.

These particulars narrow the field and he will get PC Barnard to cross-reference them with local missing persons' cases as soon as he arrives. Hitesh opens his notebook to compare these details with what the St Mary's parishioners told him.

Hitesh misses his early-morning phone calls from Manju, always a thick layer of cheerfulness on top of her fear. *Will you be catching any bad guys today, Hit?*

*Mum, I'm not out on the beat any more. I'm safe in the office. I need to go now. Bye, Mum, bye, bye. I'm going now, bye.* He had always been pulling the phone away from his ear as the questions continued. There is no one to call him this morning. He feels a slight ache to think of Darshan waking alone in their house in Kingsbury. The purple paisley bedspread was still there when he last visited.

Hitesh emails the Cirencester DCI an update. He wants to start another round of interviews with Upper Magna's older residents but only he and Barnard are available. The rest of the force has been pulled away to staunch the flood of drugs running into the county from the capital. He is running through logistics and drawing up a plan when the station officer calls through from the front desk.

Hitesh sees Anna Deerin waiting in reception. She is sheet white and her hair is still wet from the shower. Her leggings are pulled halfway up her shin on the right side, and a fat plaster is stuck on her narrow leg. Hitesh feels fear rising.

'Are you all right?

'I thought it would just be night staff.'

Hitesh shakes his head. 'Come through. Andy, could you get some tea, please?' He leads Anna past the station sergeant and into the office. No one else is there yet so he takes her over to his desk and pulls up a spare chair. 'What happened?'

Anna does not say anything for a moment. She strokes her wrist with her thumb, over and over, the way one might soothe a dog. When she speaks she is composed. 'I woke at about three o'clock this morning. Someone was knocking on the front door. I couldn't see who. Then they started dragging something over the walls outside – I think it might have been a shovel. That's what it sounded like, anyway. Then they began banging on the door. Hitting it.'

'They were trying to break in?'

The gardener is quiet again and looks away. Hitesh can see her ribcage moving, up down up down, quickly, like her breath is short. He can feel her contained panic, and wonders if she can hear her own heart beating, pounding like his does before an arrest. He wants to tell her she is safe now, that here she will be safe.

The sergeant brings them tea and a few shortbread biscuits from the interview suite. Hitesh watches as silvery islands form a film on the surface of his tea. They are silent for a long time before Anna speaks again.

'I don't think he was trying to break in.'

'Why not?'

She looks at Hitesh with a clarity he is beginning to recognise. 'He broke the bedroom window and reached through to open it from the inside. But then he didn't come in.' He. Anna had not seen the attacker but neither of them are in any doubt.

'He didn't manage to climb through?'

'I don't think he intended to. It was to show me he could.'

Hitesh rubs his eyes and leans back in his chair.

'Is it about her?' Anna asks. About the Fallow woman.

'It's likely. Too much of a coincidence to be unrelated.' Hitesh looks at her again. She has slowed her breathing nearly to normal. He weighs it up. 'The coroner sent the report. She's British, no children.' He pauses. 'Shot in the head.'

Anna looks away. 'Anything else?'

Hitesh opens his hands. 'She broke her arm as a child.' Anna glances down at her own. 'They'll look to see if she's local, but it'll be a while before we get a result.'

'And no one in Upper Magna knows who she is?'

'Apparently not.' Hitesh thinks he can see a flush of anger in her cheeks, pooling under the shock.

The airing cupboard had been cramped, stifling. After the first hour, Anna had known every beam and groove, and the way the stain from a past leak made a long finger from the pipes down to the carpet. The muscles in her back and legs had burned and she had been able to feel the blood from her shin crusting between her toes. But she had stayed and waited and forced herself to imagine each scenario so that she could plan for it. The silence had taken on its own texture, deep and resounding. When Anna had finally moved, the creaking boards had sounded like her own limbs crying out, damning her as she limped from the cupboard.

The dark had been almost leavening, let out into the cold morning through the broken window. Quarter to five. Anna had surveyed the broken glass. She had turned on all the lights, had taken the note from the kitchen cupboard and discarded it. Then she had showered; she had washed under the lukewarm trickle of water and looked at her body where blue veins wormed under the skin; she had traced the subtle dips and curves of bone and viscera with her fingers, the hollows under her jaw and at her back, above the kidneys.

For the first time in her life Anna had felt how thin the line is between civilisation and violence. The barrier between harming and not harming, between killing and not killing, and known that it is nothing but an understanding. She had known that once someone decides to disregard consequence, there is nothing to stop them picking up a knife. She had dressed and continued to shiver.

Anna sits in the police station, across from Hitesh. His face is worn, both sharp and blunt at the edges, and even as she tells him what has happened, she watches the subtle shifts. She realises it was a relief to find him here, that all the feelings that had laid heavy and jumping as she had crept from the cottage to the village had been reduced to a sediment bumping along the bottom of a stream. She wants to crawl into his lap and sleep there, or invite him home and into her bed. He is a man, a kind, strong one, and if he is there then she will be safe. And the humiliation is blistering.

That had been their design, whoever had done it – to show her she is not safe.

'Is there any way – can this not be known widely?' Anna loathes herself in a way she has not for a long time.

'I'll see what I can do. I'm sorry, this shouldn't have happened.'

'You couldn't have known.'

'Look,' Hitesh is tactful, 'it must have been terrifying. I can look into finding you somewhere different to stay until we've settled things at Fallow.'

'I don't want to move.' Her tone is fiercer than she intends and she calls herself back. 'Thank you. I wanted to report what happened, but I want to go back.'

'I don't think you're safe there.'

'Maybe not. But it's my home, my decision.'

Hitesh looks at her frankly, sternly almost, but she does not flinch. He relents. 'All right, I can't force you.'

Light slides over the face of Fallow Hall, over the limestone that was bought with sugar money, with human misery. It drips in through the sash windows. It slides across the floorboards and carpets and up the walls pock-marked with portraits. It is the same daily path the sun has taken since the last Ice Age raised the hills and dug the valley, and humans picked their way across the new landscape.

In his room, Lord Blackwaite opens his eyes on a new day and watches the dust motes in their endless dance. He rises and dresses. He combs back his grey hair, winds his father's watch and places it on his wrist. Like the sun, he traces his daily path. He descends the grand staircase into the hall, and crosses to stand before the photograph on the wall.

Hitesh realises the discomfort he feels is self-consciousness, something he thought he had lost long ago. He opens the car door for Anna, and knows that inside she will read more of him; no child seat, clean but not pristine like some men's, no smoke but no doubt old coffee. He does not think there is old sweat from the gym, but perhaps he wouldn't notice any more. All he can smell as he climbs into the driver's seat is Anna's grass-freshness.

They leave the village in silence, the hum of the car heater filling the space between them. A weak morning sun irradiates the empty fields and for a moment Hitesh does not understand why he is here at all, with these dead women and these threatened women, why everything did not end with Manju.

A deer darts into the road. Hitesh brakes and the two of them lurch against their seat belts. The deer looks bemused and leaps into the bushes on the other side. 'Fucking hell,' he rubs his eyes, 'are you all right?'

Anna begins to laugh, and with it, something shifts and Hitesh begins to laugh as well. 'These lanes are a death trap.'

'Why did you move to Magna?' Anna asks.

'Needed a change.' He watches the road closely. 'Mum died.'

'I'm sorry.' She does not elaborate with condolences, to try to soften something that cannot be softened, as people so often do in their goodwill and their awkwardness.

'And you – why Fallow, really? It's isolated. Particularly without a phone or a car. You might as well have moved to the Hebrides.'

'I like that. It's nice not to owe people your company all the time.'

Hitesh laughs. '"Two paradises 'twere in one, to live in paradise alone."'

'Shakespeare?' Anna sounds surprised for the first time.

'Marvell. I did English at university. The first of many small rebellions.'

'The second of which was to become a police officer?'

'First I was a brickie for a bit. I'm not sure which my dad despises more. Then again, if I'd become an accountant he'd have asked why I wasn't a lawyer. And if I was Prime Minister, why I wasn't God.'

In his peripheral vision, Hitesh sees that smile, a small thing, like a bird flitting between branches. Around the car, the English hills roll into the horizon, pestered by the last clinging mist. Anna smells so much like the leaves and fields that Hitesh has to check that the window is not open.

'Why the police, when you could do something less dangerous, or at least better paid?' she asks.

Hitesh breathes out slowly, almost a sigh. 'I wanted power.'

Anna does not reply. She rests her head against the car window and watches the end of the dawn. Finally, 'Most people direct it outwards.'

Hitesh glances away from the road, across to her, then smiles too. 'You could get a cheap phone if you wanted one, couldn't you?'

'Then I'd have to pick it up.'

## May 1967

I know the view from this window better than I know my own face. As I've grown from child to teenager to woman, my face has stretched, blemished, cleared, shifted. But since I was six years old, I've stood at this counter every day – at first on a little white wooden stool – and looked out of this window. And out there, the seasons have conducted their regular procession, and every day I have seen the lawn run up to the copse and the stream, the birds conducting their business, the weather cursing and beatifying the grounds. I could tell you every feature in this frame, each speckle of moss on the stone pots.

Sometimes Mother stands next to me to help prepare meals, but I have been in charge of feeding the family since about fifteen, since Mother has even less interest and capability than I do when it comes to food. 'There's a reason I was housekeeper, not a cook,' she tells me each time she chars the meat or renders good produce inedible.

And there are three meals in a day. I have stood at this spot for so many years of my life that it sometimes feels like this view is really my mind. As I am peeling and chopping and rolling out pastry, the daydreams, the thoughts and grudges and longings work across my mind's eye, with the grass and the trees and the stream behind them always. Holding them up, cradling them, drowning them. Sometimes it's hard to separate what is me and what is the land, and when Mother comes to talk to me, it takes me a moment to pull myself out of it and answer her.

I am standing there now, peeling potatoes, dropping the skins into a colander in the sink. It's hot, even down here in the vast kitchen that was built before refrigerators, and is therefore at the back of the house, tucked as far from the sun's reach as possible. My gingham dress is getting sweaty so I try to pull it away from my body and make a starchy handprint. 'Oh, for God's sake.'

'Language. Blaspheming is common. Would you make some tea, please?' My father is in the doorway.

'Yes, Father.'

As I fill up the kettle, I can feel him turning away to go back upstairs to his study. Perhaps I have been staring at the view for too long, but I have to ask him now, or perhaps I never will.

'It's just so hot at the moment.'

'Quite stifling.' He stops and returns. Already he knows something is coming. The arch of melted skin on his brow bone lifts, quite as though there were still an eyebrow there.

'I picked some flowers for the hall table vase this morning and they've already gone over.'

'Hmm.'

'Nothing lasts in this heat.'

My father's face isn't monstrous to me any more. Apparently when he first came back home, I would not stop screaming. I was only one at the time, but I still feel guilty, since having your own child bawl herself blue at the sight of you, when you yourself are fresh from war and newly disfigured, well, that must be distressing. Now I know the notches and lumps and shiny, solidified puddles of his skin and the expressions they make. I know the disapproval his bad eye can convey from under its half-sheath of a lid.

'Father, I'd like – can I have a birthday party? Mother said you had parties all the time – before.'

He frowns. 'What makes you ask that?'

'It would be a nice way to meet young people. I would organise it all – it wouldn't be any extra work for you or Mother.'

'Are you looking for a husband? Or a boyfriend – we live in modern times, I suppose.'

I am looking for a way out.

'It's quiet without Sprat around.'

'Not long and he'll be back for the whole summer. Plenty of company for you. I appreciate that your Mother and I aren't thrilling.'

'Is there really no way that I could—'

'I have said no. That's final.' Father nods and turns and leaves.

What a goddamned child I am. I am going to be twenty-four and I am standing in the kitchen begging my own father for a birthday party. I ought to be able to pack a bag and leave Fallow forever and find some life of my choosing. But of course I can't. When has life ever been so simple? If I walk out of the gate and into the village – what then? A train or a bus – where to? Where would I stay; how would I earn money; could I ever hurt Mother and Sprat, or even, really, Father that way? And what really is wrong with my life here? Boredom, loneliness. What could possibly justify such dramatic action? A feeling that my life is wrong does not seem like enough.

If I left without a plan, when I eventually found myself face to face with the authorities, they would pat me on the head and return me to the home I had so foolishly deserted.

No. If I am ever to leave Fallow, it will be with my legs open, married. And so I must find a husband. None has been offered, so I must drag one out of thin air. I'd like to give Jane Austen a slap for the stupidity of her country house romances, but then perhaps I would hug her also, because she died a spinster after all.

The kettle boils and I steep a pot of tea and put a couple of biscuits on a plate because it will be a while before dinner is ready. Mother still insists we dress for it, which is madness. Last week I tried to serve spaghetti Bolognese-style, and the week before, a sort of mild chicken curry I found the recipe for in *Good Housekeeping*. But both were met with tight-lipped disapproval, and today I have retreated to the safety of beef consommé and Dover sole.

I go upstairs and knock on the study door. When Father calls me in, I am determined to pretend nothing has happened. I put the tray on the right-hand side of the bureau and tell him dinner will be at eight.

I have nearly reached the door when he calls me back.

'Darling?' His mouth is lifted in a smile. 'I'm sorry if I seem harsh sometimes, old-fashioned. I certainly don't intend to be. Where would we be without you?'

A ballerina.

PC Barnard has been busy with background checks, and Hitesh's inbox is full of summaries. He sits with a mid-morning coffee to read them.

Anna Jane Deerin: twenty-seven, born in Kent; moved to UM nineteen months ago; previously sales assistant for ten months; prior to that, trained and worked as a ballet dancer with the London Royal Ballet for nine years.

Hitesh is unsure if he is surprised by this. It makes the discipline of Anna's existence more explicable; she does not flinch at a garden that must need her every waking hour. The physical hardship of it. And yet, to draw a line between tutus and subsistence farming requires some animating force, something more decisive than the convenience or inertia that sweeps most of life forward.

Manju had seen deeply into humanity, whether in spite or because of her job as a hospital administrator, Hitesh had never known. She had told her son as often as he would listen that people are patterns. They are not only the repetitions drawn on the surface – the cycles of similar jobs, relationships, behaviours – but also their underlying drives. Sometimes an action comes along that appears uncharacteristic, and yet, beneath the surface is that same *tick tick tick*, the same belief or idea or even inarticulate feeling that is at the base of that person – 'and it usually explains what they're doing. It's almost always of a piece, dika,' she had said, wagging her finger, 'though most of the time people have no idea that's why they're doing what they do. Deep in their inner workings, they think they're good or bad or un-loveable or that the world is a carpet for them to tread on, and whatever they're doing they act accordingly.'

Hitesh still thinks of that advice, if that had been what it was, during the course of policing.

He wonders what Anna Deerin believes about her life.

He wonders what he believes about his.

'It isn't Celia Foster.'

'You're sure?' Reverend Watts brings tea over.

'I'm sure.' Hitesh moves a stack of parish newsletters to the side of the kitchen table to make space for the tray. 'Celia – I mean, I can't tell you much for privacy reasons – but she's okay. On paper, at least. Three kids and a semi-detached in Didcot. You could probably find her on Facebook, if you wanted to.'

Watts looks stunned. He runs a hand across his silver head. 'She's all right.' He chuckles. 'She's just been around all this time? I'd make an appalling detective.'

'Yeah, she's never gone very far – no more than an hour in the car, give or take.' Hitesh drinks his tea. 'It's a good thing you stuck to ministering your flock.'

'Thank you – you didn't have to take the time to come and tell me.'

The rectory kitchen is much the same as the hallway and sitting room Hitesh had passed through; homely, stuffed with books and papers. He had assumed that the rectory would be like the concrete, purgatorial buildings he has spotted tacked onto city churches. As far as he understood it, priests moved on fairly quickly and rectories were less homes than a place to rest the physical body. But Reverend Watts has been at Upper Magna for some forty-five years, and his very being is etched into the wallpaper.

'I'm sorry about the mess. Brenda comes twice a week but I'm a grown man, I ought to be able to keep a house myself.'

'It's all right. I find it isn't as easy as it looks.'

The reverend glances at Hitesh's bare ring finger. 'Ridiculous that men should need mothers all their lives.'

'Hmm.'

Beneath Hitesh's feet something moves and he jumps and bangs his knee on the table.

'Oh, good heavens. I'm so sorry, I forgot he was even there. David!' Watts chastises the golden retriever who has woken from his nap.

David puts his chin on Hitesh's knee and looks up at him with rheumy eyes. His breath is warm and noisome, and Hitesh is nearly overcome by the impulse to bury his head in David's fur. He strokes him instead. 'Hello, I didn't know you were under there. I hope I didn't step on your tail.'

David wags his tail and nuzzles his nose into Hitesh's hand.

'Stop it, there are no biscuits for you,' Watts scolds cheerfully and the dog is so big that his rear sticks out the other side of the kitchen table, where the reverend pats it. 'Honestly, he's a hoover.'

'David's an unusual name for a dog.' Hitesh does not want to turn away. The dog is happy just because he's there.

'Well, it was a bit of a silly joke to myself, really. David was a biblical king – a spiritually complex character. A far shout from this lump.'

'Thomas Wyatt paraphrased his psalms, I think.'

'I'm very impressed, DI Mistry.'

'I'm afraid I don't know anything much about Christianity. Just the poems.'

David goes to slurp from his water bowl, and Hitesh wishes there was a dog waiting for him at home. 'Do you get a lot of people like Celia asking for your help?'

Watts frowns. 'Sadly. I'd say you don't know all the misery that goes on behind closed doors, but I think as a police officer you're probably uniquely aware of it.'

'I think it's stranger seeing it in a wealthy place.'

Reverend Watts nods. 'There's plenty of poverty lurking about where it's harder to see. But the wealthy folk, they've got their share of problems, barely concealed beneath the surface. If Hendon is anything like the seminary, they'll have taught you to sniff out sadness.'

Hitesh meets the reverend's gaze. The clouds are moved by the breeze and a handful of rain scatters across the kitchen window.

'Yes. It's a difficult habit to lose.'

Watts tuts at himself suddenly. 'I'm sorry, you really didn't come here to be sermonised at. It's such a relief to hear Celia is okay. Thank you.'

Hitesh gets up to leave. 'I'm not sure I'm used to Magna yet.'

'Think of it as a change of pace. And I hope you won't find it wearing if Magna takes a while to get used to you.'

Hitesh had not credited Watts with this sort of acuity. 'My skin?'

'Believe it or not, in this century, people here might *think* they don't think it matters, but underneath it all, some of them still won't have shaken the idea that you're different. Not entirely. I'm very sorry if you get any stupidity because of that.'

'They can't be any more racist than coppers. Bye, David.' Hitesh bends down to scratch behind the retriever's ears, and David grumbles affectionately. 'I wanted a dog when I was a boy, but my parents were having none of it.'

'Well, this morning he ate his own faeces so I'm tempted to say you can have him.' Watts looks at the dog fondly. 'But I'll keep him for now.'

Hitesh is coming up the path. Anna glances at the clock on the kitchen wall. He had said he would come at one o'clock, and it is one o'clock now.

The cottage is filled with cakes cooling on window sills, on the countertop, on the fold-out dining table. The air is warm with butter, sugar and vanilla. It ought to be a pleasant haze.

Anna hesitates, then puts the kettle on. Her front is streaked with flour, but she still looks pretty and bright. It is how she appears at market. She catches her reflection in the window and looks away.

Standing on the front step, Hitesh holds a square of plywood. 'One of the PCs found an old noticeboard – it should do until you can get a new window.'

That morning, they had stood in the cold, dank bedroom as he took pictures of the shattered glass and had had the decency not to examine the airing cupboard where she had hidden.

He had not lingered, only told her he would come back with something to board up the window.

In the dense, sickly atmosphere of the kitchen, Anna wishes he was not there, or at least that she was not there, hollow and fraudulent.

'How are you feeling now?' he asks.

'I'm all right, thank you.' She can see that he does not believe her, because it is not true.

'Is this all for market?' Hitesh glances round.

'They're popular.'

There is an awkward beat, the ease they found this morning lost. The kettle boils and Anna makes tea.

Hitesh watches her. Rather than a series of distinct actions, her movements are fluid, like the waves coming in and out.

'I understand you were a ballet dancer?'

She looks surprised but not embarrassed. 'That's right. I was with a London company. Have you ever been to the ballet?'

'A couple of times. I went with friends at university.' Hitesh tries to keep out of the way as she fetches cups and milk, but the kitchen is as cramped as the rest of the cottage and there is nowhere to stand that is not inconvenient.

'Did you like it?'

'It was very impressive, physically. I'm not sure I really understood the worlds they described.'

'The classical stories are usually about women suffering for love. And romanticising slavery, there's often a bit of that mixed in there.'

Hitesh laughs, the air between them light again. 'That's a pretty scathing assessment of something you spent years doing.'

Anna smiles and shrugs. 'It's true. And those same ballets are also exquisitely beautiful. It's not easy to disentangle. Not that that's an excuse either.'

73

'So why did you stop?'

'I tore a ligament; I can't dance en pointe any more.'

'That must have been difficult – for it not to have been your choice to stop.'

Anna pauses. 'No, it's okay, I was finished with it.'

Hitesh watches as she returns ingredients to their cupboards, and tries to catch a trace of a limp, but there is nothing.

Anna hands him the tea and asks if he would like cake, which he declines. She leans against the counter.

'What's stopping him from coming back tonight?' Hitesh asks her.

She looks down at her tea. 'Not a lot.'

'Last night makes the investigation more urgent, you understand. Clearly someone still has a stake in events.'

'I understand.'

'What will you do if it happens again?'

'I don't know.'

'I'm not saying— It's not your responsibility. You ought to be safe wherever you are. But being out here by yourself, without a phone, even – you're vulnerable if someone wants to do you harm. And seemingly they do.'

'I know that. But I'm not getting one and I'm not leaving.' Her hands are shaking.

'All right,' Hitesh softens his tone, 'all right. I can't make you.'

'It's not that I'm not scared.' She looks at him. 'I am. But I'm not going to change what— I don't want to change what I've chosen here.'

Hitesh wants to ask what it is she has chosen. 'All right, okay.' He puts his mug down. 'Shall we get this window fixed?'

The bedroom had been bright without a window in its frame, but as soon as they place the board over the hole, it could be midnight. There is a single bulb illuminating them as Hitesh holds the board in place and Anna balances on a kitchen chair and drives nails through it and into the timber frame. It takes a long time, but Hitesh does not rush her or say anything about the dozens of jobs she has no doubt are waiting for him at the station. He holds the board in place patiently and asks her questions between the hammering.

'Do you miss dancing?'

'Yes. Sort of. Ballet is about pursuing perfection, and I miss that. But then perfection is also about pleasing, and I don't want that any more.'

'Want what?'

'To pursue pleasingness.' Anna hammers another nail in.

'And pleasingness is – what? Innate to ballet because you're performing for people?'

She pauses. 'Pleasingness is innate to being a woman and we perform for everyone. Ballet just takes it to its logical conclusion.'

Hitesh laughs but she sees he is neither appalled nor confused by what she says.

Anna pulls another nail from her back pocket and leans to position it. From the dining chair, she can see the top of Hitesh's head where grey hairs streak the black. She is curious.

'Were you close to your mum?'

'Yes. I know that's odd for a man in his thirties.'

'It's not odd. Are you close to your dad?'

'I call him twice a week.'

Anna gives the board a tentative push with her palm. It is sturdy. She climbs down from the chair, a head shorter than Hitesh again.

'Will you get it replaced soon?' he asks.

'I will.' Already she misses looking out of the window onto the garden. 'How will you find out who she is, the woman in the garden?'

'I don't know. The process isn't… linear. The parishioners at St Mary's have given me some names to follow. I'll start there.'

Anna's hand tightens around the hammer. She can feel again the nausea and the dry-grit fear. She breathes like she used to before going on stage, as though if she could control her breathing she could control everything. Hitesh waits.

'You know that Fallow Hall has a trust now?' she says finally.

'Lord Blackwaite said something about it.'

'I was thinking, the members must know a lot about the estate – who worked here, lived here, that sort of thing. I know they went through a load of documents while they were setting it up – it's how they realised they were meant to have a gardener here at the cottage. And they're all locals.'

'Worth speaking to, then. Who's on the Trust, other than Lord Blackwaite?' Hitesh gets out his notebook.

'A retired judge named Michael Caulfield; a woman called Eloise Fitzhugh; Paul Wolsey, he runs some local care homes; and Reverend Watts.'

'Watts is on the Trust?'

'Not many people know the area better than him.'

'I just came from the rectory. He didn't say.'

'He probably doesn't see its relevance.' Anna shrugs.

'Maybe.'

Anna watches his face. 'If you're here long enough, in Upper Magna, you'll find there aren't easy distinctions. It's too small a community. Soon you'll be policing friends, maybe even family.'

'That doesn't sound very comfortable.'

'I imagine it isn't.'

'How are you managing for meals, Darshan?'

'I'm managing.'

'Really?'

'Yes. Lunch at *mandir*, Tuesday, Wednesday, Thursday. Monday and Saturday – takeaway. Friday, Sunday – ready meal.'

'Ready meals aren't meals.'

'If you had married when we asked you, I'd have a daughter-in-law to help now.'

'Grow up, Dad. Women aren't there to cook for you.'

'That's how family works. That's natural. Man does the work; women cook, look after the family, kids.'

'Mum worked too. You still treated her like a servant.'

'I treated your mother like a princess—'

*Click.*

From Anna's cottage, Hitesh drives once more to Fallow Hall. He is admitted promptly this time by the housekeeper, Pauline, who has an accent like Barnard's and blue-rinsed hair. In the corridor, she stops to point out some historic features. For the first time, Hitesh feels he can linger to look at the house, and the general impression of stateliness settles into its details – a heavy couch and framed mezzotints, a display cabinet full of Wedgwood. Some of it is worn but all of it has been kept spotless. He looks at the thick, textured wallpaper and wonders if it is fabric; he's unsure if he is allowed to reach out and touch it, or if such a thing is not done.

'It must be hard to clean,' he observes to Pauline.

'I have been known to hoover it – carefully – on occasion,' she chuckles. 'This is the drawing room. Make yourself comfortable here and I'll fetch His Lordship.'

She cannot be much younger than Lord Blackwaite, Hitesh thinks, yet Pauline cooks and cleans and dusts for him; an accident of birth saw her born in the village and he in the Hall. The housekeeper is proud, though, Hitesh can see. He watches her retreating back, a ramrod straighter than most twenty-year-olds'.

In the drawing room is a low sofa and an armchair, a coffee table with a vase of wildflowers, perhaps bought from Anna Deerin. The walls are papered in a blue floral print, which has faded and become spectral. But it is the windows that Hitesh covets. They line the room, nearly floor to ceiling, and let in more light than should be possible on such an overcast day. For a moment Hitesh can see the house from inside and out at once, a pale and irreducible monument in the violent green, crimson and amber of the hills in autumn. He lets the vision fill him up, and feels intoxicated. Is this what Lord Blackwaite sees when he looks at his home, at his land? Is this mastery or humility? There is a numb tugging at the edge of Hitesh's mind and he shakes himself and turns away from the view.

'Inspector, you're back.' Lord Blackwaite has appeared with unexpected grace.

'We've had further information about the body.' Hitesh reaches out to shake his hand. 'She was murdered, as we suspected, and that murder took place within the past thirty to seventy years.'

Still grasping Hitesh's hand, Lord Blackwaite pales. 'I think perhaps I had convinced myself it was a much older body. That is… quite disturbing. Within my lifetime.'

'I understand. With that in mind, do you have any more relevant information?'

The older man rubs his eyes in a gesture Hitesh is surprised to recognise, then slumps into the armchair. His face droops and his skin is so waxen that, for a moment, he too is corpse-like. Absentmindedly, he invites Hitesh to sit down.

'Are there any women who you lost track of? Who dropped off your radar?'

'They aren't odd gloves, Inspector.' Lord Blackwaite sharpens. 'One doesn't just lose women. Mother died decades ago, and my sister emigrated to Canada when she married. That's it. I've no wife or daughters. No one else to *lose track of*.'

Hitesh had thought the news had unbalanced Lord Blackwaite, but he had been wrong. He jots notes. 'Is your sister still alive?'

'Catherine? I – I believe so.' A look of guilt passes across his face. 'We lost contact years ago. Moving to Canada back then wasn't like now. No email, no long-distance phone calls to speak of. We wrote letters to begin with, but you know, slowly they peter out, and you forget who last wrote to whom.' He flicks the guilt away. 'Life moves on, I'm afraid.'

'Any other women – staff, housekeepers?'

'Dozens, over the years. But at the risk of repeating myself, Inspector, I would know if someone close to the family – close to Fallow – had met a tragic end. You'd do well to broaden your field.'

Hitesh wants to shout at him that he is a suspect, that for half a century, his land has been a woman's grave. 'Rest assured, we're investigating all possibilities. And you've never married, Lord Blackwaite?'

'Have you, Inspector?' Lord Blackwaite drops the veil from his hostility. 'I don't see that this has any bearing on the investigation. It is simply intrusive. If you cannot keep your investigation within bounds, I shall be forced to file a complaint with the Chief Constable.'

Hitesh could return the threat, accuse him of obstructing an investigation. But it would be the last time Lord Blackwaite would cooperate; give information; perhaps the last time he would provide refuge to Anna Deerin if she asked. Instead, Hitesh swallows it, buries it, as he has been taught since birth, and stiffly assures Lord Blackwaite it had not been his intention to give offence.

Lord Blackwaite is still flushed, and it makes his grey hair seem almost white. 'I don't wish to appear insensitive, really I do not, but this couldn't have come at a worse time. We are trying to launch a fundraising campaign over Christmas, with a gala and carolling. No one wishes this could be resolved quickly more than me.'

'A gala?'

Lord Blackwaite takes a deep breath and speaks calmly once more. 'You aren't from around here, Inspector, I don't expect you to understand. But if this house collapses, a piece of history collapses. Local jobs are lost. What would happen to Pauline? To Ms Deerin? Fallow is a lynchpin and not to be treated with contempt. I want justice for this woman you've found, of course I do, but she will not live again once the case is solved. If anything happens to Fallow, real people *now* suffer the consequences.'

Hitesh gets up to leave, afraid of what he will say if he does not. Through the window, the land jeers back at him.

At the door, he pivots to where Lord Blackwaite is still seated. 'Anna Deerin's cottage was attacked last night.'

Lord Blackwaite's face drops. 'What happened? She wasn't harmed, was she?'

'No, no, she wasn't. A window was broken. Do you know who might have done it?'

'Absolutely not. How appalling.'

'I'd appreciate some discretion. I'm sure Ms Deerin doesn't want all of Upper Magna asking her about it at the market on Saturday. She'll already have questions about the body.'

For the first time, Lord Blackwaite is quiescent. 'Absolutely, Inspector. It's been a shocking week for the girl.'

The chickens are raucous beasts. Anna loves that. Loves them. She opens the gate to the coop and lets them out into the kitchen garden, where they go immediately to scratch in the vegetable patches, turning up worms and grubs and gurgling happily to themselves. She sits on the ground to watch them, occasionally hops up to pull Odette off the cabbages.

They move like dinosaurs, with a little lurch and bounce, the odd pause to scratch or shit. Eventually, Margot tires of adventure and comes to perch on Anna's lap, scaly legs tucked into a V, round body balanced on top. Anna loves their surprising weight. She strokes Margot's feathers, over and over, soothing them both, then checks the bald spot where Odette sometimes pulls out a feather to assert her dominance. Margot coos mournfully.

'The police have gone now. Or did you prefer it when you had company?'

'Bwaaaak.'

'Hmm.'

Anna keeps stroking her copper feathers, and Margot's eyes begin to close with pleasure, until finally she dozes off.

Anna sits there a while, feeling her back seize up but not wishing to wake Margot. She watches the bobbing heads of the other five, and smiles as they clamber over and under in their quest for bugs. The wind ruffles the leaves of the overhanging birch, the hens tussle over a beetle. She feels a certain calm re-settling. The garden knows its rhythm.

'Not there, girl.' Anna stands suddenly and sends Margot squawking. She runs across to where Odette has found the empty patch. 'Not there.' She picks her up and puts her gently back with the others.

As Hitesh reaches the grand hall, Pauline is making her way through with a tray of tea for them.

'Are you off, Inspector?'

'Yes. Thank you, though.'

Pauline puts the tray on a console table and escorts him back towards the door.

'Have you been here long, Pauline?' Hitesh smiles down at the tiny figure. She has been dusting and her scalp is flecked with lint.

'Oh well, I'm not a day over twenty-eight, but forty-odd years now,' she cackles.

'Has the Hall changed a lot in that time?'

'Well, yes and no.' She waves a hand. 'Places like this don't change that much in themselves. I suppose the big shift was opening to the public for the first time. That's when I started here.'

'What about the family? Has that seen much change?'

'Oh, the Blackwaites have been here forever. A wonderful family – there wouldn't be an Upper Magna without them.'

'They're that important, then? Is Lord Blackwaite... well liked?'

Pauline stops and puts a hand on his arm. 'I don't know what he's said, but he's a very good man, Inspector, he's always treated staff like me very well. He's old-fashioned. Just that generation – our generation, really. Please don't mistake it for being uncooperative—'

They are at the front door and Pauline will not remove her hand until he pats it, and promises he is not upset with Lord Blackwaite.

'What happens when he – I'm sorry – when he passes away? What will happen to the house then, since he didn't marry and have kids?' Hitesh asks.

'Oh, that's a bit above my pay grade. But I think that's what the Trust is for, you know. So there's something in place.'

'What's that?'

'What's what?'

'This?' Anna crouches and strokes the weed with tiny white flowers. Its leaves are little heart-shaped paddles.

Jenny is from the West Country and the other British housemates rib the accent that contrasts so strongly with her swanlike grace. But Jenny is lovely and warm-natured, and she does, in fact, know all about plants and farming. 'That's shepherd's purse. It's a bit early in the year, but London's its own climate.'

The two ballerinas huddle over the scratch of green in the cement square that passes for a garden in Dalston.

'Do you reckon the landlord would let us put a veg patch in? I miss growing things,' Jenny wonders. She puts down her protein bar and reaches to pluck a heart from the stem. Carefully, very carefully, she splits it open with her nail. Inside are hundreds of microscopic dots. 'It's not a leaf, really, it's a seed pod.'

Anna's toes curl in delight. She takes it and holds it where a narrow slant of sun finds its way down into paving, and examines all this latent life.

*June 1967*

The bus! I don't think I have been this excited about a bus journey since I was a child. I feel like swinging my legs under the seat. The sun is streaming in through the windows and warms my cheeks, which I dabbed with blusher as soon as I was out of sight of the house.

God bless Mother. God bless her. She insisted she needed a pineapple for a birthday upside-down cake. A pineapple that certainly could not be found in the village of Upper Magna. Grudgingly, Father had agreed that I should go to Cirencester, and while I was there, that I ought to go to the haberdashers and order fabric for the dining-room curtains. He would trust my discretion as to the design.

'You won't go with her, Margaret?'

'I can't very well ask her to make her own birthday tea. No, I'll organise things here and we'll make the cake together this afternoon when she's back.'

'All right, don't stay out too long though. And don't talk to strangers. There's more and more in Cirencester now. Mr Walker said a negro family moved into Sheep Street last month.'

'I'll be back by lunch, Father.'

And so I was dismissed. Freed for the morning.

The bus rumbles into town and I hop off at the agricultural college. It is familiar from Sprat's visits to his friends there, when I have gone with Mother to collect him sometimes. My own paltry schooling took place in one of the pleasant, unambitious girls' schools placed thoughtfully out of the way, somewhere in the countryside we couldn't get impregnated or wander off. After that, my schoolmates had quickly married, or gone to London on the giddy trail of a secretarial course, but my own requests for further study had been firmly denied, and the friendships of girlhood had withered like dropped petals.

I want to take in as much of the day as possible, and the walk from the outskirts is part of the pleasure. The air is full of pollen and the dragonflies that afflict this watery county in summer. I am smiling ear to ear, and stop in at the bookshop, then the shoe shop, just to browse.

There are young people here. Working and enjoying their leisure. And I feel like another species to them. I don't know their music, the films they've seen. Upper Magna doesn't even have a parish film night. I receive books in the post, and that is my lot. Outside the Corn Hall is a group of teenage girls, applying eyeliner with an expertise I cannot comprehend. I'd kill for a pair of jeans like the ones they're wearing. Isn't that ridiculous? The girls look so modern. Like the sixties might actually exist for them. I'm stuck in an A-line skirt that reaches past my knees but which Father still eyed with suspicion before I left.

I don't think Father has been to Cirencester for a decade. Perhaps he has not been since the war. I don't know. People do stare, even in Magna, even after all these years have passed. Missing limbs are perhaps easier to gloss over, but the burns that mar my father's once handsome face – well, these force them to confront the horror of those years, and know that perhaps they are still with them somewhere, that they might come again.

I cross the street so that I'm not tempted to talk to the girls and embarrass myself.

Father knew what to do with Sprat, a boy. Authority, experience, the right education. But his daughter? All he can do is sequester me. Protect my innocence and throw away my future.

If Father left Fallow sometimes, would he still be the man he is? Would he still be all dourness and tradition, those flecks of temper that leave me shaking? Perhaps, and I'll never know. Perhaps this is what all fathers are like and I am straining against nothing. Perhaps I ought just to be grateful for the roof over my head.

I acquire the pineapple from the greengrocer and next ought to be the haberdashers, but first I want to stop for refreshments because I'll be damned if I let any pleasure escape me today. I'm not bold enough for the pub, so I step into the hotel and they inform me they are serving coffee in the dining room.

The coffee is not that hot, but the millefeuille slice the waitress brings is something special. A far cry from anything I have dredged up at home, it seems in that moment to represent everything life ought to be. I am by myself, in the dining room of an elegant hotel. No one knows me here, and I could call myself anything. Wear anything. Do anything.

But that is the sugar rush talking.

I pay the bill and turn myself back out onto the street, humming 'Happy Birthday', and that is when I notice him looking at me. I look away, aloof like Mother has always encouraged. But, like a puppy with no control over itself, I look back to see if he is still looking. And he is. In his hand is a brown paper parcel – a book, since he has just stepped out of the bookshop.

'What have you bought?'

'Le Carré – who can resist a spy story?' His voice is rich, his accent unfamiliar.

'I've never read him.'

And he has fallen into step beside me. Just like that. I slip somewhere between euphoria and panic.

'What do you like to read then, ma'am?'

Timothy McArthur is Canadian, the same age as me, staying here with relations while he studies crop management at the college, then he plans to go back and manage the family farm in Vancouver. His hair is chestnut brown, and he stands two inches taller than any other male in Cirencester. He is courteous and attentive, and says nothing crude about the fact that I have started walking and talking with a man I do not know, treats it as normal to the extent that I wonder if it might be in Canada. Hell, it might be normal in England; I would not know.

When I tell Timothy it is my birthday, he insists on stopping at the baker's and buying us both an iced bun. We walk down to the stream to eat them, talking all the way about ourselves and our lives. On the bank, he sits close to me, and brushes the crumbs from my sleeve, and I blush so violently I feel dizzy.

When we finish eating, there is a beat where it is clear he is thinking of saying goodbye. But I cannot lose this – whatever it is. I would grasp silk on a breeze today.

'Would you like to go for a walk? It isn't a big town, but I'd be pleased to show you around.'

'That's awful kind of you.' He smiles.

I wonder if he is just being polite, but then he pulls my arm through his and takes my hand. It feels nice. I like how large his hands are.

Anna loads the market goods into her handcart carefully, methodically. This mode of transport cannot be rushed. A car would be easier, but she cannot afford one, and anyway, she does not want one.

If there is one thing that Anna is sure of, it is that the world is burning. It is more certain than this project she has, of clearing her vision, about which she so often feels doubt. She knows that the world is burning and that not enough people are putting out the fires. In the garden, she has brought the wildflowers back, and with them bees, butterflies, hoppers, things with many legs. At the weekly market, she sells her goods in paper bags, composts everything she can so that she does not have to buy peat. She no longer eats meat, dairy – in fact little that does not come from the garden.

Ultimately it won't matter; plastic and fossil fuel subsidies will still choke the sea and haul up the tides to drown the people who are too poor to move. Parents will carry their children miles seeking refuge from the heat, the sickness, from the poverty. Their mothers will love them, will see them starve in their arms. It is not even a matter of time.

But she refuses to have this blood on her hands. She will not. She will have her garden and it will be a world as it ought to be, even if nothing else is. She knows that her project and this project that the world ought to share are linked. Because if we treated things fairly, Anna knows, neither would need to be undertaken at all.

*June 1967*

He is warm and wet, I can taste him.

How did we get here? I have known him for a morning.

I have never even kissed a boy before, and he is a man, heavy on top of me, and it feels good. The grass is cool on my back and as he enters me the pain is sharp and still so sweet that it leaves me gasping. He puts his tongue in my mouth so that no one will hear us behind the trees.

This is it.

It is wet and hot and cold and I don't know what can be left of the world after this pain and the unbearable sweetness.

If they are to be fresh, the cakes can only be baked a day or so in advance; the flowers cut from the meadow and the greenhouse, the arbour; the fruit and vegetables harvested all at the last moment. Anna enjoys the intensity of the labour, the satisfaction she feels when she looks at all her wares and can say, *This is mine; I have made this.*

She had made things before. With her body, her movement. In the small hours, Anna fears she is hollow, but in the daylight, she sees that she has always been generative. It was different then, though. Communal, crowded. She had woken, got ready with her housemates – all dancers – gone to class, to a rehearsal, another rehearsal, perhaps even a third, if that is what the schedule on the corkboard had told her to do. She had dressed, gone on stage, performed the night's show, returned to the dressing rooms with her fellow ballerinas to laugh, or cry, or dissect the night's performance. Again, then over again. What had been created had been beyond her control, because she had been but a piece of it.

Then, as Anna had repeated the flex of her foot, the opening of her shoulders, the turnout of her hips, in perfect uniformity at the barre, she had let her gaze fall to her training bag, and nestled inside, the book she had found in a charity shop, which named the flowers. Shepherd's purse. Then the row of thin, beautiful women had performed their arabesques, and in the mirror they had seen their grace and their flaws.

It had been addictive, rigid, thrilling.

Slow, seasonal, microscopic. At last, Anna pulls the cart of goods onto Upper Magna's market green. She wonders if the villagers have realised what it means for them. She thinks not. The woman in her garden was buried whole, but now is bare bones, and over the years, the rest of her has leached into the soil, crept up through the roots of plants, into their fruits, into the ground, again and again. In the cart ahead of her are carrots and leeks and squash from the vegetable patches. One way or another, the people in the market have all tasted her.

Anna has only herself now. What she cries for and what she longs for, alone in her cottage. Anna has so little power, and what she has, she will use for this woman.

*June 1967*

It is half past one. If I run for the bus, I can be home by two, and feasibly claim it is still lunchtime. As I round the corner, I can see it waiting at the stop, a few elderly shoppers shuffling onboard. I start to run but pain shoots through my lower body and I have to stop. I think I might be sick. By the time I have limped to the stop, the bus is long gone, and I think I might have bled through my knickers, into my nylons.

When I catch the next bus, I realise I have bought the pineapple but forgotten the curtains, and I will have to telephone the haberdashers to place our order while Father is out walking, and hope that what they send is not too hideous.

The autumn sun casts an easy haze over the morning. Stalls are being erected all across the village green and their roofs form a miniature village inside Upper Magna. The flapping of the tent plastic makes Anna nauseous and she tries to push aside the *snap snap snap* as they twitch in the breeze. She sets out two tables, one of flowers and fruit and vegetables, one of the cakes and biscuits she carefully removes from their Tupperware and places on plates and trays. Once she is done, she walks to the other side to see how it will look to customers. It is perfect, sweet and bountiful, just imperfect enough to be authentic. She has seen more than one customer take photographs for their social media, faces upon faces.

Another stallholder passes close behind Anna, and she jumps. Her hands are shaking so she weaves her fingers together and sits in her canvas chair.

The first customers begin to trickle in, most of them dog-walkers who have been out early. If Anna was commercially minded, she would sell gilets and welly socks. She greets her customers warmly, has biscuits for the dogs.

'How are you doing now, dear? Dreadful shock for you, finding that.'

*Snap snap snap.*

'Is it true? Did you really dig a skeleton up?'

*Snap.*

'Anna, I'm so sorry. How are you coping?'

*Snap.*

Business swells as the morning wears on, and people dribble from their houses onto the green. They wave to one another and to Anna; they exchange gossip and business and the titbits of daily life. This is how a community functions, Anna thinks, how the village coheres into something more than people living in the same place. She is a thread in this tapestry, when she is at market. She greets her customers by name, and answers their questions, asks after their families, parcels up their food. They ask her how she is, offer her their sympathy. They are kind.

*Snap.*

Anna knits her fingers together again.

'It's not normal not to need anyone, the way you don't,' a boyfriend had once told her.

'I need people.'

'No, you don't. You don't need me,' he'd said. She had argued, but only because he'd named what she had always feared was freakish in herself. He left her soon after that.

Anna packs fruit for the vet, and smiles as she hands it to him. Hands over a tiny piece of the Fallow sister.

Who could Anna let herself need here? For decades, someone – probably more than one person – has lived with that violence or at least the knowledge of it.

She watches the vet lift a pear to his mouth. Perhaps it might work like a fairy tale. Perhaps the murderer will eat of the fruit of the garden, of the Fallow sister. Perhaps then they will be compelled to tell the truth, to speak their guilt out loud.

Anna scans the crowd and wills someone to open their mouth.

Eloise Fitzhugh approaches the stall.

'Good morning, Mrs Fitzhugh.'

'Oh, Anna, I've told you to call me Eloise.' Eloise's white hair lopes gracefully across her head, secured by hidden pins so that it appears to defy gravity. All of her is soft and floral, a human primrose with a pale silk blouse beneath her jacket. If Anna still danced she would make a study of this woman, more radiant than the sun.

'Now then, what have you got here?' Eloise picks up the apples to smell them, murmurs that nothing will ever compare to fresh fruit, 'grown just a stone's throw away. There's something so wonderful about that.' She turns to Anna. 'You look as beautiful as ever, but tired, my dear. I can't imagine that this week hasn't been tiring for you, amongst many other things.'

'It has been.' Anna nods. 'It's too strange to absorb.'

Eloise's face creases in sympathy. 'Some things are so strange they feel like a blow to reality – that's almost the worst thing about them; they make everything less solid.' The older woman turns her replies with the same care that has worn her gaze to velvet; the sort of care that has been learned so deeply that it is inseparable from her being, her breathing; this pleasingness.

Anna feels a swell of affection and fear. 'The Fallow Trust will be all right, I hope?' she asks.

'Oh, it's kind of you to think of us, but I can't imagine it will throw things too off course, however much Lord Blackwaite is worrying. We're meeting next week but I can't see that we won't be able to hold the gala or the carolling.'

Anna stares down at the table. 'People can be ghoulish – you may find you do well from it.'

'Sadly, I think you may be right, my dear. It doesn't exactly appeal to people's best instincts.'

Anna takes a breath. 'I'm struggling to grasp how anyone kills a woman, but also how no one knows who she is.'

Eloise looks troubled in turn. 'Quite grim to think of, really. She might have been about my age now if she had lived.'

'It's a terrible thought.'

They pause their conversation while Anna serves the GP, and when he leaves, Eloise looks uncomfortable.

'What is it?' Anna asks.

'Oh, it's nothing. Nothing at all. It's just awful how your brain begins to make an encyclopaedia of everyone you've ever met and who they might have been and what might have happened to them.'

Anna lets silence pull the thought from Eloise, like gravity.

'I don't know why she's just popped into my head now. Perhaps you look a little like her.' Eloise strokes her scarf. 'Elizabeth. A lovely girl – very funny. In fact, she was Lord Blackwaite's girlfriend – fiancée – for a time, then she disappeared quite suddenly. Just left the scene without any explanation, even though she was very popular. I think Edmund broke it off but we didn't like to ask.'

'When was this?'

'Oh, I don't know. The sixties, maybe? But please, don't read anything into it. She almost certainly ended up married to some rich American; she was very beautiful, had a title. What I mean is that it's awful you even begin to have these thoughts.'

'I suppose the lack of information leaves a void to fill.'

Eloise nods and reaches over the table to squeeze Anna's hand. 'Now, look after yourself, dear, do.'

'And you.' Anna squeezes back. 'Say hello to Peter for me.'

Before Eloise has turned away, Anna's hands begin to tremble again. She nods to the other side of the green, where the Fallow sister watches.

The morning rolls on, suffocating. Anna chats and serves, all the while struggling for breath. Each time she is asked, she expresses her shock, her sadness at finding the body. She gives Magna what it needs.

Hitesh wakes late. That is something to be said for being childless, wifeless, motherless; there is no one to wake him at the weekend. He gets up slowly, feeling his knees creak from running. Is he a young man any longer, he wonders; when does middle age begin?

He begins to make coffee then decides he should go to the market, since it has become apparent that policing Magna will depend on knowing its residents, rather than on the city's anonymity. The coffee will be better anyway.

It is bright out, and the market begins only a few steps after the end of his street. There is a bustle, which he realises he has not missed, and he makes his way to the coffee stall.

The solid blonde lady who runs it offers him a single origin roast, alert to the trend for the artisanal. 'There you go, love. Oat milk?'

When he arrived, it had amused Hitesh to realise he was suspicious of English hospitality staff. He missed the Italians and Poles and Romanians of North London. It is a prejudice he must work on.

'Yeah, please. How's business?'

He drops into the patter that he has learned over the last ten years. The stallholders are all friendly, chatty, although he wonders if it would be different if he didn't have an English accent. The handful that know he is a police officer ask him about Fallow, are appalled when he tells them it is true, and offer to keep their ears to the ground. The coffee is good and he begins to feel a sort of ease in his surroundings.

The stalls are colourful, and the people well, he thinks. Even the elderly seem less attenuated than their city counterparts, as though the fresh air and their wealth have formed a protective varnish.

As Hitesh approaches it, he realises he has saved Anna's stall for last. He hangs back and watches. With her customers she is graceful, poised, charming. Deferent, yet untouchable. It has the magnetism of a performance and people are drawn to her without knowing it. He waits for a lull and crosses over.

'I thought you were done with pleasing.'

'Not at market.' Anna shrugs. 'I can't be hanged as a witch.'

'Of course – who would look after the chickens?'

She smiles, but not like while he had been watching. Then her face is intent. 'Eloise Fitzhugh came to talk to me. She said Lord Blackwaite had a fiancée in the sixties; no one knows what happened to her.'

'Certainly he didn't marry her.' Hitesh nods. 'I'll look into it. No doubt endear myself further to Lord Blackwaite.'

'I suppose it's easy to piss people off in your job.'

'I ought to have a market stall instead,' he says wryly, and she laughs. Hitesh hesitates. 'What about now?' he asks. 'Do you please people differently?'

'You make it sound like prostitution. Everyone makes themselves agreeable sometimes. But no – I'm not trying to please you, if that's what you're asking.' Anna frowns. She looks different with make-up, he realises, and cannot tell if he prefers it.

'That's Paul Wolsey.' Anna looks over his shoulder and Hitesh turns to see a man in his fifties with a limp-looking woman on his arm. 'He's on the Hall Trust.'

Anna raises a hand to wave to him, and he waves merrily in return.

Hitesh feels a surge of anger. 'Somebody knew her. You see them all talking to one another, it's not possible that no one knows.'

Anna nods. 'Someone knows.'

Her face changes, beatific once more, and Hitesh finds a woman in expensive sportswear at his shoulder.

'Morning, Louise. Can I tempt you?'

'I'm always tempted.' Louise tucks back her honeyish hair and surveys the table of baking. 'Oh, but I always end up back at the lemon cake. It's the best for miles around.' She turns to Hitesh. 'I could get fat on these. They never even make it to Monday in our house.'

Anna packs the cake up for her, and Louise flirts with Hitesh, enjoying the protection of her wedding ring. 'Take care, Anna,' she says, blowing a kiss as she leaves.

'I see you're not so inexperienced at pleasing,' Anna teases.

Hitesh grins and cringes. 'All right, that's fair.'

They watch the crowd together for a moment, then Hitesh turns to her again.

'How about the nights – he hasn't come back?'

'Not yet. Maybe he won't.'

'Hmm.'

'I'm not leaving.'

'I'm not asking you to. But don't dig, Anna. Don't involve yourself any further.'

She shrugs.


'I don't understand why he's such a—'

'Ah, ah, ah – he's your father. You might not like what he's like sometimes, but he's still your father.'

'But Mum, why is he so unreasonable? I was never going to be a doctor. What does it matter what his stupid Asian friends think? Most of them never went to uni at all.'

'He's just scared of change, dika.' Manju pulls on a pair of Marigolds and with a flick of her hand, tells Hitesh to do the same.

'English is a good degree. It's a top university.' Hitesh pulls his gloves on. 'Can't he just be proud of me? I scored highest in the year.'

'Hitesh, dika, the simple truth is that most of the time people have no idea what they're doing or why they're doing it. Your father doesn't know what an English degree is – he can't see how it's going to make you money, or support a family, and that's what he's been brought up to care about. He's not right; but he's never going to understand that he isn't right. *You* have to understand how hard it is for him to change. Now come on, if you don't learn how to clean a loo, no one's going to show you in halls.'

'What do I do first?'

'Bleach first. Round the rim – right round. Then the brush, like you're cleaning teeth.'

'Like this?'

96

'Good – that's good. I'm proud of you, you know that.' Manju gives him a nudge with her shoulder, and he can smell her perfume and her cooking. 'Don't tell your father I showed you how to do this. I don't need the bloody headache.'

'Ms Deerin – Anna?'

Anna is packing away when Reverend Watts reappears. 'Hello, Reverend. Are you all right? Did you forget something?'

David wags his tail and snuffles at her hand. She gave him a treat earlier when his master bought fruit and vegetables, surely she'll give him another one now?

'Oh, I'm perfectly all right. Actually, I wanted to ask whether you were?'

Anna's heart sinks. She had hoped that she was done with these questions for the day; she is so close to returning to the garden and to solitude. To the space to think. 'I'm doing all right, thank you, Reverend. It'll take a little while before I adjust. But no lasting damage, I think.'

The reverend waits while she feeds David, then tilts his own soft, grey head and catches her gaze. 'If it were only a matter of adjusting, I wouldn't be so worried for you.'

Anna turns back to packing away, surprised by the challenge. 'It's not nice. But what can you do?'

'You can talk to someone about it. And if you don't have someone you can talk to, you can find me at the rectory.'

'Thank you, Reverend, I appreciate it.'

Watts waves away her politeness. 'I'm not asking because I'm trying to smuggle God in, Anna. And I'm not supposing that a seventy-year-old clergyman is your ideal confidant. But if you're short on options, then do consider it a back-up.'

Anna stops tidying and meets his eyes. 'All right then. Really. I will come if I need to. But it'll be more for David than for you.'

Watts chuckles and rubs David's ears. 'Sadly, I believe that's how most people feel.'

This time Pauline shows Hitesh to the orangery. It is an exotic structure bolted onto the back of the Hall. Pauline tells him that one of the Blackwaites' forebears had returned from India with a taste for the heat, and had built this glasshouse, full of sunburst ironmongery, palms and hothouse flowers. It is nothing like the India Hitesh visited as a child, which was hectic, stifling, loving, chaotic.

Hitesh waits while Pauline fetches Lord Blackwaite. The heat in here, even in deep autumn, is overwhelming. He can feel it under his skin. Outside the glass, the hills are a cool green and once more he wants to sink into them.

Then it comes from nowhere, the grief that consumes him. He feels like he's drowning, and at the same time, that he is in a void, sealed off from his own life. Manju is gone and nowhere. He will never see his mother again. Never hear her. Even her body is gone – not rotting in the ground but ashes that have dispersed in the wind so that no trace of her remains. She exists only in the memories of her husband and son. Her red cardigan, which is empty. Nothing can change it, and nothing ever will.

The beauty of those hills? It is pointless, because no one person can see them for more than a moment. They have been viewed by a thousand eyes in the snatch of brief lifetimes. The hills' beauty outlasts the human with ease, dispassionately. Those ridges watch them fall like flies when the summer is done, confident no human will live to see their death.

Hitesh finds himself doubled over, choking. It hurts to breathe, if that is what he is doing. Could he stop now – could it stop?

'It's a Saturday, Inspector, and the third time this week that you have—'

Hitesh straightens up, but it is too late; Lord Blackwaite has seen him.

'I'll give you a moment.' Lord Blackwaite turns and shuts the door.

'Fuck.' Hitesh dries his face off, tries to open the orangery doors for air, but finds them locked. *Fuck.*

With deep breaths, he pieces himself back together, thinks of the woman in the grave, of the questions he has, of the enforced blankness that has sustained him since Manju's death. Then he is angry with himself. He has given Lord Blackwaite a wound to probe, and has no doubt that he will. Hitesh gathers himself as quickly as he can, smooths his hair and jumper.

The door reopens and Lord Blackwaite holds a tray, no doubt prepared by Pauline. 'How are you feeling, Inspector?'

'Fine, thank you. I've been under the weather, but I'm all right.'

'Hmm.' Lord Blackwaite puts the tray down and gestures to the rattan armchairs. 'A close friend, or…?'

Hitesh sits uneasily. 'My mother.'

'Ahh.' Lord Blackwaite pours tea from a pot. 'I found it difficult when my own mother passed away.'

Hitesh accepts a cup and saucer.

'One adjusts. I wouldn't say *recovers*, but one adjusts.' Lord Blackwaite sits back. 'The winter will be hard, but it should ease again in spring.'

'Thanks.' Hitesh drinks.

'So, what can I answer for you this time, Detective?'

Hitesh hesitates, still dizzy. 'I believe… I believe you had a fiancée in the sixties. No one has suggested anything – I just need to eliminate lines of inquiry.'

Lord Blackwaite smiles drily. 'Who's been gossiping to you, then? I ought to have written you a list of every woman I've ever come across. It was Lizzie, Elizabeth Millhaven. She was a darling girl.'

'You didn't marry her, though?'

Lord Blackwaite suppresses his retort, and Hitesh can see him replacing it with patience. 'No. No, I spent a good many years wishing I had. But not everything works out the way you plan, Detective. Perhaps you know that. We didn't keep in touch, I believe that's a modern thing, but I can tell you she married a few counties across and died of breast cancer two decades or so ago. One hears about these things in the end.'

'I see.'

'She's not in the garden, I'm afraid. I can't tell you who is.'

'Right. Thank you.'

Hitesh burns his mouth in a rush to finish his tea and leave, but this time Lord Blackwaite escorts him to the front door. 'Take care of yourself, Detective. Let the countryside heal you, if you can. It has wonderful powers.'

'Thank you, yes.' Hitesh leaves as quickly as he can.

At the cottage, Anna finishes unpacking from market. In her mind, she orders and reorders the events of the last few days. Under the thoughts, she feels her hands and back aching. The aching began the day after she moved into Fallow Cottage, and has not stopped since. Idly, she twirls her wrists and pulls her shoulder blades back.

But she ought to stretch properly. So many years' dancing have taught her that self-preservation is daily work.

Anna rolls out her tattered yoga mat in the living room. She does not usually draw the curtains. Today her hand hovers by them, uncertain. She leaves them open.

Lying on the mat, she examines the cracks and cobwebs on the ceiling. The spiders do not bother her, so she has left them where they are, and watches them as she pulls one knee to her chest, then the other, and rolls out the hours that have collected in her spine. She lets her thoughts follow their chosen path, to the places she expects them to go, and to the people she did not.

Hitesh follows the road back down the hill towards the village. The rain starts, a light patter that sits on the fibres of the jumper that was warm enough this morning. He has a mile to cover; if he walks fast, he can be home before the rain reaches his skin. He feels his knee straining. Hitesh does not know what he expected from Lord Blackwaite, but it was not compassion.

His phone rings and he sees it is the station. 'Hello?'

'It's Barnard.'

'I didn't know you were working today.'

'Yeah, but I'm not on nights, so it's not all bad. Got some news on the Blackwaite family.'

'I was just there. What is it?'

'Lord Blackwaite was telling the truth about his mum – she died of natural causes in 1968. His sister, Catherine, who he said moved to Canada—'

'Yes?'

'Well, she probably did, but we can't find a record of it. The Canadian embassy have checked for us too, but a load of records from that period have got lost – nothing was ever digitised.'

'So it could be her?' Hitesh stops walking.

'It isn't her.'

'Why? Are you sure?'

'Because Lord Blackwaite's DNA sample finally got logged along with the victim's, and there's no overlap.'

'They're unrelated.' Another possibility evaporates, and the woman is still as much a cipher as the day Anna Deerin dug her up.

Hitesh looks at the mizzling sky, then turns and walks the other way.

*July 1967*

Is there anything more female than waiting?

The grass outside the kitchen window is parched yellow. On the counter is the beef I am meant to be mincing. The blood smells old and dank. Not fresh like from the human body. I feed it into the hand grinder.

It isn't love. That would be absurd. I knew Timothy McArthur for only a few hours before we had sex. But it is like I have been shaken awake to my own life; the sense I have of being trapped has intensified, and I can feel the fresh air and the suffocation at the same time.

The handle of the grinder is stiff and I lean my weight down onto it.

Timothy has promised he will wait for me in the woods at the bottom of the hill this afternoon. The first time we tried it, he got delayed and I waited there for an hour, thinking he had got lost or decided not to come. When he eventually arrived, I nearly cried with relief.

This time I hope he will be waiting when I get there, and I count down the hours on the clock. But of course, Mother or Father might always stop me at the last minute, ask me to perform a chore or an errand that I cannot convincingly offer a reason to delay. Will Timothy wait for me then? Or will he stay ten minutes and take himself back to Cirencester? Will the possibility of sex keep him waiting, perhaps even the possibility of me – is that too much to hope for?

The handle moves suddenly and the beef splatters through into the bowl beneath the funnel. Red gristle spits up onto my apron, onto my cheek. It is repulsive and compelling.

I have thought about telling Mother. I am not used to

keeping secrets from her, and when I see her marching about performing her chores with that loving efficiency, blouse sleeves rolled back and pinny tied on, I cannot help feeling shame. But I can no more tell her than walk on water.

Every time I see the new blue-and-white-striped curtains of the dining room I smile to myself, and feel a twinge of pleasure and of fear.

Hitesh raises his hand to knock on the cottage door. He sees the gouges in the wood and calls out her name instead.

'Anna? It's Hitesh.'

The chickens cluck petulantly from their coop, asking why he won't feed them. He calls her name again.

'I'm here.'

Hitesh jumps. Anna is behind him, in leggings and a heavy fleece zipped up to her chin, with a bucket in one hand.

'It isn't Lord Blackwaite's mother or sister. No common DNA.'

'But it could be his fiancée?'

'Perhaps. He assures me she died of cancer, far from Upper Magna. We'll check though. I thought you'd want to know.'

'I do.' Anna nods.

'I'd have called, if you had a phone,' he explains, suddenly unsure of his presence. 'Sorry, I shouldn't have come.'

'Have you ever fed chickens?' Anna asks. She opens the door of the coop and the clucking grows frenzied. She takes a handful of grain from the bucket and throws it in. The chickens dive forward before the pellets hit the ground.

She offers Hitesh the bucket. 'Take a handful, here, then put your hand out – flat.'

The grains are cool on his palm. He crouches; the birds lunge forward, unafraid of him, pecking his hand so forcefully that he almost drops their food. He laughs.

'Can you tell them apart?'

'Like they're people.'

'I think – I want to know who might have been out here,' Hitesh offers another handful to the birds, 'apart from the Blackwaite family. Who would be in the woods, in the cottage – why would anybody be here?'

Anna empties the bucket into a low feeder. 'It's a place for when you don't want to be seen. Even more so since the cottage wasn't occupied when she was killed.'

'People meeting secretly? An affair?'

'Maybe. Pauline said there have been dozens of staff at the hall over the years. Plenty of them vulnerable.'

She walks round the back of the cottage, Hitesh trailing behind, and lets them in through the kitchen. They wash their hands and sit at the cheap, rickety table. Anna offers tea and Hitesh declines. 'I didn't come to make work.'

It is cold in the cottage. He rests his hand on the radiator next to him, but it is barely lukewarm.

'Maybe I'm following my prejudices in assuming this woman is something to do with the Hall.' Hitesh follows the train of his thoughts. 'Maybe it's just chance, or another connection we haven't spotted yet.'

'Maybe. But it feels like she belongs to Fallow.' Until now, Anna had not articulated this feeling, even to herself. Now she says it, she knows something of it has been creeping in her marrow, growing all the while in certainty.

'Mm.'

Hitesh is distracted, and Anna wonders what has happened since that morning. 'I'll get you a towel.'

Hitesh is about to refuse, then realises the rain has gone through to his skin. Manju would have scolded him for forgetting a coat, fast in her belief that one caught a cold when damp. *It's a virus, Mum, you can't catch it from rainwater.*

Anna goes to her bedroom, still darkened by the chipboard window. She examines what she is feeling, lets it sit there. She goes back to Hitesh and hands him a towel and a jumper. 'It should fit.'

He does not ask whose it was. She boils the kettle while he takes off his old jumper and puts on this new one. When she turns around, he has folded the towel neatly on the back of the chair.

'Did you go up to the Hall?'

'Yeah. Lord Blackwaite was pleasant, for once.' He accepts a mug of tea. 'I was… off colour.'

'Tell me about her.'

'Really? Am I that easily read?'

Anna laughs. 'You have a beard, not a mask.' She pauses. 'Have you talked to anyone about your mother?'

'Clearly I'm a worse copper than I thought.' He looks at his mug. 'Not really. Dad – Dad is a dick, and he's been widowed. Friends… I don't know. I talked to Manju when I needed someone.'

The jumper Anna has given him smells of the outdoors, of her, of fresh air and chlorophyll.

'Do you plan never to talk about her?'

'It's less about planning. A lack of opportunity, maybe.'

Anna waits, an invitation.

'Mum was… kind. Loving. I never saw her angry – properly angry, I mean. And she was an Indian woman of a particular generation; she did everything that was expected of her – cared, looked after me and Dad, and the house. Worked part-time as well. I think she lived a life that you're trying not to. Pleasing people.'

'Was she happy?'

'I think so. I think she accepted it. I don't know if she had a choice not to. I hope she was happy.' He can feel it

105

burning in his ribs again. 'I don't know – you don't need this—'

'I asked.'

Outside the rain picks up again, hurling itself against the kitchen windows. The room becomes colder still.

'I don't know how I got to thirty-five, and I could leave London with no one to say goodbye to.'

'It's easy to do if you aren't paying attention.'

There are plenty of single beds in Upper Magna, Hitesh thinks. Lord Blackwaite. Reverend Watts. Perhaps they are where he is heading.

'What about you? Don't you miss your friends, your parents?' he asks her.

'No one I couldn't live without. I see my parents sometimes – visit them. Birthdays and things. But I was always training or performing; they got used to not seeing me. They're happy to love from a distance.'

Anna knows that this sounds cold. She has always been able to make friends, but always been able to shed them when she needed. She wonders again if there is something wrong with her.

'What would have happened if you hadn't been single, young, no dependents? Would you have been able to come to Magna?' Hitesh frowns.

'If I had been your mother?' Anna asks. 'No. If I hadn't been white. And if I had been gay, or trans, or an immigrant, or disabled. Maybe even if I had been a little fatter. I wouldn't have been allowed near the garden. I know that. I know what I benefit from.'

Hitesh pulls the sleeves of the jumper right down. He has got chilled without realising. He looks at Anna, without an ounce of fat on her body, and she does not seem to feel it.

'Is it as different as you thought it would be?' he asks. 'A life out here, not having to answer to anyone?'

'I'm not sure. Sometimes it doesn't look radical enough, when I try to see it from the outside. But then the point is not to see it through others' eyes any more.'

'It seems radical to me. The self-sufficiency, the isolation. It's monk-like.'

The rain beats steadily on the window. Anna looks at Hitesh's hands on the kitchen table, still and folded.

His voice is quiet and urgent. 'What if there isn't anything underneath, once you've stopped having to please? Once you've worked out who you are, separate from what you've been taught? You strip away all you've learned about pleasing and how to see and think, but that's how we're made, human to human. What if there is nothing underneath? What if you dig and dig and there isn't anything – not even bones?'

Anna feels the shock of her thoughts from his mouth.

The jumper belonged to a fellow dancer, left behind after a night together. It fits Hitesh. He has a young man's body, Anna thinks, but a face that has been worn down.

She tells him what she answers herself. 'Then I'll know.'

Anna dreams of dancing. Her legs are turned out at the hips, that unnatural position so natural to her. She can swing them high, low, turn on a penny. She sweeps her arm downwards, nearly brushes the floor with her fingers, the stage which smells like soot. The gauze of her skirt drifts over the movement of her body, is pulled this way and that by the grace of movement. The bodice pinches but she can barely feel it in the heat and elation. Her bent waist contracts and pulls her upright, arms trailing, as though her body is beyond her control. But it is not.

The orchestra reaches its crescendo, leading her, willing her, carrying her through pain and joy. She carves an arc through the air, crosses impossible space with a leap. The audience in the dark beyond cannot hear how hard she is breathing and the thud as she rolls through her foot to land. To them, she is born to move as light. She smiles, transitions to the next step, partakes of their rapture. The music trails, becomes tinny. The shrill minor of the violins pulls up, abrupt, changes, scrapes, scutters, begins to knock, to bang, over

over

over

Anna wakes covered in sweat. She listens and listens and waits until she is sure the dark is really empty.

'Justine, lovely Justine, thank you.' Paul Wolsey accepts a cup of tea from his PA.

'Thanks,' Hitesh murmurs as she places his on the desk. The PA retreats, hips swaying. Hitesh suspects she is aware of how Wolsey's eyes follow, and wonders if the effect is intentional.

'So, Detective Mistry, scandal in Magna! A body.' Wolsey smiles.

'That's right. I'm speaking to all the members of the Trust. I understand you might have some insight into the estate – perhaps a sense of where we should be looking for answers.'

Wolsey rolls his eyes. 'I had hoped that was something the *police* might have some insight into.'

'We don't have a magic wand – we talk to people. I presume you had a close look at Fallow Hall's records when you set up the Trust?'

'Naturally.'

'And did you come across anything of concern?'

'Nothing undue. I've taken over a number of care homes in my time, and older businesses always have something awry. But Blackwaite had done a decent job, all in all. Some minor administrative fixes to be made, but that's it.'

'The Hall has been open to visitors for a few decades now – I presume there was an accident or complaint log of some kind?'

'Oh, absolutely. And I looked at it in quite some detail. Part of the risk assessment we made. I insisted on indemnity insurance against any past claims. But to be honest, no one's done anything worse than break an ankle in the last forty years. No mysterious disappearances to tempt you with,' Wolsey chuckles, lining his mug up on the coaster.

The businessman's office is a pleasant room at the back of the flagship care home he was pleased to walk Hitesh through, greeting staff and charming residents as he went. He has a Mac and a filing cabinet and chintz curtains around the windows that admit a pleasant burst of light. Wolsey is a pillar of the community.

'The thing that's been at the back of *my* mind: that cottage Anna Deerin is in, where the body was found – when I was a teenager, it was the deserted shack you'd go to for a joint or a shag. Half of Magna's teenagers lost their cherry there, myself included.' Wolsey laughs to see Hitesh's discomfort. 'No need to be a snowflake, officer.'

'I'm sure the Trust appreciates your straight-talking,' Hitesh says drily.

'I know when to be honest, and I know when to be earnest, Mistry. What I mean is that if a lovers' tiff or a druggies' argument went awry, that'd be the place it happened. With a bit of luck, you pop the body in the ground and no one finds it for a few decades. Not until Ms Deerin picks up a shovel, anyway.'

A pillar of the community.

'Right,' Hitesh switches tack, 'and what happens to Fallow when Lord Blackwaite dies? He has no children to inherit the property.'

'Quite. He had a bout of high blood pressure a few years

back and I suppose it must have set him to thinking – nothing certain except death and taxes, etc. That's when he approached a few of us about setting up the Trust. Getting a structure in place, stealing a march on mortality, if such a thing is possible.'

Outside the window, a resident moves slowly across the courtyard, arm in arm with a vacantly smiling carer.

'Don't you find it odd that Lord Blackwaite didn't marry?' Hitesh continues.

Wolsey guffaws. 'Clearly you aren't lawfully wedded. A lucky miss, if you ask me.'

'I was under the impression it was what the gentry did – marry, pass on the estate and the name. I can't imagine it's too hard finding someone willing to marry you if you have a country pile and a title?'

The businessman reflects. 'Mm, true. He's never said so directly, but I get the impression he had his heart broken once, and never quite recovered. Rather *romantic.*'

Hitesh ignores the disdain in Wolsey's voice. 'Was it Elizabeth Millhaven?'

Wolsey tuts. 'Callow youth. I might be older than you, but I'm certainly not old enough to know who Blackwaite's *amour* was.'

'Any staff problems you're aware of, current or historic?'

'Any more straws to clutch at?'

Hitesh stands and pulls his coat on. 'Right. Thanks for your time, anyway, Mr Wolsey.'

'Very good; stop by again, Officer,' Wolsey chuckles. 'Justine? Will you see Detective Mistry out? And ask Wilson to check on our new resident in room eight – I didn't like the state of that armchair, she won't be comfortable in that.'

Hitesh can hear Wolsey humming to himself as he boots up his computer and returns to work. When he gets outside,

Hitesh texts PC Barnard. *Run check for an Elizabeth Millhaven – probably under a married name now, possibly deceased.*

*Yes boss. Wi-fi down. Will add to list. Coffee machine also down – want anything from Costa at petrol station?*

Hitesh smiles despite himself.

'We're hiring again.' Pauline rolls her eyes. 'I'm too old for this gala business.'

'We both know that's not true.' Anna raises her eyebrows. 'Anyway, don't you always use the same recruitment firm?'

'Such innocence. There will never be enough cleaners. It's not a job people *want*. It's a job people do. And this is a one-off job – they'll spend half the pay on the petrol to get out here and back.'

Anna makes a note of the width of the mantelpiece. 'So who will you get?' She crosses to the double doors of the ballroom and asks Pauline to hold the end of the tape measure. 'Separate garlands, or a single large one to run across the top? I assume these will stay open during the gala?'

The housekeeper squints up at the frame, envisioning. 'A single one, I should think. There'll be someone who needs the work. Always has been, eventually.'

'One of your tragic casual cleaning women?' Anna ventures, and Pauline harumphs at her.

'Yes, I expect so.'

The women move across the room, measuring with care around heavy gilt frames and mirrors.

'You need to find a husband, Anna, my love.'

'I don't need a husband, Pauline.'

'It's not natural to live alone in that spidery old cottage. You need somebody to go home to. I have Mr Pauline; I don't spend all my time here, with all due respect to His Lordship.'

'I have the chickens.'

'Sometimes, I wish Mr Pauline was a chicken,' the housekeeper muses, and their giggling fills the dormant ballroom.

'I suspect a husband might be more trouble than he's worth,' Anna says.

'You might be right. I remembered one of my sad women.'

'Mm?' Anna says, pencil in her mouth as she measures. She feels the hairs on her neck rise.

'Annette. She was a miserable one, God bless her.'

'Annette what?'

Pauline looks archly at her. 'Waring. See, I remembered.'

'Why was she miserable?' Anna asks, and pretends to be interested in her notebook.

'Well, that was its own mystery. She was always crying – we caught her at it all the time. Whenever you went into a room she was cleaning and she wasn't expecting you – eyes all red. We thought she must be, you know – pregnant. But the whole season went by and she never got any bigger, straggly creature that she was. So I suppose it couldn't have been that.'

'I suppose not. But her husband was no good?'

Pauline shrugs expansively. 'Not a husband. I don't think it was anything so formal. We'd become very liberal by the eighties, you know. Boyfriend.' She lowers her voice: 'A terrible shit.'

Anna raises her eyebrows again.

'Goodness knows what he was up to, but he phoned the house most days, demanding to talk to her. None of us liked that. But then one day, he turned up here, out of the blue. Started yelling at her.'

'About what?'

'Haven't a clue. We all assumed it was something to do with drugs.'

'What happened to her?'

112

'The Virgin Mary came down and carried her away. No, my love, she just didn't come back one day. Happened all the time. Like I said, cleaners.'

'Do you want one?'

'I'm all right, thanks.' Hitesh sips his pint and Barnard withdraws the pork scratchings. Hitesh can see the series of thoughts passing over his junior's face: has he caused offence? If his boss is Muslim, then why is he drinking? Hitesh feels the nagging weight of explanation; I was raised in a Hindu household, I haven't believed in anything since childhood, it still seems strange to eat flesh. But it is tiring; he does not want to explain himself.

He moves the conversation on. 'Where are the farm equipment thefts at?'

'Caught a couple of guys, actually, on a traffic stop. Willers noticed seed hoppers on the back seat.' Barnard seems to know what seed hoppers are.

'You got them back to the farmer?'

'Yeah, it was a good job actually.'

'That's good, that's good news.'

'And the Fallow case?' Barnard asks.

'Still nothing substantial.'

'Does that happen often? Like, it just peters out?'

Hitesh shrugs reluctantly. 'Yeah, it can do. Did you find Elizabeth Millhaven?'

'Not yet. Some of the checks still need to be done manually.'

'Mm.'

There is the hubbub of sociability all round. Most of the Cirencester force is at the pub, half of them vaping heartily in spite of red-ringed posters. Hitesh wonders who can be on duty tonight and how everyone is meant to be getting home at the end of the night, in a place with no public transport.

Everyone here seems to have known each other for years. They are trading stories, asking after one another's families, cracking in-jokes. It is a sea of white faces, even whiter than it was in London. At his old station, he, the Somali hijabi, and the Ghanaian officer had become friends, almost despite themselves.

Barnard pulls him over to stand at the bar with a couple of the other young officers. He lets their easy buzz drift past him, dips in where he can so that he does not seem standoffish. Work, relationships, Netflix, force gossip. Perhaps Hitesh needs to try harder; if he is to make a life here, then surely he cannot hold them at arm's length forever?

'What's the local gym? Running on these roads is doing my knees in.'

'For the love of God, don't use the police one in Cirencester, boss. You'll get athlete's foot just looking at it.'

'Trust Barnard, he'd know.'

'Try Malmesbury, that's all right.'

Their circle banters on harmlessly. Then one of them, Simons, touches on politics, then it is only a matter of seconds before it becomes protests, then stop and search. 'You know who's a wrong'un; we aren't just using it willy-nilly like the papers seem to think.'

'It was overused in London. On Black people,' Hitesh says.

His colleagues look uncomfortable, the same way they did in London. He knows he should say more, and he knows they will avoid him if he does. Before he can decide, they have whisked the conversation on, past difficulty. And as ever, he has not done enough, has only stepped away instead of stepped in. Poor Barnard looks faintly embarrassed by his boss.

'Do you play cricket, Mistry?' one of the sergeants asks. 'The force has a team in summer.'

Sport is safe territory for them all.

'Yeah, I was bowler for my old team.'

'Good man. We'll have you then.'

The evening passes lightly and meaninglessly, with the assurance of the pond skater crossing a body of water; the tension will hold, and it will never fall into the deep water that is underneath.

It is hot. The sun shines with rare fury on the October afternoon, and Anna finds herself peeling off her coat and standing at her stall with only a short-sleeved blouse and the warmth on her skin. She can see the other stallholders doing the same, and the market-goers stripping off jackets, stuffing them under arms, or into paper bags full of purchases. She smiles to herself.

Then Anna sees him. She has been looking since morning, and now catches sight of him moving among the villagers. Some stop to talk to him now, and she watches the way he listens. He, too, has been reduced to a T-shirt.

Eventually Hitesh reaches Anna's stall. 'What is this weather? I thought autumn in the country was all about "mists and mellow fruitfulness".'

'Sorry, some false advertising on our part.' She smiles, then she turns and calls to Alex Johnson on the neighbouring stall to watch her own for a few minutes. She turns back to Hitesh. 'I need to talk to you.'

Hitesh follows her as she walks away from the crowded market green, towards the church and the stream. Without a fleece or coat, she is even smaller than he had realised. There are tiny flowers embroidered on her blouse collar. By the time they stop walking, they are both sweating, and Anna leads them under the lychgate of the church, where they stand in the shade.

'What is it?'

115

'I went up to Fallow Hall and spoke to Pauline again. There was a woman named Annette Waring in the eighties. She cleaned the Hall during one of the peak seasons.'

Hitesh tilts his head and thinks for a moment. He can see the note in his book. 'One of the parishioners at the bridge morning said they had a cleaner called Annie back then. Something about drugs.'

Anna's face opens. 'Pauline said the same. Her boyfriend was a piece of work. They all thought he was using.'

'Was Annette?'

'Pauline didn't say.'

Hitesh looks resigned. 'She might not have been. Plenty of women end up in prison supporting a partner's habit.'

Anna tells Hitesh all she knows, about Pauline's unnoticed and uncared-for women.

'Did they report Annette's boyfriend to the police at the time?'

'Apparently it wasn't the done thing – and they didn't think the police would care about someone like Annette.'

Hitesh looks pained. 'We've always liked our victims pure. And one day she just didn't come back?'

'Apparently.'

He takes his phone out and makes a note of what she has told him. 'Paul Wolsey said the cottage was used by addicts when it was deserted. Maybe he was close to the mark. I'll look for Annette in the system – she's not listed as a local missing person, but she might still have a record.'

Anna nods. 'I should get back to the stall.'

She leaves the shelter of the lychgate, but Hitesh calls her back, his tone lower than before. 'Anna – did you go up to the Hall to find out more?'

'Yes.'

'Don't. It's not your job. You're putting yourself at risk.'

Anna is standing on the path, in the full glare of the sun. She lifts her hand to shield her eyes. 'Would you have found out about Annette if I hadn't?'

'I don't know, but it's not worth it if you get hurt.'

'That's my choice to make.'

She is so tiny and so immovable. Like a limpet that would resist the whole force of the sea. He starts to speak, stops, starts again. 'I can't physically stop you, but just – it's my conscience you're on, okay?'

'I'll be careful.'

Hitesh looks at her with weariness and fear.

*When I was waiting outside the electronics shop, I noticed that the door did not close properly after each customer. Because the door did not shut, the bell did not always ring to alert the sales staff when a new customer entered. After watching for some time, I decided to slip in. The bell did not ring, so I was able to place two small radios in my handbag before exiting the shop. Someone must have spotted me, because shortly after, the sales assistant ran out and stopped me. I sincerely regret what I did.*

— Annette Waring, sworn statement
given at Cirencester police station,
2.25 p.m., 25 August 1983

'It isn't her.'

'What do you mean?'

'The statement – she would never have spoken like that. And she could barely write. She's said it in her own way, hasn't she, and someone's taken it down and made it all neat and nice.'

'It's likely,' Hitesh admits.

'It's what happened,' says Nick. 'Tidied away so she didn't bother no one, even on paper.'

Hitesh sits uncomfortably on the garden wall. 'Are you sure you don't want to go to a cafe or something?'

'I've gotta finish this job today.' Annette's brother is re-plumbing a bathroom in the period cottage they perch in front of. 'Is this – is this to do with that body you found a few villages over?'

'I don't want to worry you. We just know Annette worked at Fallow Hall for a while.'

'Yeah, and it was around the time she disappeared.' Nick is suddenly angry. 'It's taken you this bloody long to find her. I knew something had happened to her – I knew it.'

Hitesh reaches a hand out to calm him. 'It might not be her. We don't know yet. Tell me about her, tell me about the last time you saw her.'

'Eighty-four. She was cleaning still, where people would still take her. Her health was poor – and her mental state, you know.'

'Did she have a boyfriend?'

'Yes,' Nick spits, 'Mitch. Worthless. It was for him, all the stealing and the petty stuff. He was like a leech on her. One of a series. Even came to me looking for her when she disappeared. I told him where to go.'

'He didn't know what happened to her either?'

'No, useless cunt. Said he'd gone to meet her after work but she never turned up.'

'Did you tell the police she'd gone?'

Nick shakes his head, grudgingly. 'Didn't see the point. She disappeared, she reappeared. I thought she'd come back eventually, until she didn't.' The tears drip down his cheek, disbelieving. 'I didn't make the connection with that body at Magna.'

Hitesh rests a hand gingerly on the plumber's shoulder. 'It might not be her. Let me get someone to check the DNA of the remains against yours. Put your mind to rest – one way or the other.'

'Ha,' Nick is mirthless, 'we aren't related.'

'I'm sorry? On the statement, you're listed next of kin, as her brother?'

'I was and I wasn't. Fostering. We were both in care and got placed with the same long-term family. Ten years together. Not blood, but when you don't have anything, you find something.'

Hitesh looks at Nick, his flushed skin, thin hair grey around the temples, and the belly of someone who lives on what he needs now, not trusting in the promise of tomorrow. The workman is openly crying.

'I'm really sorry about Annette. Whether it's her or not. She deserved better.'

'Fuck off,' Nick snaps. 'You're only investigating because you don't know who that body is. If you knew it was Annie, you'd scribble a note saying it was an old druggie and move on. She wasn't worth a thing to anyone when she was alive – no one was interested in helping her.'

Hitesh doesn't say anything. He waits while Nick takes deep breaths.

'She had too big a heart, Annie did. She never learned to stick up for herself.' Nick wipes his nose on his T-shirt.

Anna breathes her mother in and wonders how a human can smell so much like a cake, all vanilla and butter. She lets her face rest in her mother's biscuit-brown hair. Eventually, her mother releases her shoulders and holds her at arm's length to look at her.

'Darling, you've got so tanned in the sun! The outdoor life is suiting you.'

'It's suiting me very well, Mum. Happy birthday.'

'I can't believe you came all this way.' Her mother's eyes glisten, and Anna finds herself leaning in to hug her again.

'I've been a bad daughter, it's the least I could do,' she murmurs, and her mother gives her an affectionate bat on the arm.

'You're here now, and what a lovely surprise.'

They are standing outside an Italian trattoria in Canterbury, and Anna's father wears the same proud smile he has had on since he picked his daughter up from the train station.

'Oh, you are pleased with yourself, Richard, aren't you?' Caroline giggles, and pulls him down to give him a peck on the cheek. 'What a lovely surprise to have organised. Come on then, do we have a reservation?'

Anna follows her parents inside. It has been five months since she last came home, and she notices the tiny progressions of late middle age. Her father's shoulders stoop a little deeper than they did. Caroline, never athletic, now moves more awkwardly, her right hip pulling under her Joules dress. It is like a bow being drawn across Anna's chest.

A waiter ushers them to a table with a linen tablecloth and a candle in a wine bottle, and hands them menus, but Richard and Caroline can barely keep their eyes off their daughter. Anna gives her mother the wreath she twisted together from dried lavender and rosemary.

'It's going straight next to the breakfast bar. When did you get so clever with your hands?'

'I always liked crafts, didn't I?'

Caroline chuckles. 'Hardly, my love. When you were ten, I spent a fortune on a little sewing machine for your birthday. I don't think you ever even opened the box.'

Anna frowns. 'I don't remember that.'

Richard orders a nice bottle of wine and pours them each a glass. 'To Caroline. And to Anna's unexpected second career.'

They raise their glasses.

'Tell us all about everything,' her mother implores.

The waiter brings antipasti, and Anna tells them what she can. That the stall at the market is going well. The names of the fruits and vegetables she is growing. She describes the cycles the plants move through, the rhythm of the week, and she can see their polite incomprehension.

'Gosh, it sounds like just as much work as when you were dancing, poppet. You really do pick these jobs.' Her father shakes his head affectionately.

Anna asks them about their lives in retirement, insurance and teaching now nightmares from long ago. They describe the lives of family and friends, the events of day trips, and she knows they are happy, but that she could make them happier. They drink up every moment of their daughter, and she pours as much of herself as she can.

'Well, it's lovely to see you eating something more than salad or soup these days,' her father says when their main courses arrive.

Anna swallows and nods.

Over *melanzane* and *orecchiette*, they reminisce about her childhood.

'Do you remember when we went to Mallorca? You were only about eight and you performed that little show for the other guests on the hotel terrace? They were in raptures. I think that waiter, Juan, would have adopted you if he could have.' Her mother is misty-eyed.

Anna moves the pasta around her plate. 'When I was little, did I do anything that wasn't ballet? Was I interested in nature or anything?'

'I mean, you loved Panda, but you never took any interest in what you saw when we were walking him.' Her mother tucks her hair behind her ears and screws up her face as she thinks back. 'We did encourage you to try other things, in case the ballet didn't work out. But I can't say you ever really warmed to any of them.'

Her father nods. 'Just ballet, poppet, and reading.'

'You've always been focused, darling, if that's what you're getting at,' her mother explains.

Anna hesitates, and her father notices. 'It's part of who you are – a bit of intensity, that's what all the greats have, isn't it? Nothing to worry about,' Richard says.

Anna smiles. 'Nothing to worry about.'

When at last they have finished their tiramisu, Anna says she will get the restaurant to call her a taxi back to the station.

'No, Anna, surely you're staying the night?' Her mother takes her hand. 'It's hours on the train, and you've only just got here.'

'I couldn't find anyone to look after the chickens in the end,' Anna says apologetically. 'I'm really sorry. I've had such a lovely evening,' she reassures them.

They try half-heartedly to convince her, but they know before they start that they have lost. 'Maybe, soon, we could come and see the garden? We can stay in a local B and B, if there's no space in the cottage?' her mother asks.

'Of course,' Anna says, 'I'd like that.' She pauses. 'You know I love you guys, don't you?'

Caroline's face crumples for a moment. 'Of course we do, darling. We've never doubted that.'

'We worry about you, sometimes. Not being able to call,' Richard says.

'I know. I'm sorry. It's very quiet out there though, nothing much to worry about.'

'We'd be happy to get you a phone, if money's a bit tight?'

Anna fudges something about signal and changes the subject. She feels ashamed.

*

Annette Waring barely exists on paper. Hitesh has been searching. There are arrest files for the petty crimes that were never enough for her to go to jail for, each with a statement that, as her brother had complained, was not in her own voice. He finds a single sheet stating that she has aged out of the care system; the rest has been lost, including her birth certificate. When Hitesh asks them about her, the parishioners who had mentioned Annette at bridge morning were surprised to learn her surname.

He submits a warrant requesting personnel files from Fallow Hall. Lord Blackwaite sends back a terse note that maintenance and cleaning staff were paid 'cash in hand' until 2000.

Hitesh convinces Nick to file a missing persons report and promises to keep looking.

Barnard finds that an Elizabeth Millhaven married and became Elizabeth Jones. Between call-outs, he begins to run down the list of one hundred and fifty-eight feasible Elizabeth Joneses.

Upper Magna passes through October, creeps forward on crisp-leaved toes, drags the damp and gloom of November in its wake. The stone cottages turn a mottled, ailing grey; the narrow roads choke with Land Rovers twice a day, no one daring to walk any distance now. On Saturdays, the markets are subdued; Magna-ites scuttle between the stalls buying supplies before seeking shelter again, leaving the stallholders to shiver.

Hitesh runs most days and returns home cold, aching and bitter. He visits the other trust members. Watts. Graceful Eloise Fitzhugh. Michael Caulfield, who was once a fine judge, but who Hitesh suspects now has early dementia. None of them can tell him anything new, anything about Annette Waring. He keeps looking for her in all the places he knows.

And he follows the other names that Watts' parishioners have given him, and one by one, finds them living and well, or dead and briefly explained. He begins to pick up other cases, helps investigate an aggravated burglary in Cirencester. One weekend, Hitesh travels home to see Darshan for Diwali, and they sit together in silence, watching the news. Later, while his father is pottering downstairs, Hitesh goes up to his parents' room and sits on the end of the bed. The room is exactly the same as it has always been. He pretends for a moment that Manju is there, somewhere out of view. Briefly, he is comforted, then the emptiness is weightier than before. He goes to his childhood room and sleeps like he is dead. Before he leaves, he arranges food deliveries for his father and fixes the slates that are threatening to come off the roof. They argue about Darshan getting more help, and part without arranging for Hitesh to come again.

Anna works outdoors in the short hours of the light. There are many miserable days when her fingers freeze, damp inside her gloves. The garden is fallow in the true sense now, stripped of fruit and greenery. Instead there is mud and maintenance, the cleaning out of the chicken coop, turning the compost heap and mending fences. There are at least the evergreens to keep her company, and the ivy to reach out and welcome her with its tender curls.

She spends many hours in the kitchen, making preserves and Christmas cakes, chocolate logs and mince pies to sell. Her fingers bleed as she weaves mistletoe and holly into wreaths. From the kitchen window, Anna can see the wintering earth, Persephone kept deep in Hades, and the empty grave of the Fallow sister. In the morgue, her remains are unclaimed and alone.

Sometimes she finds herself looking through the kitchen

window at the path. Every so often – perhaps one day in ten – she sees Hitesh approaching, dark head bent down. Then he looks up and through the window and smiles, or calls her name so that she knows it is him. He comes to talk, sometimes about the body and often not, and though he does not say so, she knows he is checking she is safe. Then Hitesh leaves, and Anna has only the chickens for company. She swings through the arcs that have come to characterise her thoughts. I am feckless for having left a life that kept me warm and safe, when Annette and many others never had the chance for such a life at all. I have caused my ageing parents pain. I would have gone mad if I had stayed, sixty long years stretching ahead of me, and never knowing if the husband and children I am yoked to are the ones I have chosen or the ones I have bent myself to fit. I am alone. I am in danger. I can wear heavy boots and warm fleeces and feel every inch of me on this glorious earth and know that I have chosen it. I will find her name.

Slowly, the end of November approaches, and with it, traces of festivity begin to peek out. The butcher in the village takes orders for Christmas turkeys, the cafes are trimmed with tinsel, and the tree erected on the green. At St Mary's, endless Advent and carol services are hustled in between the bridge mornings; the primary school rehearses for the upcoming Nativity. The sweetest, roundest-cheeked pupils are chosen to be Mary and Joseph. Gloria and Geoff Finchley cajole and josh coins from all they meet on Magna's high street, and despite the inward sighs of their victims, change the lives of a pair of Syrian children they have never met and never will.

The market revives, buoyed by stalls selling glühwein and anglaspel. Alex Johnson has got engaged, and talks loudly about his 'missus' to anyone who comes to the pottery stall.

Reverend Watts catches Hitesh outside the post office one

day and invites him to walk David with him. The two men talk
and there is a loosening of their being alone.

On creeps winter, on creeps Christmas.

It is the fifth of December, and the gala is in four days.


'Tables through to the dining room, if you please. Take care
with the tight turn at the end of the corridor.'

Fallow Hall is lit up with activity. Lord Blackwaite strides
through the corridors, master of his domain, in command of
the troops that have rallied to him.

There are caterers, vintners, deliveries of table linen and
cutlery. Pauline has hired two Polish women, Ewa and Renata,
and in their tabards and jeans, they will spend days cleaning
every room the guests will see. Starting in the hall, working
through the library, dining room, drawing room, ground-
and first-floor bathrooms, gallery and salon, they will scrub
and hoover and brighten, mostly silent, occasionally chatting.
Tomorrow, Renata will bring her ten-year-old, who will sit
quietly playing games on his mother's phone, eating crisps and
apples.

Fallow responds to Lord Blackwaite's touch, rouses itself
to something of its former glory. It remembers when it had
servants who slept in the attic, when the kitchen was full of
bodies and voices, labouring to feed and water their masters.
Like a creature waking from a long hibernation, Fallow
stretches its limbs and flicks out its claws one by one.

Pauline is Lord Blackwaite's able lieutenant, and she brings
Anna to meet him in his study during a lull in the mustering,
deposits her there, and with a final flourish turns back to the
melee.

'Good afternoon, Lord Blackwaite.' Anna is soft-voiced,
but he can see the work she has already undertaken, notes and
samples in her arms.

'Ms Deerin, thank you for coming.' Lord Blackwaite puts down the lists he has been consulting. 'My mother organised these galas before I was born, but I must say that when she talked about it she made it sound quite effortless.'

He grimaces theatrically, but looks younger than Anna has ever seen him. There is colour to his skin, an almost feverish light in his eyes. He takes the arrangement of flowers she is carrying and places it on the coffee table, then stands back to admire it.

'Excellent – and this is a sample of the table decorations?'

'That's right. I'll do twelve, one for each table, and swags for the front entrance columns. Do you want anything for the console tables in the hall?'

'More of these, along with some hellebore and mistletoe wreaths for the internal doors. Is that too much for one person? I know you don't have anyone to help you.'

'It can be done.' Anna jots her instructions in a notebook.

'Thank you. You don't know how welcome it is to have someone I can depend on. Fallow needs people like you.'

'It's a pleasure to be able to help.'

'Now, Ms Deerin, you may regret that, since I have a favour to ask of you. Please, sit down – I'm so used to being on my feet at the moment. How rude of me.' He ushers her to the sofa.

Anna sits and traces a silk flourish in the upholstery. The whole study smells of dust and jasmine, of the piling-up of years and lives into the fine patina that speaks of itself with quiet, fierce, unrepressed authority.

'Now, as cottage gardener, you're a representative of Fallow. Not in the formal sense, but as someone in its orbit, working with the estate – and a wonderful representative, I might add; I hear so many good things whenever I'm in the village. I wondered if you might act as a sort of informal steward on

Friday? Make sure everyone has what they need; knows the way to the facilities; no one is left without someone to talk to – that sort of thing.'

'Making people feel welcome – at home?'

'Precisely – that's exactly what I meant.' Lord Blackwaite is pleased by her responsiveness. 'There's a future for you here at Fallow, you know.'

'I hope so, I really do,' Anna says, and he nods, pleased. 'Don't worry about seeing me out, Lord Blackwaite. I'll bring the flowers up on Friday morning. I can hang them myself.'

'Simply brilliant. I'm very grateful, Ms Deerin.' He smiles warmly, and there is something charming about seeing him so energised.

As Anna threads her way through the house, she has to avoid deliveries and piles of equipment that have been stacked in the corridors, the plastic crates and cardboard boxes incongruous against mahogany and Wedgwood. She can hear Pauline issuing orders from the drawing room, and the steady hum of voices organising themselves.

Anna reaches the entrance hall, and finding it empty, pauses to exhale. Behind her, the staircase has been polished to a high shine by Ewa and Renata, but in front of her is the wallpaper that is rough and psoriatic with age. Anna reaches her hand out to feel it. She cannot tell if she is overawed or disappointed by Fallow Hall, sometimes. From the garden, it is ever-present, a god on the horizon. To be inside it and see it rendered solid and almost knowable, for it to exist for others, is a strange thing.

Anna checks that she is still alone, then examines the walls of the entrance hall. Each of them is thick with the history of the house. There are etchings of the grounds; portraits of inhabitants; shields and medals and tokens; lush wall hangings from the Middle East; curved scimitars from a warrior race, by implication, conquered. This house is beautiful and as much a face as that which Anna wears to market, a mythmaking shaped by its inhabitants, and which shapes them in turn.

Anna wonders what it was like for Lord Blackwaite growing up here, and in a niche, she finds a cluster of photographs. One is of a school rugby team and she searches for a young Lord Blackwaite. The figures' faces are all so dour, so unlike the children they are, and she cannot spot him. But he is in the colour photograph next to it, a young man. Handsome, straight-backed. There is an element of mischief in his eyes that the years have rubbed out. Next to him is his mother, proud, and a young woman, his sister.

The girl is pretty, round at the edges of her face, eyes wide-set and her chin pointed. She wears a thick roll-neck and a pleated skirt.

The world is on its side in the moment of the unknown becoming known, and the colours drip backwards, dizzy.

This woman, grown now, perhaps out of that shy body and naive smile.

She is safe in Canada. Estranged from her brother by years and geography. Anna knows this.

But Anna knows this also, knows her.

As sure as anything she has seen under the sun. This girl was in her garden. This woman has been in the soil in her hands. Anna has cried for her.

Catherine Blackwaite.

Anna says her name aloud and listens for the reply.

This woman is Catherine Blackwaite.

Hitesh and Reverend Watts watch as the figures scurry away down the side alley at their approach, scattered like a flock of pigeons.

Watts sighs and shakes his head. 'Poor souls.'

He draws his gaze towards where David is sniffing the bins of the Chinese takeaway.

'Leave that now, David.' He grips the dog's collar and moves him gently but firmly away from the dregs of some sweet and sour pork. David grumbles but allows the two men to lead him away from the high street and into the park that gives out onto the fields. Hitesh's evening walks with them have gained regularity as autumn has worn into winter, and now they all know the path they will take, even in the five o'clock gloom that has descended.

'It's not as though Magna never used to have drugs, I suppose,' Watts reflects. 'The eighties happened here as well.' He opens the crossbar gate at the back of the football pitch and stands back to let Hitesh through. They take the track around the edge of the uncut meadow.

'But not on the scale of county lines?'

'Mm. There's something about the late-stage capitalism of it all,' Watts exhales, 'identifying a market in rural isolation, bosses divvying up risk, and ten layers down, some lad gets sent out from London carrying goodness knows how much heroin to sparrow some vulnerable soul.'

'Cuckoo.'

'What?'

'It's called cuckooing when dealers take over a house.' Hitesh zips his jacket up even further. He understands, now, why everyone here possesses such an array of unattractive outerwear.

'Yes, cuckooing, of course.' Watts stops to untangle the lead that David has managed to wind between his front paws. 'And these days, you can be down and out, and still able to tap a message into your phone, and five minutes later, you've scored a bag of the powder that's ruining your life; that's probably going to kill you. What a… I don't know. A waste. A travesty of human invention.'

They pause while Watts unclips David's lead so that he can trot alongside them, veering off here and there to investigate an interesting smell, or flop onto his side and loll in the long, wet grass.

'You think if Annette Waring was still around, she'd get mixed up in something like this?' Hitesh asks. It comes naturally to his mind's eye.

'Mm.' Watts sounds defeated. Hitesh glances across; the older man's gaze is fixed on the rutted ground as they walk, distracted. 'She sounds like the sort of person who gets preyed upon. Easy pickings. Easily lost.'

'Yeah. Are you – are you all right, James?'

'Hmm?' Watts looks up, startled from his reverie. 'Oh. Some days priesthood weighs heavier than others, I suppose.'

Then the dog makes a break for it. A blur of surprising speed, he is suddenly haring off towards the treeline.

'David, stop!' Watts shouts, panicked, and begins to run. 'Hitesh, there's a busy road that way, there's a gap in the fence—'

Watts is slow, but the policeman is already moving. He can see the field perimeter and the flash of passing headlights behind the hedgerow. He picks up speed quickly, cutting across the grass with long strides, eyes fixed on the buttercup-yellow of David's fur.

'David, come back!' Watts is shouting far behind him, but Hitesh does not waste his breath.

The gap closes.

He can feel a stitch pulling in his abdomen and ignores it. With more vigour than he knew he had left, he runs towards the animal that is as close as Watts has to a child.

But he is not going to make it. David is nearly at the road now. Hitesh cannot cover the distance in time.

'David, no!' Watts' voice is anguished. Hitesh gives a final push, but it is futile; he is too far away. He can see the gap in the hedge and the tarmac beyond.

At the last moment, David changes direction and plunges his face into a carrier bag of old sandwiches tangled in a hawthorn bush. He begins to bolt them down as quickly as he can, until Hitesh reaches him and collapses on the grass, restraining him in a bear hug. David is overjoyed to have a human on the ground with him, and wriggles and licks Hitesh's face with glee.

Watts comes limping to a stop, and clips David's lead on before his knees fold and he lands on the grass, next to them both. Watts cradles the dog's head. 'What were you thinking? You could have been killed!'

David wags his tail madly. At the edge of his vision, Hitesh sees Watts' lips move in silent thanks.

The two men, soaking and still breathless, pull David along the boundary to the bench in the adjoining field. David licks and clacks his chops happily, flicking long strings of drool back and forth as he catches up the final crumbs of the sandwiches.

'I think he ate some plastic, James.'

'Not for the first time. It'll digest. Thank you. I don't know what I'd have done if—'

Hitesh shakes his head. 'It was the sandwiches. He'd never have gone into the road.'

Watts wipes his forehead with a hanky. 'Well, that was the cardio I'm always promising myself I'll do.' They laugh and slump back, recovering their breath. 'That's enough exercise, I think – let's go home.'

They walk in silence for a while, and Hitesh can see Watts sinking back into his own mind.

'What's going on, James?'

Watts looks confused. 'Like you said, David caught the scent of sandwiches – you know what retrievers are like. One whiff of food and they're off.'

'Not that.' Hitesh is meaningful. 'What's going on?'

The priest looks across at him, thin, grey hair plastered down in the damp evening, and suddenly he sighs. 'It catches up with you when you don't expect it – this life. A life of helping others, putting them first and such – I knew what I was signing up for. But sometimes I think I didn't expect it to be such a zero-sum-game.' They walk on in silence. Watts shifts uneasily. 'I – I never wanted to keep secrets.'

'No.'

'I was told something this week. In confession.'

'What?' Hitesh asks before he can help himself. Watts raises his eyebrows. 'Of course, you can't say, can you?'

'No, I can't.'

'But you wish you could?'

'Of course I do. It's – it's not something I want to keep to myself. It really isn't.'

Hitesh makes his guess. 'Is it about Fallow?'

'I can't tell you,' Watts implores.

It is. Hitesh shakes his head.

They cross the football pitch and play area and emerge back onto the high street. David has enough sense or shame not to try the takeaway bins again. The street is empty – the dealers have chosen somewhere else to work for the night.

Hitesh feels the anger welling up, and presses his hands deeper into his pockets. 'Someone was murdered. I know you have a duty when people – confess, or whatever they do. But there's a duty to the dead woman, too.'

Watts is pained. 'It's not that. Not exactly.'

'Then what?' Hitesh presses.

'I want to tell you, believe me. With every fibre of my being

133

as a man. But as a *priest* – I can't. I can't break the confessional seal. That's my burden to shoulder.'

Hitesh refuses to meet his eyes. Their footsteps fall heavily on the narrow pavement, and they are forced into single file past the overhanging fuchsias of cottage gardens.

They reach the gate of the rectory and David leads Watts towards the front door. Hitesh remains on the street. Finally, he looks at his friend's face. 'I understand you can't tell me. I do.'

Watts nods, and rests his hand on David's head. 'The person who confessed – I've told him to come to you. I told him to come and tell the truth.'

'I hope he will.' Hitesh turns to leave, then pauses and turns back. 'Look after yourself, James. You're not alone.'

*August 1967*

I have never been scared of spiders. You can't be, growing up somewhere like Fallow. But Timothy, in spite of valiant efforts to appear otherwise, is terrified of them. The old gardener's cottage is held together only by moss and cobwebs, and I evict all the spiders I can before he arrives.

As across the other fields of my life, I have become accustomed to waiting. I settle on the mass of cushions and blankets we have slowly accumulated since I rediscovered the cottage. I wonder if I ought to set out the flask and mugs I've brought, but my lover could be a while yet and I do not want midges to drown in the whisky.

This mock home is not something I intended. It happened accidentally, as so much else. Even this radical, rebellious, secret affair has collapsed back into the only model I recognise. Is there any other way between men and women, anything other than sex and housekeeping?

And why must I wait for him, like some faithful hound?

Not once has Timothy been here first. Nor even on time.

He has a wristwatch but he is always late. And when he arrives, I'll forgive him because he'll kiss me and tell me I'm beautiful. And because I want sex too. I won't jeopardise it with anger. And the cycle will begin again.

I rearrange the pile of blankets so they will ease the cold and discomfort of the dirt floor.

But there it is. The anger is creeping in anyway.

It starts with Timothy but soon has spread to my father, who has clipped my wings so decisively. Then slowly even Mother gets caught in my anger's grasp. My kind, stubborn mother who has always been my ally in this place. But she has failed where it counts most – she has never demanded a future for me from my father; she has only shielded me from his anger when I have tried to claim one myself.

There is a temptation here and now to get up and leave forever, to walk out of the cottage and keep walking, whomever calls me back.

But like any and all aspects of my anger, it is futile and hurts only me. Where would I go?

The door creaks open and my body is awake before he has even stepped over the threshold.

'Sorry I'm late, beautiful. There was traffic on the road out of the village. Didn't think you'd want anybody seeing me duck in here.'

He strokes my hair with his warm hands and the anger mixes with desire and makes the taste even sharper.

They are shards of a broken jar that resist all attempts at reassembly. Whichever way they point, they are jagged. Anna can see the skull in her hands, and slowly Catherine Blackwaite's face regrows its flesh over the bone. Anna shakes her head and tries to read. It is not possible it is Catherine. There is the DNA.

135

She turns over the pages of an art catalogue, leaves still glossy, but the corners ragged from whatever life it lived before it reached Magna's Oxfam. They show plates from Renaissance frescoes, and Anna finds herself skimming faces, looking for features, for who is feeling what, and who meets whose gaze. She wonders what Catherine became. What her new life in Canada was. She tries her hardest to paint Catherine a story, a life after Magna. Anna shuts the catalogue abruptly. She fidgets, moves restlessly. Sends an email full of bland love to her parents, checks on the chickens. Sweeps the shards away, gathers them up again. She puts on her coat.

Hitesh is surprised by a knock on the door, something that has never disturbed him before here in Upper Magna. He is washing up, and slings the towel over his shoulder.

Anna. To find her on his doorstep is disorientating. He has visited Fallow Cottage half a dozen times, but she has never come here; she has never existed, for him, closer than the safe distance of the market green. She is not wearing make-up, and has on the thick waterproof coat he has seen her wear in the garden.

'Anna—'

'Sorry, I know it's unannounced. Is it all right if I come in?'

'Yeah, of course.' Hitesh steps back to admit her.

For a moment, he is indecisive. In the lounge there is a sofa with a few books on the second seat, and nothing else. In the kitchen is a table and chairs, pots and pans, but still a stack of boxes he has come no closer to unpacking. They go into the kitchen and he makes a half-hearted apology before she shakes her head. 'You've seen the cottage.'

And it is true, and she is not his mother, and she has always known he is alone.

'Are you all right? What's happened?'

'Nothing. The DNA samples you had done – is there any room for interpretation, or mistakes?'

'The testing is done by people, so there's always room for error. But it's rare,' he replies.

Anna is strung with energy, her eyes bright and liquid. 'I was at the Hall, talking to Lord Blackwaite about the gala. I saw a photograph of his sister, Catherine.'

'What did he say?'

'Nothing. He wasn't with me.'

'What was important about the picture?'

She does not reply straight away. She is agitated. Hitesh is resting against the counter but she has not taken the chair he pulled out for her. Instead, she is holding its back, rocking onto the balls of her feet and tensing her shins and calves until her legs form a long and perfect line to her abdomen. Once, twice, to a phrase she does not know she is hearing. Hitesh sees her for a moment in her past life.

'Anna,' he tries to tether her. She notices what she is doing and stops.

'I think it's Catherine Blackwaite.'

'Who? The body?'

'Yes.'

'Why?' Hitesh takes the towel off his shoulder and sits at the kitchen table.

Anna is needle-sharp. 'You're trying to make me sit.'

'Is that a bad thing?'

'Just tell me to sit.'

'Sit down.' His voice is as even as it always is when he speaks to her. He is not upset by her appearance at his home, long after work hours. He has not dismissed her or Catherine Blackwaite out of hand, which Anna realises only now is what she had feared. She sits.

'It's not something I can explain. It sounds hysterical. But when – when I found her, I held her skull for a while before I went up to the Hall to phone the police, to phone you. The distance between the eyes, the narrow jaw – it was her.'

Hitesh watches Anna. 'What's she like?'

'Young, innocent-looking, light hair like Lord Blackwaite. It isn't something—' She trails off.

'Tangible?'

'No, it's not tangible. It's… impressions. It's also contrary to one of the only hard facts you have.'

'Yes.'

'But I can't put it aside. I've tried. It keeps coming back.'

Hitesh gets out his phone and brings up the photo of Annette that Nick Waring sent him. It is blurry, and Annette's features fade into the middle ground of some barbecue in a park. She holds a can of something and her thin hair is tied back.

Anna scrutinises the picture, zooms in to examine what little record exists of Annie Waring's face. 'No. It isn't her. The cheekbones are too low, and her chin is wider, and…' She shrugs.

'You don't feel it.'

Anna shakes her head. 'I'm – I'm sorry Annette hasn't been found. I hope she's alive still.'

Hitesh can see a line of mud beneath her index nail. She is more shaken now than she was at the graveside or in the night. He puts his hands in his pockets.

'I was going to come and see you tomorrow,' he says. 'I had a meeting with the area DCI this morning – case reviews. Because there hasn't been a substantial lead, the case is being closed.'

'What?'

'We've hit a dead end with enquiries about Annette Waring. Elizabeth Millhaven, or Jones as she became, we haven't found her yet, but we have nothing except her gender and proximity to suggest a connection. And the tests show it wasn't Catherine. We have no other leads.'

'That's how quickly this woman can be put aside?'

'From the DCI's perspective, the case is decades old, the perpetrator might be dead. Right now he needs resources to deal with county lines.' Hitesh meets her eyes. 'I'm sorry. It's not my call.'

'No.' Anna looks away. He watches her moving and rearranging it all in her mind.

'Are you okay?'

She frowns. 'She's being left again.' The guilt flowers in Hitesh's chest. 'It's like letting her rot a second time.'

'I'm sorry.'

They sit in silence.

Anna shakes her head. 'I don't understand why – I don't know how to reconcile reality with the conviction that it's Catherine. With her face.'

Hitesh spools and unspools what he knows, tries to disentangle it from the guilt he is feeling, then exhales slowly. 'What if I had the sample re-tested?'

'To put my mind at rest?'

'To put my conscience at rest. And because I want to know if you're right. I want to know if it's Catherine.'

'Your tests have already said it isn't.'

'And it probably isn't. But mistakes are possible. You aren't stupid, Anna. If you feel something this strongly there's a reason. Whether it's because it's Catherine Blackwaite or because there's something we don't know yet.'

'And if the DNA test comes back the same? Won't you look foolish – to your colleagues, I mean?' she asks finally.

Hitesh shrugs, smiles. 'I'll have to do it quietly, especially now the case has been closed. I don't want to get shit for wasting resources. But there's something to be said for not seeing yourself through others' eyes.'

Anna laughs and allows herself to close her eyes for a moment on all the madness of these months. She hears Hitesh scrape his chair back and turns to watch him fill the kettle. His house was easy to find – he had mentioned he lived off the village green. She knows Magna, and Magna knows her; she had asked Tom Wilkes as she crossed the road, and he had told her where the policeman lived.

Anna wonders what she had expected in coming here, whether she had hoped her unfounded certainty would be set back in place, soothed away. Or perhaps, really, she had wanted what she feared; had she wanted Hitesh to use his power to tell her she was wrong, to set her forever somewhere outside these new uncertainties and cast her aside?

Hitesh is already unpicking Catherine Blackwaite, thinking about how to get a re-test under the radar. It is not until the kettle boils that he realises he has only unpacked the one mug, the one he washes and reuses each day. He washes it again and makes Anna tea.

She looks gaunt and dark lines extend beneath her eyes. She looks older than the first time he saw her. He places the mug on the table and pushes away the smell of grass.

'If I can get a solid new lead – if the DNA result comes back as Catherine – then I can get the case reopened.' Hitesh's face creases with concern. 'You need to stop looking, though.'

'I won't.'

He turns away and picks up the tea towel to dry the dishes. 'I know.'

'Darshan, have you got extra help in yet?'

'You haven't called all week. Why am I answering to you, huh?'

'Get some help.'

'Stop bloody interfering. You've moved away. What does it matter to you, eh?'

'I'm your son, I care. Why does everything have to be a fucking argument?'

'You're never here. Stop chewing my head.'

'Dad, get help or I'll arrange it for you. You need to—'
*Click*

Anna has already evened out her skin with foundation and powder; now she picks up a pen and lines her eyes with great care – at the top and at the bottom to make them wider still, doe and appealing. After, her eyes, her cheeks. A wash of colour so that she appears to blush, and red lipstick, which will remind men of fucking.

She examines her reflection with curt horror and satisfaction. She wonders if the nervousness she feels is only reflex, because so many nights she had applied her stage make-up, blotted out her features and painted them back better. Always seeking perfection. Madonna and whore. Artist and muse. Ready to step into the excruciating thrill of that performance.

The gala is no stage, and perhaps that is all she needs to remind herself of. But she can hear it.

The fall was nearly silent except for the sound of the tear – a ripping noise which was quiet yet surely audible. Anna's gasps of pain followed many long seconds after. Her fellow ballerinas gathered round, recognising a bad fall.

Georg was learning over her, handsome face contorted by guilt and fear. But it was not his fault, nor really hers. Sometimes gravity just stakes a claim. A rehearsal, at least, not on stage, in front of an audience.

The physio could not tell her if the damage had been so catastrophic because of this single event, or whether the years of use and repeated impact had already weakened her ankle. It is something Anna has asked herself often since her fall. Flex, lift, turn, smile, relevé.

Why had she wanted it in the first place? What had prompted her to choose a life that was poorly paid, gruelling, rigorous and beautiful? After a long while, Anna had had to accept that there was no traceable moment in her childhood. All the girls at school had dreamed of being actresses or dancers; Anna had simply been talented enough, single-minded enough to achieve what had enchanted them all, and finally had become the pink-clad ballerina on the music box.

Years away in Fallow Cottage, she can look back on the artistry, the athleticism and the commitment with a measure of awe. There had been warm-ups, classes, stretches, rehearsals, costume fittings. To watch some of the dancers was to witness raw flesh made holy, transformed for a few minutes into light, into feeling, so that the air asked permission to hold them. Anna had been a mere First Artist, and yet this world had been all she lived and breathed.

Perhaps, then, it had only been natural to ricochet from one extreme to the other. If she had failed to transform herself with air, then she would use the earth. And if she had failed to attain the perfect womanhood of the ballerina, then she would try to strip back any trace of what the world expected. It had been sudden coming and had not. Repeated and acute. If since childhood she had trained herself relentlessly to be pleasing, to dance well, to put the kettle on, then since childhood she had reviled it in herself.

During her convalescence, when Anna had had to hobble around on crutches but before she had formally retired from the company, she could no longer keep the two forces in balance. Underneath her smile was white-hot anger, and when she could no longer stand it, she quit the company.

The job at the department store was the first thing that came along. Anna was not qualified for anything outside of ballet. She had resisted her parents' suggestions that she move back home, but swapped her house-share for a foetid studio flat so that between shifts, she could come back to her own space. To read, draw, think, work through the pain of her exercises without her housemates' sympathetic murmurs.

At the store, Anna was stationed in the perfume section.

'You're so elegant,' the floor manager had thrilled, 'you'll be successful here.'

Anna had been. She had sold to women, to their boyfriends and husbands. Between customers, she had practised taking her face on and off as smoothly as possible. She made a game of waiting until the last moment before putting it on, then winning the customer completely, selling to them, taking it off as soon as their back was turned. She examined that face in every detail, made a microscopic study of the pleasingness she had always lived.

She found it in the grooves of her nails, filed to a delicate oval. In the way she let customers talk over her. In her flat stomach and her softened voice. Sometimes she caught herself trying to please the spiteful rota manager, not for a favoured shift, but because what else had she been taught but to be *nice* and to please others at the expense of herself?

The perfume section sat opposite the returns desk, and Anna had stared at that sign for more hours than she could count. Return. She noticed it, then forgot it, then noticed it again. It took root in her mind, and twisted there.

Return. *Return.*

From whom, to whom? Return to where?

What is being returned? A pair of ill-fitting shoes, a face, a life.

Return, *remeo, revenir.*

143

And where did Anna wish to return to?

Can we return at all? To anything.

It had been the tool Anna had been looking for. She had dug with it; she had excavated.

Anna stopped seeing friends, all of whom had been fellow dancers. She missed them a little, but not enough. She especially did not call the men who had occasionally spent the night, bodies pressed together in the search for meaning. Her parents she had reassured, then pushed back to arm's length.

And then she had seen the advert for Fallow Cottage. And she had known where to return to.

Anna looks at herself in the cracked mirror above the sink. The cottage has no full-length mirror, but it does not matter, because she has worn this gown to enough arts fundraisers to know what she looks like. She leaves her hair loose, a dark tangle of ivy around her face and neck, because that way her beauty appears more natural, as though it is something of which she is not conscious. And that is what people want.

Anna puts on her perfume and takes a final look. She has applied a thin layer now, of glamour, sex, innocence – whatever it is, it will license her to move through that evening's world. It will let her get close enough to ask about Catherine; she will charm them enough that she will be allowed to stay at Fallow Cottage.

She hears it again, that tearing sound.

Each of the eighteen eyes is a bright light cut out of the darkness; three storeys, six across, uniform in their hauteur. They watch the guests arriving, from the bottom of the hill to the very moment they pass through the portico, whereupon Fallow's eyes lose sight of what is inside it.

At the threshold, the freezing night air evaporates; the glow of the chandelier robs everything of its edges, makes it soft, invites Hitesh to bathe in its warmth. Suddenly his coat is gone, and there is a glass of champagne in his hand.

The hall is thick with people as a sea with fish, and they shimmer and ripple in their silks and refinements, bunching together to talk, flowing past one another, greeting, joking, eddying. Hitesh finds himself unaccompanied in the entrance hall, and yet, borne on this tide and in this warmth, feels more at home in the Hall than ever before. He is a guest now.

The general flow is leftwards, towards the east wing, and Hitesh drifts along in it, until Lord Blackwaite breaks off from an older woman to approach him.

'I'm so glad you could make it, Detective, so very glad.' Hitesh's host is lighter and brighter than his years. His black tie fits immaculately, a breathing layer of skin that a tailor pieced together decades ago, a skin that slips seamlessly back on tonight. His hand is firm in Hitesh's.

'I'm pleased to be here. The Hall looks wonderful.'

'Truly, it's a beautiful place. I was sorry to hear that the case was closed – but I'm glad that you're finally seeing Fallow as it should be seen, as a part of the community, as something that can bring us together. Now, I'm afraid I must keep gladhanding, but see that you aren't left without a drink.' As he turns to leave, Lord Blackwaite flags down a waistcoated young woman and Hitesh's glass is topped up to brimming.

Ahead of Hitesh is Watts' silver head, deep in conversation with Eloise Fitzhugh's pale golden crown. The two men arrived together, yet Watts has been swallowed up even quicker than Hitesh.

'But why have I even been invited? Lord Blackwaite already thinks I'm invading the sanctity of the Hall – his privacy, or his reputation, or God knows what.'

'That's precisely why he's invited you, Hitesh,' the vicar replied wryly. 'You're new to Upper Magna, and you're fairly senior in the local police force. But most of all, you've come into conflict.'

Watts had been deft with the bow tie, leaning over the younger man's shoulder and forming the loops and knots that Hitesh had repeatedly tried and failed to achieve.

'I don't understand.'

'Lord Blackwaite is a gentleman. In both the literal and the spiritual sense. He knows in his heart of hearts that you aren't interfering for your own gain, that you are carrying out your duty as a police officer. Edmund was performing what he saw as his duty as the guardian of Fallow Hall, and in the course of performing that duty, he lost his temper with you. He needs to invite you to the gala to demonstrate that he understands you too are acting out of duty; that you have a role in Upper Magna; that you're *both* gentlemen. There you go, you look positively handsome.' Watts turned Hitesh to look in the mirror of the rectory hall.

'Thanks, I'm glad one of us knew how to do that.'

'It's not all dog collars, you know. Don't play with it, it'll come undone.'

Now, Hitesh steps into Fallow's ballroom and inhales. Its grandeur is a shock; where in daylight its glory had been faded, tonight it is transubstantiated by the presence of human bodies, greenery, the smell of perfume, sweat, champagne, the glow of the chandeliers, and the twinkling of lights on a Christmas tree that grazes the cornices and reaches out with wintery, proprietorial fingers.

Hitesh scans the room, and to his surprise, finds he recognises a number of people. His new Chief Constable has chosen to wear dress uniform instead of a tux, and occupies a corner with a military gentleman; there is the wine importer from the St Mary's bridge morning; faces he recognises from the market. And yet these well-off locals are at the lower end of the social spectrum here tonight. The village is wealthy, but Fallow Hall and Lord Blackwaite have swept in another stratum again; there is real money here, and power. The evening suits; the jewels in the women's ears and on their necks; the cut-glass voices and polished European accents, these guests are wrapped in a fine tissue of assurance. These are people to whom the world responds, and to whose needs reality bends itself.

*Look at where I am, Mum.*

'Not a bad turnout, is it, Mistry?'

Hitesh finds Paul Wolsey at his side. Hitesh is surprised by how tall he is, shoulder to shoulder with him – less the old lech than a successful businessman.

'It's certainly impressive. How are the homes?'

'Well, time hasn't stopped. People are still getting old, so I'm still making money.'

'What a spiritual outlook you have.'

'Have you nicked anyone for the body yet?'

'Not yet.'

'Impressive. I'll be sure to call for you next time I'm in trouble.'

Hitesh senses that Wolsey will take no offence in being told to fuck off, and he is right, Wolsey just laughs.

'You should ask your boss for more resources.'

'I think the station is focused on getting a working photocopier first. Maybe some more manpower in a few years.'

'Very good,' Wolsey chortles.

'What will the Trust do with the money raised tonight?' Hitesh asks.

'Some urgent repairs, first of all. But beyond that, financial security will allow us to plan ahead; we can invest in making this the foremost heritage business in the area. There's more appetite for it than ever – *the English countryside*,' Wolsey snorts. 'Edmund's done well getting these guests. A title still impresses a lot of people, you know. Englishmen, but foreigners particularly. We've landed some rich Eastern Europeans and a few Spaniards looking to add cultural philanthropy to their portfolio. A clutch from Dubai and China, too.'

'Fallow looks so picturesque, I had no idea it was such a *business*.'

'Don't be naive, Mistry. These places have always been businesses. From the first brick. The people who built them were dick-swinging and making friends in high places. Don't be misled by their age.'

'You've opened my eyes to the truth, Paul.'

Wolsey is amused by Hitesh this evening. 'What are you looking for then, Mistry?'

'What do you mean?'

Wolsey nods towards a well-groomed woman in velvet.

'Jesus.'

'Hypocrite. I've seen you hanging about Anna Deerin. Or are you looking for dick?'

'I've heard human beings might be worthy of respect, Wolsey,' Hitesh retorts, then is embarrassed at this naiveté coming from his mouth.

Wolsey sees his bait has been taken and guffaws. 'We can't all be so morally upright.'

'Fuck off.'

Wolsey shrugs, his face oddly serene. 'I may not be *a good man*, Mistry. But I spend all day giving old people a good death. I can live with myself.'

'Well, that's all right then. I'm sure St Peter won't mind.'

Wolsey gives an equable smile and looks Hitesh in the eye, 'Every worker I employ respects every resident. If they don't, they're out on their ear. Now, I'd fuck Anna Deerin given the chance, but if she was a resident at one of my homes, she'd be treated like royalty.'

'Really? Is that how you justify yourself? You're shit to women but it's okay because you're Mother Teresa once they have dementia?'

'Sounds about right.' Wolsey claps Hitesh on the shoulder and makes his way into the crowd, grinning from ear to ear.

Hitesh feels dirty and foolish, but that was Wolsey's intention, and he tries to push it away.

A crowd is beginning to swell at his back now, and Hitesh moves further into the ballroom. Through the hubbub of voices is the sound of a string quartet playing an intricate, woody harmony that pleads and promises before dipping below the waves again, and siren-like, it draws Hitesh forward. He can see the musicians under the Christmas tree, heads bowed, sawing at their instruments, and he wants to hear the next phrase. The sound is purifying, after Wolsey. He threads his way towards it, but midway finds himself in a circle with Watts.

'Hitesh, this is the Right Honourable Judge Phelps, and this is Lady Arnling, Ambassador to Nepal.'

Watts is at his ease, boyish and ebullient. Today, at least, priesthood weighs less heavily. The reverend already knows the judge, and they bounce one off the other, to the delight of Lady Arnling. Watts introduces Hitesh and his role in recent events, to a flurry of questions, and Hitesh does his best to keep up with them.

Eventually, Watts steps in to parry for his friend. 'You can't ask that, Charles, it's not one of your bloody trials. Speaking of which, have you adjudicated on that fraud case yet?'

'Oh, don't get me started. About two minutes after I'd pronounced judgement on an eighteen-month case, they lodged an appeal.'

'All this misbehaviour pays your bills, though, doesn't it?' jokes Lady Arnling.

'*Alleged* misbehaviour,' Watts says sternly, and they burst out laughing.

Hitesh is buoyed to see his friend this way. He drinks his champagne, and watches his companions' interaction, their cadences, the cut of their clothes and the subjects of their conversations, an anthropologist in their midst.

A judge, an ambassador and a priest go to a party.

But then, a judge, an ambassador, a priest and a policeman go to a party.

Hitesh is here too, adding his anecdotes and making them laugh. Lady Arnling asks him whether he has any family locally, any children.

'No? A catch like you? Well, I'm sure you won't have to wait long.'

And the judge, the ambassador and the priest see no reason he should not be part of this world, take a wife, put down roots. He flushes with disorientation, and something he fears is pleasure.

*Should* he put down roots? What had he expected in moving to Magna, really?

A waiter tends to the circle and refills their glasses. *Thanks, thank you, oh wonderful, cheers.*

The alcohol tickles Hitesh's bloodstream. He had been running away, there had been no question about that. At his leaving do, his Met colleagues had clapped him on the shoulder, an unspoken acknowledgement that in leaving the city, he was admitting he was spent, that he might as well be sold for glue.

'If you're looking to buy, don't go with Watsons on the high street. Not only are they terrible, but everyone knows that Watson Senior is embezzling.' Lady Arnling rolls her eyes.

'Don't tell me that,' Judge Phelps groans.

'Sorry, sorry, no shop talk!'

Hitesh laughs.

He is thirty-five. Will he spend the next fifty, sixty years here in Upper Magna?

'Go with, um... Thorpes, that's the one. Thorpes in Cirencester.'

'Sometimes I think I entered the Church to avoid dealing with estate agents,' muses Watts.

'Frankly, it was a good decision. One we all ought to have taken,' Phelps agrees, 'though I'm surprised Watson hasn't tried to convince you to sell the rectory yet. *Prime location, structurally sound, excellent access to God.*'

'It's not exactly a family home; I nearly broke my neck coming down those stairs this morning.'

'Oh well, pop a conservatory on, you'll be all right.'

As each of Hitesh's relationships had petered out, Manju had looked quietly despairing. Once, near the end, Hitesh had tried to reassure her that he would have children one day, 'There'll be grandkids.'

'I won't know, dika, I'll be dead. I just don't want you to be alone.'

There had been no plan for what would happen once Hitesh had run away; he has been pushing the future out of reach.

In the shifting crowd beyond Watts' shoulder, in the smears of colour and light, something makes his stomach tighten. His understanding catches up with his body but by then it is too late – it has been unearthed. Something he has been so careful to bury, even from himself, and suddenly, it is revenant. It flutters and slices.

Hitesh wonders if he will be able to bury it again. He wonders if she knows.

Anna sees Hitesh glance over and meets his eyes fleetingly.

'So, what do you do, Thomas?' She lifts her chin up.

Eloise Fitzhugh's son is tall, fair like his mother, and

exceptionally good-looking. 'I'm an art dealer, for my sins.'

'Do you specialise in anything?' she asks.

'The Italian and Northern Renaissances. Some of us aren't creative, we can only make money from the beauty of others.' He grins. 'Mother tells me you're a ballerina.'

From the corner of her eye, Anna sees Eloise and her husband. Every so often, Eloise glances over, not, Anna thinks, without some hope.

'Was a ballerina. I'm retired now. Out to pasture.'

Her dress is midnight blue and skims her collarbones modestly, but at the back, it falls away, leaving clean flesh from nape to small, before the material gathers again and drops to the floor.

Thomas's gaze is subtle. 'I haven't been to the ballet in too long. Not since *Giselle* last season. Did you ever dance as the Wilis?' Anna had. Ethereal, draped in white tulle, one dead girl among many. 'I'm sorry to have missed it. Mother tells me you're bewitching Magna now instead.'

'Digging up weeds and shooing crows. It's not quite fine art.'

Thomas shrugs. 'Don't tell my colleagues, but there's more to life than art.'

'Your secret is safe with me. What was it like growing up in Magna?'

Thomas is warm. 'Idyllic. Climbing apple trees in autumn and cherry trees come spring. You know Mother – there were stews and crumbles and a spotless home.'

'Sounds like an Enid Blyton story.'

'Precisely like a Blyton story. I think my brother married the closest thing he could find to our mother. Kept the fiction going.'

'Not you?'

Thomas gazes across at Eloise, full of affection. 'No. No, she should have had more time for herself instead of spending all her energies on us. Don't get me wrong, I'm eternally grateful, but it seems old-fashioned to look for a partner to replicate those gender roles.'

Anna tilts her head. 'Unfair, but not uncommon.'

'Sadly. Magna, of all places, doesn't move very quickly.' Someone is gesturing to Thomas from across the room. He sighs. 'Business calls. I'm so glad to have finally met you.' He offers his hand and she grips it lightly.

Anna catches Eloise's eye. The older woman adopts a mock innocent expression. *Who, me?* she mimes, and they both laugh.

'Anna?'

As she turns, she realises she knows his voice now. 'You look smart, Detective.'

'Watts had to help with the tie. Next time I'll get one on elastic.'

'Like at school.'

'Primary school. It's about the right level.' Hitesh grins. 'You look – pleasing.' She raises her eyebrows, and to his embarrassment, he blushes. 'Stop it.'

Anna drinks to stop herself laughing, but she has not had alcohol in a long time, and it makes her dizzy. She draws herself back. 'Some of the people here tonight have been around Magna forever; their families, too.'

'Full of gossip, then.'

'At the least. Will you ask the older guests about Catherine Blackwaite, if you get the chance?'

'I will. Don't put yourself in harm's way, Anna.'

She gestures with her toothpick arms. 'I'm standing still.'

Hitesh sighs and Anna can see all the lines around his mouth and eyes.

'Are you enjoying yourself, at least?'

'I think so. I think it's a nice evening.' He frowns.

'It's a strange sensation. But I hear you're allowed to be happy.'

'I don't know. It feels – dangerous,' Hitesh half jests.

'You should move somewhere quiet, live off the land, find yourself,' Anna says mischievously, and he cannot help but laugh.

Anna excuses herself to help Eloise and threads her way towards the trustee and the group of glamorous women she is entertaining. She can sense Hitesh watching as she crosses the room, and it feels like needle points.

This is Fallow Hall. This is its past and its destiny. This is how it was reared and how it will be fed.

Lord Blackwaite breathes deeply and looks upon his work. The ballroom is only as light as it needs to be, that is the secret – people should need to stand close to one another to talk, to exchange intimacies. Blemishes are softened and faces made luminous by shadow. Conversation flows between these esteemed guests, and the evening looks effortless, as it ought to. Arranged correctly, the guests do not see the labour and the sweat. Power is the suggestion that it could never have been another way.

Edmund takes stock of the waiters' effectiveness in keeping glasses full. They are doing well, and he will use this firm again next year. The cleaners, too. Anna Deerin's flowers are perfect. Of Fallow. Elegant. And yet in their dark lustre, they speak of something potent.

He scans the heads of the crowd from his vantage point by the ballroom doors. There she is, Ms Deerin. She is talking to the local MP; to Mr Velasquez, who has already pledged sponsorship; and to Allan Armand, whose hedge fund he has high hopes of securing a donation from. She is charming them, because she is a charming girl. Lord Blackwaite is far too old to have any designs himself, but her spindly grace is of a piece with Fallow, less vulgar than the current trend for breast and buttock. Sex ought to be whispered, not shouted, in his opinion.

She seems to be telling them an anecdote, and her audience is listening, rapt. Lord Blackwaite senses that Anna Deerin understands this place and its worth like he does, in her marrow. It is why she is here and not Keith McCarthy, the groundskeeper. Keith appears, clips bushes, smokes, goes home. He is pleasant enough, but being pleasant is not enough, not for Fallow. Lord Blackwaite has raised it from nothing, from starvation. Its diet is one of care, of intelligence, of commitment. In her walled garden, in the orchard, in the wildflower meadow, Anna Deerin has offered that, and he is grateful.

Lord Blackwaite shifts his gaze. Eloise Fitzhugh, Paul Wolsey, Reverend Watts; he can see his trustees pulling their weight. He consults his mental checklist again, then sights a lone guest and strikes out to integrate her into the fold.

His blood feels hot, hotter than it ever did as a young man. He can secure Fallow tonight: if he can make a success of this evening, if he can convince these guests to give generously, then he can ensure that history does not hinge on an old man's blood pressure, and that Fallow will not die when he does.

These are the stakes.


'You're right.' Anna listens carefully, head inclined.

'The garden must be a strange sort of place – living history. Ground where a lot of things have occurred. As I'm sure you're well aware, after the last few weeks.' Christine is a retired Classics professor, down from London for the gala. She stands at a right angle to Eloise's other friends, who all stopped working when they had children, and now lunch and volunteer. The circle defers to her short grey hair and elegant spectacles.

'I often think about the women who have been here,' Anna says, 'so many, over the years. Big and small.'

'There must be a lot of stories we'll never hear,' Eloise murmurs.

'Quite,' Christine muses. 'What can one truly recover?'

There is a moment of collective recognition, grief, that ripples through the women. In the warmth of the ballroom, their shoulders hunch and they look into their glasses and to one another.

'Some sad lives, I expect,' one of them says.

'Not least Lady Blackwaite,' says another of Eloise's friends, a kindly lady in purple brocade. 'Gosh, that was terribly sad, poor woman.'

'What happened to her?' Anna asks, wide-eyed.

The gong sounds for dinner and the guests begin to be ushered from the ballroom towards the dining room. Hitesh is borne on their tide, content to be led. They pass through the corridors and he can smell the old wood and the lacquer from the cabinets that line the walls. Then they are in the dining room, every bit as grand as the ballroom, the friezes a riot of centaurs and laurel. Hitesh is seated at one of a dozen long tables laid with white linen and gleaming cutlery, and before long he is joined by the man Anna was talking to.

'I'm told you're a copper.' Thomas Fitzhugh's handshake is firm.

'Don't hold it against me.'

'We used to get drunk in the fields when we were teenagers and it drove the local PC mad,' Thomas laughs. 'I'm pretty sure the farmer knew, but us being there kept burglars away, so he let it slide.'

'It'll be nitrous oxide now, so he might be less keen.'

'Ha, yes well, from the state of the pavement outside the gallery each morning, I'd say he was getting off lightly.' Thomas radiates easy charm.

'London's a beautiful place.'

The table begins to fill up round them, and they stand for the arrival of each lady, like Hitesh was taught as a recruit. On the table, between Hitesh and Thomas's name cards, is *Amber Delaney*.

'Amber!'

'Thomas!'

The gallerist leans in to kiss the new arrival on both cheeks. She is tall and toned and her hair is a caramel tumble. She moves with a self-possession that cannot be taught.

'Stunning.' Thomas stands back to admire her. 'Where is this from?' he gestures at her red silk gown.

'Dior, darling.' She mimes fanning her face and they burst into giggles, a joke from long ago. She composes herself and pushes her hair back with a clean flick. 'And who's your friend?'

'My apologies: Hitesh, this is Amber. Amber went to school with my cousin and it's a small world in these parts.'

'And somehow we've ended up living about a mile apart on the King's Road.' Amber beams, her teeth so white against her lips. 'We haven't quite escaped one another even in the Big Smoke.' She leans in and her perfume is what Hitesh imagines velvet might smell like. He pulls her chair out for her, and the three of them sit down together.

The first course arrives and Hitesh asks Amber about her life between Upper Magna and Chelsea.

'Oh, nothing terribly exciting to hear about. University, internships, lowly first jobs and the like.' She pours sparkling water for the three of them from the bottles on the table.

'Drink up, or you'll have a terrible hangover tomorrow. The champagne is good, but it's not that good.'

'Don't listen to her,' Thomas waves a hand mischievously, 'she'll have you playing drinking games before dinner is over. Anyway, she's being modest; Amber took a first at Cambridge.'

'A first in what?' Hitesh asks.

'Archaeology and Anthropology – I had a brilliant time. I ended up specialising in prehistoric burials in the wetlands.'

'Ah yes, the bog corpses.' Thomas nods.

'Well-preserved human sacrifices.'

Thomas chuckles. 'Amber specialises in wrinkly old men, you see.'

She bats him away with mock outrage. 'Anyway, I work in banking now, managing clients.'

This only makes Thomas laugh more. 'You see?'

They volley back and forth, and draw Hitesh into their jokes, spinning the golden threads of their conversation. He feels himself loosening again.

The courses are whisked in and out by deft hands, and Hitesh barely tastes what he is served, noting only that it seems to be good. Amber asks Hitesh about his life, his cottage, his work. She is interested and interesting, warm, attentive, ready to land the punchline that makes her companions laugh.

'But you can't possibly believe that, Thomas? Tell him, Hitesh. It's total bullshit!'

Hitesh finds himself teasing, needling, being gently mocked. He tells them about the drugs raids, the gossip, the things they have found during searches.

'Oh my God, that's so much worse than drugs.'

'But technically legal.'

The ballroom has become thick and heady with bodies and conversation, the shifts and lulls and excitement. A portion of Hitesh's mind is still set enough aside to watch Thomas and

Amber as they talk. They have been intimate, he can tell. They have history with each other and with Magna. They are shining, gilded, and he thinks they understand they are exceptional, but it would no more occur to them to move outside their sphere than it would a planet to leave its orbit. Fallow Hall and all its glamour is where they belong, and tonight he finds it hard to grudge them that. He is here too, isn't he?

Above the noise of the guests, someone begins to tap a glass with a knife, and with much settling and whispering, the room falls to a hush.

Lord Blackwaite stands at the top table, waiting until he knows he will be listened to without interruption. His pose is the analogue of the portrait above him, and Hitesh is caught between the desire to giggle hysterically, and solemn admiration.

'Ladies and gentlemen, thank you. To see Fallow Hall filled with such life is a joy. In fact, it is the reason I invited all of you here tonight. The joy that Fallow is capable of bringing to others is… remarkable, truly remarkable. For three hundred years, it has been a home, a landmark, a piece of history. The cycle of birth, life and death under this roof, and the lives that have been brought into Fallow's orbit: each has been indelibly shaped by this place. And it would be a travesty for that cycle to be broken. The newly established trust is the next step in Fallow's story, the link between the past and the future, and a chance to bring that joy to generations to come.

'In joining me here tonight, you are already part of this next step, and I want to thank you. Yes, your generosity will repair tiles and mend the leaks that like to spring up in an old place like this, but far more than the bricks and mortar, it will protect the legacy of Fallow Hall, and its history yet unwritten.

'So, a toast to you, a toast to the future, a toast to Fallow Hall.'

*To Fallow Hall. To Fallow. To Fallow. The future. To Fallow Hall.* The toast is half drowned in admiration and applause.

Thomas raises his glass. 'You've got to hand it to him, he knows how to ask for money.'

'Such a pretty history,' Amber laughs, 'when you don't mention the slavery and the ghosts.'

'Ghosts?' Hitesh raises his eyebrow.

'Oh gosh yes, packed to the rafters, this one,' Thomas agrees.

Amber grimaces at him. 'Seems a bit distasteful now, with that body being dug up.'

Hitesh wrinkles his brow, unsure, and the two locals take him into their confidence with glee. 'Proper sleepover material, mind you,' Amber grins again, 'star-crossed lovers, etcetera. Go on, Thomas.'

'Don't know if my version is the same as Amber's. But the idea was that one of the old Lord Blackwaites – you know, in some unspecified past – had a secret lover. Wanted to get married but, well, he was already married. Despair, longing, the whole shebang. Eventually they choose to die together – he kills her, but is stopped before he can kill himself. She returns and haunts Fallow for his betrayal. Floaty white ladies and mysterious sobbing noises. That about how you knew it, Amber?'

'More or less. It seemed very dark and romantic when I was younger, but obviously now, the whole idea is problematic as hell.' She shudders.

'Is there any truth in it?' Hitesh ventures.

They both laugh, surprised by his innocence. 'No,' Amber tells him pityingly, 'it's the sort of thing you only joke about when you don't actually think anyone has been killed here. I suppose, if anything, the body proves the story's untruth.' She is briefly the anthropology student again.

Hitesh looks at his companions in the semi-darkness of the

dining room, and suddenly they are blurred and distant. He realises he is giddy, drunker than he had intended.

Dinner is over, and he excuses himself, pushing his chair back and looking to find Reverend Watts; but the whole room is moving, shuffling, rustling with the smoothing of trousers and dresses, and nothing stays still long enough to be recognised.

A lick of cold air catches his cheek and Hitesh sees the glass doors standing open to the terrace.

The night is freezing and there is a lone brave smoker pacing up and down the flagstones that overlook the formal garden. The man offers Hitesh a cigarette and Hitesh takes it. He has not smoked in years but the stroke of ash on his lungs is a welcome balm. Then his benefactor returns inside and Hitesh is left alone.

Above the terrace is a full moon and its light strips the stones bone-white. How does it take the colour with it, where does it keep it? What is he doing at Magna – the place that is his home now? Home. Manju. Darshan. Watts and David. Thomas Fitzhugh and Amber Delaney. A ghost. A body that might be Catherine Blackwaite, might be Annette Waring, might be Elizabeth Millhaven, might never be named. Anna.

Hitesh feels it stir once more. Striding across his roiling thoughts. He has been stupid. It is something to bury again, not something to burden her with.

'Hitesh?'

He did not hear her approach and for a moment, bleached by the moon, Anna looks like her own ghost.

'Don't you feel the cold?' he asks.

'I think we got used to ignoring what we felt when we danced,' she says, and as she gets closer, he can see the gooseflesh on her arms.

'Let's go in.'

She shakes her head. 'Lord Blackwaite's mother killed herself.'

'What?'

'She didn't die of natural causes like Lord Blackwaite said. She killed herself not long after Catherine is supposed to have left for Canada.'

'Who told you that?'

'One of Eloise Fitzhugh's friends. It's common knowledge, apparently. An open secret among the older locals. Though no one's sure of the circumstances.'

'Her death certificate says heart failure. Barnard checked.'

'Are you saying that the police and doctor wouldn't lie to protect an important local family?'

Hitesh sighs and rubs his face. 'Of course they did. For fuck's sake. Thomas Fitzhugh and Amber Delaney – when they were young, there was a local tale about ghosts and murdered lovers here.'

'Does it mean anything?'

'I don't know.' He looks Anna in the face for the first time. 'I'm freezing. Let's go inside.'

The guests have already left the dining room and staff are scurrying to clear away the detritus of the meal. Anna threads her way past the tables, and Hitesh follows behind. She can feel her skin burning on the back of her neck.

In the ballroom, the quartet are playing a waltz, and the room heaves and shifts with the movement of the couples dipping and turning under the high ceiling. Anna turns and holds her hand out to Hitesh.

'I can't—'

'I'll show you.'

'I—'

'I'll show you.'

When Hitesh takes it, her hand is cold in his, and he can feel the roughness and the calluses of all the hours bent over in the garden. It is a shock to the system. An upturning. He does not remember the last time he touched another human, felt skin on his. She steps in closer to rest a hand on his shoulder, and his other hand finds her waist. She is wearing perfume, but underneath it is the relentless freshness of grass.

They begin to move, and Anna leads him in a gentle rocking to and fro. She can smell the smoke and the cold on him, his soap, and his fear. She is aware of each place his body touches hers, their hands, the light pressure on her hips and stomach, his palm on her back. She can feel the texture of his skin and his shirt.

To begin with, Hitesh tries to block it out. Not to breathe her in, not to feel her body against his. Then he glances down at her, and is caught by her depthless gaze that works to find a way under his skin.

'What do you want from Magna?' he asks.

Anna holds his gaze, even as she frowns and considers his question. She chases the truth out of herself like a terrier, he thinks.

'I don't know. But I won't be beholden to others. Or at least, I'll have chosen to be.'

'After all this – the pain, and the hardship – you might still be a wife and mother?'

'Maybe. If it's what I choose.'

'Is it worth it? Is the labour worth the reward?' he asks. Her hair grazes his cheek and a frond has come to rest on the shoulder of his jacket.

'I don't know yet.'

'Hmm.'

They barely move now, only a sway.

'What do you want from Magna?' she asks.

'I don't know yet either.'

But Anna looks up at him, and the smell of grass makes his throat tight, and they share the lie.

The guests are sated. They have been fed and watered, and the hubbub of the ballroom has loosened from its early buzz into a mellow burbling. It is the right time to approach them for money, so Lord Blackwaite scans the room for prime candidates. The dancing couples cannot be disturbed, but he pauses to watch them anyway.

The husbands and wives fold together in easy intimacy, but the politics of the other dancers is fascinating to observe. Mr Velasquez and Lady Arnling are laughing and talking as they sway; Mrs Velasquez, svelte in mauve satin, waves to them and turns back to her friend. Thomas Fitzhugh holds Amber Delaney close, his mouth pressed to her ear to tell her something. Reverend Watts is on the sidelines looking fondly on, and Lord Blackwaite follows the line of his gaze until it rests on the policeman and Anna Deerin. Lord Blackwaite smiles too. To be young again. How different would life have been if he had married Elizabeth Millhaven? With modest luck, they might have had children. A son to dance with Anna Deerin, and an heir to Fallow.

Lord Blackwaite probes the old regret to feel it ache. Nothing to be done now.

He sights Mr Armand in the corner with Mr Iliescu. There is little English money to be had, but these are modern times.

When the dance ended, Anna slipped away and now Hitesh feels cold again. He drifts through the house. There are clutches of guests here and there, snatching conversation and drinking brandy. Hitesh has not been free to roam the Hall before, but tonight has sidestepped reality, and soon he finds himself alone in the entrance hall. He ignores the portrait of the Governor of Assam and scans the walls for the photograph Anna described.

Catherine does not take long to find.

Lord Blackwaite and his sister are lanky, slim in the way people were before there were gyms, and when rationing was a recent memory. They appear relaxed with one another and the matronly woman who stands at their shoulders, the tragic Lady Blackwaite.

Where is the previous Lord Blackwaite, their father, Hitesh wonders? Is it him behind the camera?

Hitesh takes a picture on his phone. It is nearly midnight and he does not know where the hours have gone. His hand goes up to the bow tie that has miraculously retained its shape, then to rub his eyes.

There is a shout. Whether he is the rabbit or the hound, Hitesh feels the instinct across his stomach, and jerks towards the noise.

It comes from his left. Some central event, loud, and the ebb-tide sound of bystanders that trickles away.

By the second shout, he is running, weaving his way past guests to reach the sound.

They are in the corridor outside the library, two men struggling. Their arms are locked together and the shorter man is also the stronger, about to bring the other to the ground.

'Stop!' Hitesh yells, but there is too much movement, too much noise.

He reaches them, and as he pulls the shorter man away, he realises that the tall man is Thomas Fitzhugh, his handsome face distorted by drink and fury.

'Stop,' Hitesh repeats, and manages to tip the other man off balance and apart from the art dealer. He puts an arm between them.

'Nick?' Hitesh sees the other man's face for the first time. Annette Waring's brother is in a waiter's uniform, blotchy and sweating. Hitesh wants to ask what the hell is going on, but they are too angry still, and he will have no sense from them yet.

Slowly, Hitesh lowers the arm he has held out between them. 'Thomas, come and get a drink.'

'I don't want a drink, Hitesh.'

'Then come and get one for Amber.'

Amber Delaney is in the doorway of the library, shocked into stillness. Thomas glances at her. She nods shakily and holds out her hand to him. For a moment, Thomas wavers, then begins to straighten.

Eloise Fitzhugh lurches into the doorway at Amber's shoulder. 'Thomas?'

'Mother?'

Nick looks from Thomas to Eloise and his pale face splits into a guffaw. 'Your mum? Go on then, off you go, boy.'

Thomas hurls himself forward but Nick is ready and grabs at his throat.

'Thomas – stop!' Amber is screaming, but neither of them can hear her.

Nick has toppled the art dealer before Hitesh can get hold of him. They are on the floor, and Hitesh grabs Nick's jacket to pull him back, but already Hitesh can see blood on them both. Nick is bulky and strong and he struggles against Hitesh, still landing blows, while Thomas kicks his long legs and hits them both in the narrow space of the hallway.

Hitesh shifts his weight and rolls himself and Nick to the side, then he is on his feet, catching Thomas across the chest with his arm as he rises. Hitesh drags him back into the library. 'Thomas – Thomas, stop! Stop or I'll have to arrest you.'

'Who the fuck are *you*?' Thomas snarls. He is muzzled with blood and there are streaks in his fair hair. In the glut of his wounded pride, he looks at Hitesh with contempt. Then he turns to spit on the floor, a glob flecked with red, and looks at Nick. 'You need to arrest this low cunt.'

'Nick, what are you doing here?' Hitesh catches his breath. Around them, the guests watch in horrified fascination.

Thomas stares at Hitesh. 'You *know* him? He was lurking in the bathrooms, waiting for men to come in. Waiting to steal wallets and watches. I challenged him and he went for me.'

'Fuck off.' Nick turns to Hitesh. 'This drunk idiot started on me.'

Hitesh holds his hands out again. 'Wait, just – Nick, what are you doing here?'

In the edge of his vision, he sees Anna take a chair from beside a desk. She places it near enough to Nick that by instinct, he slumps his bruised body down into it.

'He killed her. He killed Annette.'

'Thomas?' Hitesh frowns. 'He was a baby.'

'Don't be stupid. Blackwaite did. He did it. Some company was hiring waiting staff so I came here to find him. Didn't realise you would be here too, did I? Had to hide out in the bathroom.'

Thomas blanches, confused. 'Wait, what? No, he was lurking in the stalls. He was looking at my watch.'

Lord Blackwaite steps forward from the crowd, spurred into motion by his name. 'I beg your pardon, this is ridiculous.'

Nick starts up from the chair. 'Is it you? Are you Blackwaite?'

'I am, and I have absolutely no idea what it is you're talking about. Are you waiting staff? Why are you fighting with my guests?'

Hitesh feels the situation threaten to spiral again. 'Nick, sit down.'

Thomas, too, has begun to wobble, the alcohol and the violence and humiliation taking its toll. Hitesh glances across to Anna, and she places another chair within Thomas's reach.

'He did it.' Nick jabs a finger at Lord Blackwaite, and his voice cracks. 'Before she went, Annie told me she was scared up at the Hall. I knew she was stealing again. I never thought she'd get killed for it.'

'Why didn't you tell me she said she was scared?' Hitesh implores.

Nick heaves with grief that has nowhere to go. 'Didn't remember it at first – too much of a shock. Then, when, when I'd recovered – what, you were going to arrest the lord of the manor because some plumber's thieving sister said something forty years ago? Yeah, fucking right. If there's going to be any justice, it's not coming from you.'

Nick lurches out of his chair and Hitesh moves in front of Lord Blackwaite, but the older man steps around him, as incensed as Nick.

'You think I would kill someone for stealing? *Annie*. If it's the girl I think you mean, then I fired her.'

'What?'

Lord Blackwaite draws himself up, formidable. 'I caught her trying to take a silver coffee pot. She looked like a godforsaken creature – one I didn't have the heart to send to the police. I told her not to come back.'

It is Nick's turn to be confused. 'What? No, no, no, her boyfriend said she was gone. She didn't meet him after the shift. He came to me looking for her.'

Lord Blackwaite looks down, torn between his anger and what he wants to say. 'I – I don't know anything about what she did next. Who she did or didn't meet. She just said something very sad about being sorry for causing trouble. She said she was going to start afresh. It stuck with me longer than I expected. She was... lost.'

*

Watts checks the graze to Hitesh's forehead, a light bruise already coming up underneath. The vicar's face is wrinkled with such care that Hitesh wants to tell him that this is the least of what he has received over the years. He can feel that there will be a bad bruise on his stomach where Thomas's heel struck him, but if Hitesh checks it now, it will upset Watts.

'Honestly, it's fine, James, stop worrying.'

'Okay, okay. I did a good job on that tie, though.'

'Can you undo it now? It won't come off.'

'Just tug the end there, like that.' Watts folds it carefully into his pocket, then turns away.

Hitesh can see his face in the gilt mirrors of the drawing room. 'What's wrong?'

'Apart from seeing two men try to kill each other? And you, and Edmund, and Amber Delaney getting caught in the fray? Someone could have died. How could the Chief Constable only issue cautions?'

'Thomas is rich, James, and well connected. Even if the Chief Constable wanted to charge him with assault, he would fight it in the courts. And Lord Blackwaite didn't want the publicity. I saw him talking to the Chief Constable. Perhaps, in a way, he wanted the same for Nick Waring as he did for Annette. Not to make someone's difficult life harder by involving the police.'

'So that's English justice, then.' The vicar looks crestfallen.

'I'm sorry, James.'

The party has ended now, and the guests have bled away. Thomas ought to have been seen at the hospital, but he refused, wincing his way into a car with the shell-shocked Eloise and her husband. Nick left in his van, thinned, deflated again by the loss he had not been able to correct. Hitesh called PC Barnard to pick up Amber Delaney and take her home.

169

Lord Blackwaite joins them in the drawing room. 'I don't know what to say, Detective.' He is pale, a frail old man, late at night. He sits in an armchair. 'Never in my wildest imaginings did I think this would happen.'

'It's not your fault.'

'I promise you I didn't touch that girl, Annette.'

Hitesh sighs. 'I believe you.' He does. He recognised Nick's desperation for what it was.

'And the Fitzhughs are a good family. Thomas is a good man. I've known him since he was born. How he could attack someone like that—'

'You couldn't know this would happen.'

'I should have known.'

'*You couldn't know.*' Hitesh feels sorry for these elderly men. 'Sometimes alcohol brings out faces that aren't there the rest of the time.'


'Wait there, I'll walk you back,' Hitesh had flung over his shoulder. Then, with the help of the Chief Constable, he had led Thomas Fitzhugh into a separate room. Anna had sat down on the grand staircase to wait.

From here, she can see Catherine Blackwaite, and the two briefly lock eyes.

Was Fallow to you this same mix of peace and uproar? What did you do here? To whom were you beholden – or did you escape it?

Did you get away?

Did you cut whatever bound you?

The last of the guests have left, and the staff have been dismissed – told to return in the morning to clear away. But not tonight. Not after the tumult and the violence.

After a while, Anna gets up to stretch and soothe herself. She is in her flats now, heels clacking from her hand as she walks round the hall. A mirror returns her face, gaunt, lipstick long gone. She ties back her hair. What will be upended next, she wonders? The Fallow sister has started some sort of domino-fall, and Magna has not reached the end of the cascade yet.

Behind her, a door opens, and Hitesh emerges. Anna has seen blood over and over as a dancer – on feet, between toes, running down the shin after a bad fall; these were strange badges of honour. But it is different to see it on Hitesh's shirt and to know how it got there, and to not know which man it belongs to.

'Sorry that took so long. What's the best route to get you home?'

'Through the woods is quickest. I have a torch.'

'Through the woods, in the dark?'

She shrugs. 'It takes fifteen minutes. If we walk on the roads it will take forty, and there are no streetlights.'

Hitesh holds her gaze, frowns, is unable to suggest an alternative.

They step out and cross the lawn, and soon the Hall has gone, swallowed whole by night. Anna switches on her torch and finds the path that cuts down towards the woods.

'Have you done this before – in the dark, I mean?' he asks.

'Yes.' Hitesh's sigh is audible. 'Don't think about it too much, you'll only worry.'

The hillside is open and still, and she can hear Hitesh's breath behind her and their feet crushing the frozen leaves against stones. The moon is high and hard and bright, and Anna turns to glimpse Hitesh's face, cut up by shadow into slivers and hollows.

'Does violence become less shocking when you see it often?' Anna asks.

'A little – I think you just become less surprised when it erupts. It's usually closer than you'd think.'

171

'It feels closer in Magna than it did in London,' she says, and her voice feels hoarse.

They reach the woodland and the gravel path ends. Anna knows which opening to take in the trees, a small gap which leads to a dirt track. Hitesh follows, and she can feel him close behind, treading carefully, uncertain.

'Choosing to live at the cottage – did you never worry about being alone?' Hitesh's voice is hoarse too, worn out from the evening.

'For my safety, or because—'

'Because most people choose companionship, one way or another.'

'I couldn't do it with anyone else looking – the new life and the garden.' She leads them through a clearing and the moon briefly lights their way again. 'Why are you alone?'

Hitesh exhales a half-laugh. 'That's different. I didn't choose it.'

The woods close again, and there is only the thin beam of torchlight. Something scurries away from them through the undergrowth.

'Yes, you did. You could have found someone by now, before or after your mother, if that had been what you wanted.'

'It's not— I don't know, Anna.'

They reach the stream and Anna crosses first, taking the stepping stones that the local children love in summer. Then she holds the torch beam steady for Hitesh and he does the same. They are out in the open again, skirting the desolate meadow.

'Do you feel guilty about not getting on with your dad?' she asks.

'Yeah. I mean, not for him, he's— But for Mum, it hurt her. She loved us both.'

'It doesn't mean you can't make people happy, if that's what you're worried about.'

'Jesus, that makes it sound bleak. I made her happy, but I made her sad too. That's children. I'm not the first son to reject his father. It's not new.'

'Then what are you afraid of?'

He does not answer. They walk on, calves brushed by the wet, clinging grass.

Then they are in the orchard, on the bounds of the cottage. He still walks behind her, slowing his long stride to stay there. They cross the kitchen garden in silence. The lights of the cottage are on, as Anna left them, and they illuminate the last steps of the journey. She switches the torch off and turns to Hitesh.

'All this power and you use it to police yourself.'

'I don't have the control you have, Anna,' he says softly.

He looks down at her. She is in shadow but he knows her face.

Anna reaches out and puts a hand on his chest, and watches it rest there for a moment. He does not move. She can feel his breathing, the rise and fall. She slides her fingers between the buttons of his shirt and feels his skin burning. He waits.

'Anna, you don't have to. It's not why I—'

She begins to unbutton his shirt. He lets her, watching her dark head as she undoes each one. When his shirt is open she puts her palm on his chest again and he can feel the calluses.

Hitesh reaches down to kiss her. He is going to ask her something, but she slides the shirt off his shoulders and he does not need to. He can taste her now, put his hand behind her neck, breathe her in. She takes his tongue in her mouth and when they stumble against the door he can feel her breath on his neck and his body aching in response to hers.

Anna can feel the press of his weight against her. The taste of soap and sweat and his skin. He lifts her and she knows every cord, every bone, every blemish. This is what she wants.

*September 1967*

'Just for once, couldn't you be on time, Timothy?'

'I don't see the problem, darling – it's a few minutes here and there. You don't work, what's the urgency?' He strokes my hair but I bat his hand away.

'I'm taking such a risk to be with you. The least you could do is be here when you say you will be.'

'Okay, okay. Next time, I'll be here.' He leans in to kiss me but I turn away. 'Come on, Cath, don't be like that.'

He is fobbing me off. He does not want to be nagged. He is here for a lover, not a wife.

What am I here for?

He pulls me close. 'I promise, next time. Not a second late,' he murmurs into my neck.

'I don't believe you.'

He begins to stroke my breasts, put his hands up my dress, into my underwear. I could make him wait. I could tell him, no, not till next time.

But why cut off my nose to spite my face? Anger is no barrier to love-making. If he is here for what he wants, then why should I not be too?

'Come away with me,' he mutters.

'When? Where?' I whisper back. But as ever, he does not answer, instead he keeps kissing my neck, pulls up my skirt.

I want a lover. I need a husband. I do not know if these things can be reconciled into a future, but it can wait for now. Now is for pleasure.

Anna has replaced her bedroom window. The morning is still dark but Hitesh can see across to the patch of churned earth, dead where the rest of the garden is sleeping.

'I'm sorry.'

He pulls his shirt back on. In the mirror above the basin,

Hitesh can see that his hair is greasy, and below his eyes are dark marks like charcoal.

Anna watches him from the bed, the last traces of make-up still on her face. She sits up and does not try to hide her nakedness. He has seen her now – what is there to hide? He looks away.

'What is it you think you shouldn't be doing?'

'You're involved.' Hitesh glances through the window at the grave.

'So is most of Magna, one way or another.'

'Not like this.'

'Reverend Watts is a trustee, and you're friends.'

'I'm not about to sleep with Watts, Anna.'

'The case has been shut. You're not on duty. I want this, Hitesh. I chose this.'

'It's the spirit, not the letter of it. It's not a line I should cross. None of this is.'

She climbs out of bed but does not touch him; she will not plead.

'I'm really sorry. It's not – please don't think it's because I don't want to, that I don't want you.'

Anna shakes her head. 'I'm not vulnerable. I'm not the one who was surprised to be wanted.'

Hitesh finds her eyes. 'I'll still want you when it's over.'

'And if it's not over? If you never find out who killed her, or who she even is?'

'I'm sorry.'

'You'd rather be alone than believe I might want this?'

'I'd rather be alone than cause you harm, Anna, any more than I have done.'

It is so cold. Hitesh cannot bear to see the goosebumps on her body.

He turns away and looks for the shoes he is missing. They

are in the doorway, and he leans down to retrieve them, the bruise on his stomach aching.

She watches. 'You think I'd regret fucking you.'

'Anna, if this was only sex, I'd fear it less.'

She does not flinch, she does not turn away. She watches him lace his shoes, and waits as he tries to find something to say. But he can do nothing to lessen the pain he has caused, and he leaves without the insult of trying to pretend there is.

Hitesh crosses the garden as the sun is rising. His body is cold and tired beyond measure. When he turns and looks back from the gate, Anna is wearing her fleece and leggings. She stoops to let out the chickens.

The fence post has rotted at the base, past repair. The picket fence is at the boundary of the cottage, and serves no real purpose, since it is the wire fence of the kitchen garden that keeps the rabbits out. But Anna has worked hard to resurrect the garden, and the smallest parts of it need her attention. With a trowel and an awl, she works the bottom of the post loose, then with a hammer, knocks it free of the horizontal bar. The post remains stubbornly in the ground, standing at a drunken tilt, free of anything else. Anna gets to her knees again and works the awkward angle, splintering the wood with the weight of her shoulder.

This December is wet. So cold it chokes the bones, but unable to snow as it would like. Petulant and miserable, it inflicts itself on all it finds. Anna's knuckles redden inside her gloves as she scrapes at the soil, until finally she can fit the shovel underneath the post, and presses down on the handle with all her strength. The post topples, and she drags it to the wheelbarrow, panting. She stands to catch her breath, and looks through the freezing haze at the garden. Nothing stirs:

no birds, insects dormant, even the chickens have retreated into their coop. And no human as far the eye can see.

Anna pushes wet strands of hair back under her hat. There is a dull ache behind her eyes so she waits to see if tears will fall, ambivalent towards them. They do not.

Anna can feel her body, the reddened skin on her neck and ribs, the space she had been willing to give Hitesh. The wind rips past and takes the sensation with it. She has always been alone at Fallow, but loneliness is something new, something Hitesh has left on her skin.

She puts the shovel and tools in the wheelbarrow with the post and pushes it back towards the empty cottage.

'We think they're operating out of a pair of flats, one in Swindon and one just outside of Cirencester, probably supplied from London.'

Hitesh looks at the washed-out photos projected onto the screen. Two of them are children still, seventeen-year-olds who ought to be sitting A levels.

'As you know, county lines are a priority for the force, so we are reassigning all but urgent response units for this week, until the suspects are brought in.' The DCI loads a slide assigning teams and tasks.

Hitesh rubs his eyes. This is a good thing. This takes him away from Fallow, away from Anna. If he intervenes here, he can prevent harm, maybe even do some good, push for the teenagers to be treated as gang victims instead of suspects. This is a good thing.

Back at their desks, Barnard is his usual eager self. 'Next steps, boss?'

'Do you know how to fill in surveillance requests?'

Hitesh shows Barnard, then he organises and emails, reads reports and evidence logs. He can look at all these details without feeling anything. He drinks them in. He begins to plan, calling colleagues who agree times and locations. An old DS he knows from London gives him some background and warns him about a rise in dealers possessing firearms. There are some crime scene photos and injury details, gory and unaffecting. The hours pass without Hitesh leaving his desk.

Someone opens the windows a crack on the stuffy, overheated office. Wind slips through and ruffles the tinsel hanging from the ceiling. The rain has been falling all morning and the smell of greenery creeps in. Hitesh can taste her, feel her skin under his hands.

'You all right, boss, you look pale?' Barnard is watching him.

'Hmm? The gala was a late one the other night. I'm too old for that now.'

Barnard laughs. He is twenty-three and goes out drinking and wakes up the next day fresh as a daisy. 'Time catches up with us all, boss. Amber Delaney though.' He frowns. 'She was still distraught when I dropped her back in London. I could see her pacing up and down on the phone after she got out. I stayed in the car for a while until the lights went out in her flat.'

He's a good copper, Hitesh thinks, a good man. Long may it last. Hitesh nods. 'She saw some stupid drunken fighting. I'll call to make sure she's all right.'

'Cheers, boss.' Barnard goes back to writing surveillance warrants.

Hitesh leans back in his chair, rubs his eyes again. He picks up the phone to ring Amber.

*October 1967*
'I know about the Canadian boy.'

I put the kidneys down on the chopping board, then turn to Sprat. 'Know about who?'

178

'Don't pretend, Catherine. His name is Timothy. A friend at the college studies with him.'

Timothy has talked about us then. He has broken that promise. And my pain must be visible, because the flame of Sprat's anger flickers for a second.

'It isn't widely known,' he says. 'Matthew sought me out to tell me. He knew I'd want to know.' It rekindles. 'And it's a damned good thing he did tell me. If this spread, it would ruin you.'

'Don't be ridiculous. It's near enough 1968. I have a boyfriend, I'm not Christine Keeler.'

'You're not a shopgirl or a secretary – you have higher standards to uphold. No decent man will want soiled goods.'

'Don't be such a bloody hypocrite! Are you telling me you haven't touched Lizzie Millhaven?'

He takes a step back, shocked at my vehemence. 'That – that's different. We have an understanding. We'll marry after I graduate.'

'The only difference is that you have a— a—' This is ridiculous; it has been in me so many times now but no one has ever told me what to call it. 'A member. You're a man. That's the only difference between us.'

'Catherine, if Father finds out, he'll kill you.'

'Don't be so dramatic.'

The grass outside the kitchen window is damp. Under the sill, out of view, a drift of fallen leaves has built up and begun to rot. My breath condenses on the panes.

'Tell Father about Timothy. Introduce him; make it proper,' Sprat urges.

'If I tell Father, it's over. He'll ban me from seeing him; he'll scare Timothy off. Then I'll be alone. I'll be stuck here forever.'

'Now who's being dramatic? Father's old-fashioned, but he has no intention of keeping you captive here. If you can introduce a suitable husband, he'll let you marry.'

'You don't know how he is, Sprat. You're a son, you're the heir. Of course he's reasonable to you. If I so much as want to go into Cirencester, he has to know why and when I'll be home.'

'He's just protecting you, Catherine. It's a nasty world out there. Father's an honourable man and he loves you. You ought to treat him with the respect he deserves – tell him about Timothy.'

'Edmund, please. Please, don't tell him. I can't stand being alone here any more.'

'Tell Father, or I will. And stop sleeping with this Timothy, for God's sake. He won't marry you if you're already giving him what he wants.'

With that, my little brother leaves. The kidney has grown warm under my palm and the smell of urine leaks out. I release it.

We have been discovered then. Timothy has told someone. With that, we must surely be over. Either Sprat will tell Father, or someone else will. And there can be no arguing with Father, despite what my brother believes.

If life were poetic, Father would scorn me because I remind him too much of my mother, whom I killed with my birth. But I know how he treats his second wife, the mother I know, and it is too much of a stretch to think he treated his first wife with anything more than the same terse indifference. While I live quietly keeping the house, there is nothing to complain of, but when I start with my pestering, my needs and my questions about the future, then I am another chore, a dog who does not know its place at heel.

The rectory is filled to bursting with Advent programmes, donations envelopes, and mince pies from joyful parishioners. Even as he opens the front door, Watts has to snatch David away from a Christmas cake left on the doorstep.

'David, that has raisins in it for Pete's sake. You'll poison yourself.'

'Afternoon, James.'

'Come in, come in, Hitesh. Our Lord God did not give golden retrievers a strong sense of self-preservation.'

Hitesh bends down and allows his face to be licked, then nuzzles into David's coat in return. He is so warm.

'If it's a bad time, James...?' He follows Watts into the kitchen.

'No, no, Christmas is a marathon to be paced. As you say, it's good to have company that doesn't need something from me.'

Hitesh moves a stack of papers and settles on a kitchen chair. 'Well, that isn't strictly true.'

'Really? What can I do for you?' Watts puts the kettle on, then rummages in the cupboards, trying to find the teabags his housekeeper has bought.

'Does the church run any programmes for youths? Education or well-being or anything?'

'Oh, uh yes, yes we do. Not St Mary's ourselves, we're too small. But the south-west branch has programmes I can access. Why do you ask?'

'A police operation. Some kids might need support.'

'Send them my way, when you're ready. I'll see what I can do.'

Hitesh watches the vigour with which his friend moves. 'The Church keeps you young, James.'

'It alternates. Ages and renews me, I think.'

'You feel better, then – about things? About the confession?' Hitesh asks.

Watts pauses, milk in hand. 'I do, thank you. I – I still can't tell you about—' He waves his hand. 'But I feel better about things now. Though you don't.'

Hitesh shifts. 'What do you mean?'

'You *don't* feel good about things – you look grey.'

'Tired, I suppose, worn out.'

Watts brings tea to the table and feeds David a digestive that disappears in one. He opens up the parcel of Christmas cake. 'Marjorie, dear Marjorie. Every year she leaves one.' Watts cuts a couple of slices and passes one to Hitesh. 'Down, David.' He gives the dog an affectionate push.

Hitesh takes a bite. He has always found Christmas cake a strange food, overly sweet, overly rich, and something people seem to eat out of duty rather than pleasure. Manju had bought one from Marks and Spencer every year to serve to guests.

'So, did you sleep with Anna Deerin?' Watts asks.

Hitesh chokes on a crumb. Watts waits for him to stop coughing. 'People are always surprised to find vicars know about sex. We are humans, after all. Did you?'

Hitesh wipes his watering eyes. 'It's not— No. We didn't—'

'And things aren't going well?'

'There's nothing to go well.'

'You don't want a relationship? You seemed to like her very much.'

'Jesus, do I have no poker face at all? Sorry.' Watts waves away the blasphemy. 'No,' Hitesh continues, 'I can't pursue a relationship with Anna. Not while I'm still trying to find out who was buried in her garden. It was a lapse of judgement on my part.'

'Anna doesn't get a say in the matter?'

'It's not fair on her. She's getting enough scrutiny from Magna as it is. The whole thing is unfair to her.'

'She's a grown woman, and she knows who you are, and why you came to the garden in the first place. Let her decide.' Watts pours tea.

'There's too many abuses of power. I shouldn't have— And I can't prejudice any criminal proceedings.'

Watts sighs and passes him a cup. 'And after you finish with the case? You'll pursue her then?'

'I don't know.'

'Hitesh, don't look for reasons to be alone. Tell your boss, if you need a paper trail, or wait if you really have to. But don't use this as an excuse not to be happy. You'll end up alone like me.'

'Jesus, James. I'm just trying to do the right thing.'

'The right decision isn't always the one that causes you pain, Hitesh – that's a mistake Catholics make.' Watts grins. 'Just let me know when to book the wedding in.'

'Can we talk about something else, please?'

David, keen to contribute, puts his front legs across Hitesh's lap and wags his tail enthusiastically.

*November 1967*

'Catherine?' Mother settles herself on the sofa next to me in the drawing room. She draws my feet into her lap absentmindedly, as she always has, and strokes them. 'You've been on another planet recently.'

'Just my time of the month, I think.'

'No, it isn't, Catherine. Not for another two weeks.'

I sigh. 'What's the plan for me, Mother?'

'What do you mean, darling?'

'Have you and Father never discussed what my future is?'

'You know your father, Catherine. He keeps his counsel and woe betide anyone interfering.'

'It's not the nineteenth century any more. I'm not a piece of property to be managed.'

'Don't cross him, Catherine. Just don't.'

'I have no say in my own life, then?'

Mother says nothing. She strokes the top of my foot like a

sick child's hair. I love the bags under her eyes and her broad nose. But she chose to marry Father, not me.

'Is there a boy?'

'Does it make a difference?'

'Women don't get a lot of say in their lives, Catherine. It's an awful truth. But one that is easier to live with if you accept it, rather than fight it.'

'One day I'll leave, Mother. One day I'll get up and go.'

She stops stroking my feet. Her face is creased with fear. 'Please don't do that. I couldn't bear that. It would break your father's heart too—'

'It wouldn't.'

'Don't, Catherine. Don't.'


The village green is packed with market tents and twinkling lights, and the choir sings 'In the Bleak Midwinter' to the bustling crowd. Upper Magna presents a perfect Christmas card, lacking only snow, and Anna thinks of her parents, who would love to see it and her. She has promised she will visit them again in the New Year. She lied and said she hadn't been able to find anyone to come and look after the chickens over Christmas. She loves her parents, but it would be exhausting to be back with them, in her childhood home, for three days of conversation and reminiscence and the inescapable emotions that must tie together children and their parents, for good or ill.

And she worries it would be easier to stay than to return again to empty Fallow.

Anna's market stall is laden with wreaths and cakes and the firework blooms of witch hazel, and a steady flow of villagers stop to buy from her. She smiles and laughs, and wishes them a merry Christmas. Among these glowing faces, Eloise Fitzhugh appears.

'Hello, Eloise.'

'Hello, Anna dear. What lovely bouquets, as always. Where do you find the time to do everything, in that garden?'

'Thank you, it has been busy.' Anna drops to a murmur. 'How is Thomas, is he okay?'

Eloise looks down at the table. 'I think so. He stayed the night, but he left in the morning before we could talk. I've tried calling him, but he just messages to say that he's fine.'

'It's only been a few days. He'll call soon.'

Eloise tugs at the collar of her wool coat. She is as immaculate as ever, but her customary radiance is dimmed. Anna wants to lean over and hold her. 'He was so swollen you could barely see his eyes. But he was angry still.'

'With himself, I expect.'

'I'm not so sure. With me, with that man he was fighting. With everyone watching. Just angry. I hadn't seen him like that before.'

'It must be frightening.'

Eloise keeps her eyes down. Anna can see her lip trembling.

'Perhaps we don't know our children as well as we would like. My husband is angry with Thomas in turn, so—' Eloise shakes her head and looks up. 'You did beautifully, Anna. You brought some youth and glamour to Fallow. A number of the guests told me they would like to see the cottage gardens. Perhaps the Trust could arrange a visit in spring?'

'I'm so glad I could be of some use, and of course they would be welcome to visit.' Anna reaches across to Eloise and squeezes her hand. 'It'll be okay.'

Eloise squeezes back. She buys flowers and smooths her hair, and when she turns to re-join the crowd and greet her friends, Anna watches to see if she can find the fault lines between the face that is pleasing and the mother in pain. There are none, Anna concludes, as she watches Eloise greet a friend and stroke her goddaughter's hair, and she wonders whether Eloise is too practised to show it, or whether it is not there. Whether, if you please for long enough, the boundaries dissolve and your pleasing face is your real one, and the only one you have.

*O come all ye faithful, joyful and triumphant,*
*Come ye, oh come ye, to Bethlehem.*

Anna listens to the choir and scans the crowd. She cannot see Hitesh. Last week she would have told him about Eloise, and asked about Catherine Blackwaite, Annette Waring, Elizabeth Millhaven. Last week, Hitesh would have made her laugh with a joke about GK Chesterton, or Paul Wolsey's shamelessness.

Instead, she watches Reverend Watts as he tries to make progress through the stalls. Each time, he can get no further than a few steps before he is stopped for a chat. His brow furrows and relaxes as he hears the villagers' news; he pats shoulders and pretends to steal the noses from children. Anna watches as he holds an elderly woman's hand. He is reassuring her about something, and Anna can see the relief spread across her face. He makes it to the next stall before he is stopped again. All the while, David wags his tail at his side.

'Reverend.' Anna greets him as he approaches.

'Ms Deerin! Have you recovered from the gala yet?'

'Almost. I thought this was a sleepy Cotswolds village.'

Watts raises his eyebrows. 'So did I, but there's certainly been plenty of intrigue of late.'

He waits patiently, and Anna meets his eyes. 'You've seen Hitesh?'

He sighs. 'I have.'

Her chest tightens. 'Is he okay?'

'Broadly.' Watts nods. 'He'd be better for seeing you.'

'I'm not the one preventing that.'

'He's a good man, Anna.'

'I know.'

'That's why he's no good at this. He's afraid he's going to hurt you.'

'That's what's causing the hurt.'

'No one works in straight lines, I'm afraid. You understand he has a point, though, about being a policeman.'

'Hmm.'

'Besides, he's used to being alone. You'll just have to be patient with him.'

'Is this how you and David got together?'

'He was carsick on the way home from the breeders, but otherwise the similarities are uncanny.'

Despite herself, Anna laughs. Then tears quickly trip to the brims of her eyes and she swallows them fiercely.

'Merry Christmas, Reverend.'

'Merry Christmas, Anna.'


*December 1967*

I thought about writing a letter, but that seemed like the coward's choice. If I am to make my own life, the least I can do is have the courage to leave the old one.

'If that is your final decision, then at least let me walk you to the gates.'

And Father had calmly gone to collect his hat and coat, and I am shell-shocked by the ease of it.

His gait is stiff next to mine, as we walk through Fallow's woods now. When did I last walk with him? Not for years. He moves slowly these days.

'I expected you to shout, Father.'

'And what would that achieve, Catherine? Other than to make you walk away faster?'

The frost is crisp and the leaves have rusted blue on the ground. I will miss Fallow, and all its beauty. This parting company is the last thing I had expected. It throws me, and I try to watch Father's face in my peripheral vision.

'Let me take your bag.' He takes my holdall from me. 'Your train is at quarter to four?'

'That's right.'

'Where will you stay?'

'There's a hostel in Marylebone.'

He nods.

Mother – Mother I did leave a letter. Whatever I do, she will stand like Penelope, waiting for my return. But unlike Odysseus, I will not be back. And to inflict on her the act of leaving is a cruelty she doesn't deserve. She does not have to watch me go, only know that I am gone.

'Will you tell Edmund for me?'

'If that is what you want.'

'He'll visit me in London anyway, I'm sure.'

We are reaching the limits of the estate now. Ahead is the old gardener's cottage. Father never did find out about Timothy.

It gives me courage. Besides, this is my last chance to know before I am gone.

'I have never made you happy, have I, Father?'

'I don't see how it's relevant to the matter, Catherine. Are parents and children meant to make one another happy?'

The sound of the market reaches Hitesh in bed. He closes his eyes again and imagines he can hear individual voices in the hubbub.

He wonders how he let it sneak up on him. The new place, the stale grieving, perhaps. But he ought to have noticed it; he ought to have dealt with it before she knew.

And then he had gone home with her.

*She led.*

*You didn't have to follow.*

Hitesh still feels desire when he thinks of Anna, and it infects the guilt he feels. Even as he regrets what he nearly did, he knows he still wants to do it, and he hates himself for that. He had thought he was a better man than Paul Wolsey, and now he has hurt her.

The radiator next to his bed is on. He is too hot, his T-shirt and boxers are stuck to him. He ought to get up and go running. But he does not move.

A physio, a doctor, another copper, a few casual relationships here and there. Anna had accused him of vulnerability. Had it been true with the others he had been with? Had he had these doubts about himself before? He struggles to think back to another world, before Manju's death and Magna and Anna.

He peels himself up to sitting and pulls back the curtain. At the end of the road, the white peaks of the tents draw a washed-out Field of the Cloth of Gold. He is about to get up when his phone rings.

'Hi Darshan.'

'Are you coming back for Christmas?' His father has never believed in greetings.

'Uh – I don't know, I hadn't thought about it.' Hitesh slips back into Gujarati. 'Do you want me to?'

'You haven't thought about it?'

'I've been busy, Dad.'

'I see. So?'

'Let me see if I can get time off. It might be hard – a lot of the other coppers have family.'

'I'm not family?'

'You know what I mean. Kids.'

His father is silent at the other end.

'I'll try.' Hitesh watches his neighbour across the road scurry back from the cold of the market. They struggle to unlock the front door with their gloved hands and knock their wreath swinging to and fro, but when they finally get the door open, the rooms inside glow and Hitesh catches a glimpse of a Christmas tree. 'What happens at Christmas without Mum?'

Manju had been the heart of their festivities, just like she had been the heart of everything in their home. She had organised the Christmas presents and repurposed Diwali lights for the tree; she had insisted on Christmas dinners that looked nothing like the ones on television, not least because she served *channa* instead of turkey. Darshan had done nothing but open all the doors at once on the cheap Advent calendars she brought home. And then last year she had dwindled in hospital and they had not remembered it was Christmas at all.

'I don't know what happens, Hitesh,' his father says. There is more silence.

'Is the cleaning lady still coming?'

'Yes, she moves things. She puts them in places I can't find them.'

'Okay. Don't yell at her – I'll talk to her.' Hitesh says goodbye to his father and lies back on his bed.

What would Manju have thought about Anna? She would have been jubilant with this... whatever this is, with the ex-ballerina. She would have been teasing, entertained, worried. She would have encouraged her son to be happy.

*Then you shouldn't have died, Mum.*

*Oh, sorry, dika. I'll just ask the gods – see if they don't mind sending me back down.*

His phones pings again and he reads the message. 'For fuck's sake.'


Anna unloads the handcart from market. It took more than an hour to pull it back over the damp and shifting leaves, and the sun is nearly beneath the hilltop. She stands under the security light mounted on the shed as she returns empty flower buckets and unsold wreaths to their places. She feels hollow, like she might make a ringing sound if tapped.

Her ears prick up at the sound of tyres on the gravel track, and there is a split second when she is going to run inside, then she recognises Hitesh's car.

Unprompted, her body loosens and she feels the sweetness in her bones. She winds herself tight again and waits for him under the lamp.

Hitesh gets out of his car and puts his hands in his coat pockets. He comes only just within the circle of light and waits.

When neither of them can find a greeting, Anna laughs bitterly. 'So what is it?'

'She isn't Catherine Blackwaite.'

It is a blow Anna is not prepared for. 'She – it's not her?'

'No. It's someone else.'

Anna had not wanted it to be Catherine Blackwaite. She had not wanted it to be anyone. But she had known it, Anna had *known* it was Catherine. What she knows is all wrong.

Hitesh reaches out then stops himself, and Anna watches him return his hand to his pocket.

'Do you look foolish to your colleagues now?' she asks.

'I'm not sure any of them are thinking about the case right now.'

'Do you think I clouded your judgement?'

Hitesh pauses, then slowly shakes his head. 'No, she makes sense as a victim. Forensic mistakes are possible. It was worth re-testing the remains.'

'But it's not her.'

'No, it's not Catherine.'

'Then who? Annette still? Elizabeth Millhaven? The lover who became some version of that ghost story?'

Hitesh shakes his head again. 'I don't know. I'll keep looking. Annette, Elizabeth, others.'

She looks away. It is all slipping, meaning and emptiness sliding over one another.

'Anna, are you all right?'

'I'm fine.'

'No, you aren't.'

'No, I'm not.'

It is dark now, outside the circle of the light. The sun has set. Both of them are only outlines. Hitesh takes his hands out of his pockets.

'I chose you, Hitesh. Freely.'

'You'll choose better next time.'


'What did the doctor say?' Anna returns her gardening tools to the wheelbarrow.

'They'll do some more tests over the next few days; for now he can be at home, thank heavens, so long as he rests in bed. But as soon as the doctor left, he asked for you.'

Pauline looks fretful. Anna has only ever seen the housekeeper inside the Hall, and in the grey daylight of the garden, she is papery and insubstantial. 'Of course, Pauline. Come inside while I put something clean on.'

Anna leaves the housekeeper perched on the edge of the sofa and goes to strip off her muddy clothes. She pulls on a dress and tights, and feels something shifting. Foreboding or promising or a chasm opening. She does not know, but she can feel it under her feet. But then, she felt Catherine too. She no longer knows what is certain, and has to corner the fear.

Anna climbs into Pauline's little Nissan and knows that the older woman needs something from her. She leans across to clasp Pauline's bird-like shoulder. 'He'll be all right. He's a strong man.'

'You're right. You're right. Nothing to be gained by panicking, is there?' Pauline pulls down the cuffs of her blouse, takes a deep breath, then crashes the car into gear and begins the bumpy journey down the track and back up the main road.

Anna wonders what it is that Lord Blackwaite wants from her and draws only blanks as they drive past the hawthorn that twists its fiery arms into the sky, the inky starlings, the frost-perished formal lawns, up to the great grey edifice of the Hall.

Everything is strange.

Pauline ushers her in, up the grand staircase, down a corridor Anna has never visited before, to the panelled door of Lord Blackwaite's bedroom. The housekeeper knocks, and Anna can taste the queasy damp of sickness before she even opens it.

'Lord Blackwaite, how are you feeling now? Ms Deerin is here.' The housekeeper pokes her head around the door.

But he is asleep.

Pauline ushers Anna in and pulls a chair up to the bedside. 'Sit here, sit here, he'll be glad to see you when he wakes up.' She pats Anna on the shoulder and totters away to fetch tea like it is the thing that will save them.

Lord Blackwaite's face is almost serene as he sleeps. He looks translucent, less than the sum of his parts; his hair is thin on the pillow and his breath shallow.

Anna settles in to watch him. On the window, the rain starts again, pattering, pattering. She follows the rivulets. If it is not Catherine, then who? Annette or Elizabeth? A ghost from start to finish? And why is Anna here; what does Lord Blackwaite want? For a second, she lets her grip slacken. She lets the waves crash and turn, and considers letting them go, feels the ease. She drifts over to the window and regards the view. There is the cottage and her garden, the beds empty, the orchard skeletal, but waiting, resting, ready to return to life again when the Earth tilts back towards the sun. A quiet place;

a burial place; the chickens' home; the place she had nearly had Hitesh; her place.

She steps back into the icy waters.

Hitesh waits in his car across from the grimy bungalows. Next to him, Barnard adjusts a pair of binoculars, then jots a note in the log. The window fogs over and Hitesh turns up the car heater.

'You didn't have to volunteer for this shift, boss.'

'I don't mind. Reminds me of when I was a PC.'

Barnard looks sceptical and returns to the binoculars. Hitesh looks again at the cottages. They are the same pretty stone as the others he has seen in the Cotswolds, but they are decaying, neglected. In the front gardens are old bathtubs and rusted Calor canisters. The walls are greening, and inside there must be mildew. They are dwellings for the poor, twenty metres and a world away from wealthy villagers and the summer tourists.

'Rural poverty, isn't it,' Barnard had explained to him. 'Cost of fuel to drive everywhere, cost of gas to heat the old cottages; all the services have been cut, health and education and everything. Rent is sky high.'

'Why don't people move away?' Hitesh had asked.

Barnard had given him a strange look. 'They've always lived here. Got family and everything.'

Hitesh had felt ashamed.

Inside the cottage, the dealers are moving about, oblivious to being surveilled. The curtains are not fully drawn, and through the binoculars Hitesh can see the cluttered coffee table on which they are weighing and packing their product. As a process, it is both shambolic and ruthlessly professional. There are lighters and bags and papers, empty cans of energy drink. Then every few minutes, a call comes in to one of the six burner phones, and the smallest lad, acting as receptionist, takes the calls and notes down orders. The other teenager cuts the heroin with laundry detergent and puts the cling-film wraps in envelopes. Behind them, an older man mills round, observing. One of the boys asks something and cringes when he is barked at; he adjusts his baseball cap and goes back to his work. The boys do not speak to one another.

'Jesus, they catch them young,' Hitesh exhales.

'They're seventeen, they're old enough to know it's wrong, boss.'

Hitesh opens his mouth to reply, then closes it. To be seen as a bleeding heart is the worst of police stigmas, a betrayal. But he knows the force would be less hard on them if they were white.

He switches the heater off. It has become stifling.

Barnard changes subject. 'Did you reorder forensics on the Fallow body?'

'Yeah.'

'Was there a mistake or something?'

'I thought there might be, but no. Back at square one.'

'It's odd that no one has come forward with a proper lead.' Barnard stretches his long legs as far as the footwell allows. 'You working Christmas, boss?'

Hitesh shifts. 'Yeah, let the officers with kids have the day. I'll go see my dad in the New Year.'

Barnard takes up the binoculars again. 'You gonna be by yourself on the big day, boss, after the shift?'

'No,' Hitesh lies, 'I said I'd drop in on Reverend Watts once he's done with his services for the day.'

'That's— Oop, here we go.' Barnard picks up the camera as one of the teens emerges from the bungalow. The boy pulls his hood up and slings a bag over his shoulder, and Barnard snaps a few shots. 'Expect they're working Christmas too.'

*

Anna Deerin is at the bedside, but his head hurts, and for a moment he does not remember why. He tries to greet her, and finds only a clumsy tongue in his mouth.

'Take it easy, Lord Blackwaite. The doctor has been again, he said you need to keep resting.'

'Was I... was I awake when he came?'

Anna shakes her head. 'No, you were asleep.'

Lord Blackwaite settles back, then realises he ought to sit up, since there is a lady present. Like his tongue, though, his limbs are feeble.

'Please don't.' Anna settles him back. 'Not for my sake.'

He would like to protest, but without her help, he does not think he will be able to get upright anyway. He waits to catch his breath.

'The doctor thinks it's an infection, Lord Blackwaite. He'll take some blood this afternoon.'

Edmund opens his eyes again to look at Anna Deerin properly. Unflustered, capable, intelligent. Yes, this is why he had asked for her. He takes a deep breath.

'Help me sit up please, Ms Deerin.' He flexes each ageing muscle, demanding their obedience, and pushes upwards. Anna Deerin slips her wiry arms under his and assists with surprising strength. He pauses for breath again. 'Thank you. Well, I asked you here, didn't I?'

'You did. What can I do for you?'

He wonders how to start. It is hard to organise his thoughts, and there is prickling shame in what he needs to ask. He pauses, looking for another way. But there it is – he has left himself without alternatives, and once you have set a course, there is no use in being coy. 'Ms Deerin, I'm old, and I appear to be sick. As you know, I don't have a wife or children. Pauline is wonderful but she is far too old to care for me, I can't ask her that.' He pauses to haul the breath back into his lungs. 'Will you help me?'

The young woman furrows her brow. 'I don't have any care experience. There are companies that can—'

'I don't want an agency worker. I want someone I know. Someone I trust. I'm not asking you to do… any of the hygiene. I can wash myself. I can go to the toilet. But I'll need someone to help me out of bed. Fetch papers. Prepare meals when Pauline isn't here. Someone to lend a hand in the running of the Hall, if I'm in bed for more than a day or two.'

Anna says nothing. He cannot read what she is thinking, and that is true of so few people. 'I won't compel you. Your post at the cottage doesn't depend on it. I am asking as a favour – although, of course, you'll be recompensed for your time.'

'If you want my help, then of course, you have it,' she agrees.

Good; that is very good, he thinks.

'Thank you. Well, that's a load off my mind. I'll ask Pauline to make up a room for you so that you can be comfortable while you're here.'

With that, Edmund can exhale. He slides back down the pillows and lets himself release the portion of his mind that has been waking him over and over since his collapse that morning. He has discharged his responsibilities now. All is in safe hands. Fallow will not fall while he lies in bed. He feels his eyes closing and this time lets them go without a fight.

The kettle is the old-fashioned kind. Made of tin, it boils on the stove and lets out an alarming whistle when the steam builds up. It makes Anna jump.

She turns her conversation with Edmund over and over.

Anna is in the kitchen, where she has never been before. It lies cold and open like a mortuary, all basins and slabs and drainage. The window beyond the sink lets out onto the land at the back of the Hall, and from where she stands she can see the lawn and the copse being eaten blade by blade by the dark.

Suddenly, the Hall is at her fingertips. She could stroll out of the kitchen and walk into every room, with full permission. If she wants to know who the Fallow woman is, how better to find out than to step in?

Lord Blackwaite has asked her to.

'I'm glad he's got someone here with him.' Dr Bradley had nodded. 'Infections at this age can turn nasty quickly. Take his temperature twice a day as standard, but don't wait if you think his temperature is going up.'

Dr Bradley had left Anna with a course of antibiotics, emergency numbers, and his approval. She had gone down to the cottage and shut the chickens away for the night, then come back up to the Hall. Now she is in the kitchen, getting Lord Blackwaite something to eat.

Anna sets out a slice of pound cake and the tea things on a tray, and pops the first antibiotic tablet from the blister pack. As she puts loose tea in the pot and pours the water over to steep, she finds her feet moving to some old steps. *One two three, relevé, one two three, plié.*

Anna ascends the whitewashed staircase to cross back from the old servants' quarters into the main house. The smell of wood and the tea in the pot and the chill in the vast, ghost-populated hall rise with her footsteps.

Lord Blackwaite has been drifting in and out of sleep all afternoon, but when she knocks on the bedroom door, he calls her to come in.

He has sat up by himself, and looks almost proud of the feat. Anna feels an unexpected dart of affection.

'How are you feeling now, Lord Blackwaite?'

'Like a frightfully old man,' he smiles, 'but a good deal better. Has Pauline gone for the day?'

'She has.'

'Will you sit and keep me company? I expect I'll drift off again in a few minutes anyway.'

Anna brushes the skirt of her dress aside and sits on the chair that has become hers in the course of the afternoon. Lord Blackwaite's breath is costing him a lot of effort but she can hear him trying to hide it.

'Are you warm enough, Lord B—'

'I appreciate the respect you have always shown me, but I think perhaps Christian names will do now.' He is good-humoured.

'Edmund.' She tries it out, much more cautious than she had thought she would be. 'Is it strange? The title, and the Hall?' she asks. 'Did you ever wish for a more normal life?'

'You know as well as I do, Ms Deer—'

'Anna.'

He laughs breathlessly. 'You know as well as I do, Anna, that there is no such thing as a normal life. Superficially, perhaps, not having the ancestral home, and whatnot. But not really. Everyone has too much rolling round in their brains, hidden away from view, for a life to be *normal*.' He looks at her.

She passes him his tea on a tray. She wonders if the Fallow sister is the woman to whom he was once engaged. 'I know. Then do you have any regrets about staying at the Hall, instead of leaving to explore the world?'

Edmund takes a sip and lets himself rest against the pillows. 'No, no I don't. My father taught me very young how lucky we were to be custodians of this place. This piece of history. It'd be like the Virgin Mary telling Gabriel, "Thank you, but no thank you". It's a gift. A duty — but that duty is a gift, if you understand.'

Anna feels that knock of affection again. 'I think I understand. Like the garden. I might be freezing or exhausted but without me it would fail. And when I think I can't do it any more, it hands me its fruits.'

Edmund smiles, wrinkles chasing each other up from his mouth to his eyes. 'Yes,' he exhales, 'when I was a boy, seven or so, the exterior wall to the east wing collapsed. Just gave way after some heavy rain. But I stayed awake all night crying in my bed, poor chap that I was. Because I realised the Hall might die. I had assumed it would always be there, but now I could see that it might fall, without care, without a caretaker. So, of course, as a young boy with a vivid imagination, I swore I'd protect it, like some knight in a legend.' His eyes cloud with fondness for the innocent young Edmund. 'As I got older I realised what I actually needed to do was to look after the accounts and repairs, and the things that aren't at all Arthurian, but are what Fallow needs, and what keeps it alive.'

Anna smiles. 'You've lost your romance. Who else would do those things, apart from someone who understands a labour of love? I was at the gala, I heard your speech.'

Edmund chuckles again. 'You understand how to make an old man feel better.'

'That's why I'm here.' She stands to take the tea tray and lets him see the smile creep into her eyes.

And that is how the next five days roll from one to the other. Anna wakes, she walks down to the cottage in the dark to let the chickens out of the coop and to feed them, to whisper them the things she has no one else to tell, then walks back again in time to greet Pauline as the housekeeper is hanging up her coat.

'So much for Tuesdays off. I am glad you're here, Anna, my love. I'd be in such a flap doing this on my own – he's never ill.'

'That's nonsense, and we both know it, Pauline. You could run a multinational in your sleep.'

The women make breakfast together and day by day, Anna drips her questions, honey-like, over their labours.

'Why didn't Lord Blackwaite ever marry, Pauline?'

'Maybe nobody ever asked him, dear. Pass the milk, would you? I don't know, I think he was perhaps a little tunnel-visioned in his youth, very focused on making the Hall work. And then you blink and your knees ache in the mornings. I don't think he's gay or anything, if that's what you mean.'

'He had a fiancée, didn't he? Eloise Fitzhugh mentioned her.'

'It rings a vague sort of bell, but I don't know really.'

'What was his mother like, Pauline?'

'Lady Blackwaite? Well, I didn't start working here 'til after she'd died, but she used to have my job, you know. She was the housekeeper for the Lady Blackwaite before her, Catherine's mother, but I think *she* died giving birth, if I remember rightly. Hard to keep track, once you go back a few Blackwaites. And then the old Lord Blackwaite married the housekeeper and along came *our* Lord Blackwaite. My own mother said it caused a bit of a stir, initially, marrying the housekeeper, but I think the Hall was pretty down-at-heel after the war, not a lot of money going round for a fancy new lady, so I suppose he saved the housekeeper's salary by marrying her! Pop that up now – he likes his toast well done, but not cremated.'

'Hang on, Catherine and Lord Blackwaite don't have the same mother? They're half-siblings?'

'Well, from what I understand, there was never any distinction made between the two. The housekeeper-cum-new-Lady Blackwaite raised them both as her own. Tends to be the male bloodline that people worry about,' Pauline rolls her eyes, 'and they shared a father and it was his title to pass on to the next male, so that's that.'

'Oh. Right.' Anna arranges the tray absently.

*

Anna takes Lord Blackwaite's temperature and keeps a neat chart for the doctor, who visits twice, and pronounces his patient on the mend. The infection retreats. Edmund's colour returns.

Anna misses the last market of the year, but she does not care. She can live on what is in the cupboards and cold-shed, on the pay that Edmund has promised. This is what matters now. Everything else hibernates.

In the afternoons, when Anna has helped Pauline with the laundry and the dusting, she keeps Edmund company. On the second day, she helps him to move to an armchair and he asks her to bring up the post. By the third day, Edmund asks Anna to read his emails to him and dictates his replies.

Anna sees that the Hall has a problem keeping damp out of the basement. Weddings are the most profitable events to host, but the most fraught. Hiring for the spring and summer season, when the Hall opens to the public, must begin in January and be finalised by mid-February at the latest. There are new income streams to be explored.

Edmund asks her to fetch this and that from his study. When he nods off in his armchair, she covers him with a blanket and soon knows his earthy scent.

When the house is quiet, Anna tidies and bakes in the kitchen. She goes to the study and looks through Lord Blackwaite's papers, as far back as she can find. Combing, searching for traces of the woman in the garden. Anna goes back up at teatime with fresh rolls and cakes. 'Pauline says you're fattening me up,' he tells her.

She walks down to the cottage to put the chickens to bed. She gives her conscience its moment of revolt; she locks it away again.

At eight, she goes to check that Edmund has a glass of water for the night and has taken his last tablet. By then, he is very tired, but he always opens his eyes to wish her goodnight and thank her for her help. She tries not to feel sad.

Then Anna goes to her room in the attic. The one she asked for. It is a beautiful place. These are the old servants' rooms, and are crisp with whitewashed walls and iron bedsteads, washstands and a dormer window. She likes her room very much and knows it would make a fortune if it was let out to holidaymakers given a chance to play at *Downton Abbey*, and not to think of the previous inhabitants and their exhaustion, homesickness, unwanted pregnancies and backstreet abortions, their petty jealousies, the grievous harms, the unfulfilled potential, the fundamental unfairness of one lot of people set below another.

On the seventeenth of December, Pauline departs for her Christmas holiday and the Hall is nearly empty, save Anna, a loose marble in its corridors, and Edmund, at a desk by his bedroom window, typing slowly on his laptop.

Edmund asks twice whether she has somewhere she needs to be over the holiday, and twice Anna assures him she does not.

On the eighteenth, he moves from his bedroom to work in his study again. Anna brings him cups of tea. She goes upstairs to strip the bedsheets in his room and finds his single-breasted pyjamas, which have been changed for a shirt and jumper. He asked forgiveness for not wearing a tie.

Hitesh's chest feels tight, and he knows Barnard feels it too. The younger officer has never done a full raid. Hitesh can see him sweating and fidgeting in his stab vest and rests a hand on his shoulder. They hang back behind the armed officers and wait for the signal in their earpieces.

It comes.

The firearms men break the front door lock with a ram, and before it is fully open they are driving forward, shouting, dominating, securing. By the time Hitesh and Barnard are across the threshold, the armed police have pinned down the two boys and their boss, and a Staffie is being muzzled. The chaos stops twenty seconds after it starts, stifled to a jarring calm.

The cottage looks just like it did under surveillance, but inside, the smell is overpowering. The acidic tang of the product mixes with the smell of bodies and winter heating, and within seconds Hitesh is nauseous.

'Okay, start securing evidence for London colleagues. Barnard, formally arrest Tolley. Williams, arrest Jameson. You two, get the dog off scene.' Hitesh issues a series of orders, drawn up in Cirencester's draughty command room.

Barnard approaches the boss, Patrick Tolley, who closes his eyes and smiles, like he is hearing a joke. Hitesh turns to the older of the two boys.

'Michael Okeke, I am arresting you on suspicion of possession with intent to supply. You do not have to say anything, but it may harm your defence if you do not mention when questioned something which you later rely on in court. Anything you do say may be given in evidence. At the station, you will be provided with free legal counsel if you do not wish to appoint your own. Because you are a minor, any and all interviews will take place with an Appropriate Adult present. Do you understand?'

'Yeah, yeah,' Michael mutters. His record says this is his fifth arrest. At his age, Hitesh had a PlayStation and revision and all his meals cooked for him.

Suddenly the boss starts howling wildly, head thrown back to the ceiling and heaving great lungfuls of breath. Startled, Barnard jumps backwards, and DS Williams spins to see what is happening. In a flash, Jameson, the younger boy, shakes a phone from the leg of his joggers and stamps his heel down on it. The plastic splinters and the boy lands a second blow to the circuitry before the officers drag him back. Tolley abruptly stops howling and shouts with laughter instead.

'Okay, okay, break them up.' Hitesh's head is pounding. 'Tolley out to the van, Jameson in the kitchen. Okeke here.'

Michael Okeke tries to stand up from where the armed officer is holding him on the sofa and is shoved back down.

'Fuck you!' Michael lashes out.

'Listen, he just said stay here, are you deaf?' the armed officer barks.

'All right, all right.' Hitesh holds a hand out. 'We'll be okay. Can you help get Tolley out?'

The officers begin clearing the room. Michael looks every inch a sullen teenager slouched on the sofa, and Hitesh wants to scold him for missing school.

He draws his breath and runs over what they planned back in Cirencester. They need evidence, and at the station, interviews and statements. Hitesh talked to the council about places at a secure children's home for the two boys, but was told the only place to remand them was the young offender institution, a place known for the staff's enthusiastic use of restraint.

Michael begins to fidget, kicking his feet to and fro. 'Can we go? I been doing this since five in the morning, I want to sleep now.'

'Will you just keep still? I'm trying to help you.'

'Fuck you, fucking joke,' Michael mutters, tucking his chin into his hoodie.

Hitesh feels his face tickling, like he's going to sneeze, and he realises it's his eyes. He's going to cry. He's going to fucking cry. He turns away. Michael watches, confused, wondering if this is a pause before some retribution. Hitesh rubs his face furiously. *Fuck's sake.* What is happening to him?

'Boss?' Barnard dips back in with some paperwork and pauses. 'Did he hit you?'

'What? No, just the adrenaline dropping. Sudden headache.'
Barnard looks puzzled, but carries on.
*Pull yourself together.*
'You look like chewed-up gum,' Michael says from his position on the sofa.
'Yeah, thanks. You look like you're facing a stretch for being really bloody stupid, so just quiet down.' Hitesh lowers his voice. 'You'll be able to sleep at the station.'
Michael rolls his eyes, but leans back without another word.

Anna turns over and the bedstead creaks. It is bitter in the attic and, even under the duvet, it is too cold to sleep. She slips out from under the covers to grab a jumper that is draped over the back of a chair, and hurries back into bed to pull it on. The cottage has never been as cold as this – it is too squat to the land to feel the worst of the night, but the attic of Fallow Hall is exposed on the hilltop, and at the mercy of the void above.

The little crescent-faced moon peeks in through the dormer window and Anna finds herself fidgeting again. She has too much energy. However hard she works in the house it is not the same as the garden, or dancing. It is past midnight and she is no closer to sleep. Her mind trips over itself, spins and glides restlessly over the woman's bones, Edmund and his illness, his half-sister, Hitesh, the Hall, Christmas, her parents, the work left undone in the garden. She sits up and looks out of the window but the angle is too high to see the cottage. The treetops of the woodlands wave gently back and she knows what she needs to do.

Anna slips out of bed. Her feet are already in thick socks, and she picks up the torch she uses to let out the chickens before dawn. On top of her flannel pyjamas and her jumper, she pulls on a second jumper, the man's one she had lent to Hitesh. She knows he would rub his face, exasperated and resigned to her actions. Then she opens the door onto the corridor and steps out into the night air. Anna listens. The silence is deep and textured with draughts and the settling of old pipes.

Anna makes her way to the servants' staircase and takes the steps slowly, emerging by the bedrooms on the first floor. The air is pure and argent in her lungs and her heart thumps painfully. Skirting console tables and potted palms, she reaches Edmund's bedroom door and presses her ear against the wood. Her own breath is staccato, but behind the door there is nothing to suggest Edmund is not asleep.

Following the weak beam of the torch, Anna moves to the end of the landing and the control box for the alarm system. The metal squeals on its hinges, and she freezes.

The seconds pass. She waits. Finally, she accepts the silence.

Anna inputs the code that Edmund has trusted her with and switches the alarm off, then she descends the main staircase on soundless toes. At the bottom, she pauses.

The woman in her garden was known to the Hall. If Anna cannot trust that, then she can trust nothing she knows of herself, and her new life is worthless.

She swings the torch beam onto the photograph of Catherine with her mother and brother. Step-mother and half-brother, she supposes, as though that changes anything. The woman in the garden is no degree of Blackwaite.

Anna turns to the east wing, walking silently under the portraits and into the library, made cavernous by the dark.

Edmund's study had held nothing of interest when she had searched it; it is a working office, only recent papers. But in the library, she had noticed a solid teak cabinet and twitched the handle only to find it locked.

Anna tries the handle again now, then steps back.

The gloaming moon picks the room out in black and grey, and she swings the torch beam over the walls, then begins to run her fingers across the underside of shelves, into the nooks and corners between stacks of books. One shelf, then the next, and the next.

Something shifts in the doorway. Anna stops.

'Hello?' Her voice is tiny and hoarse and deafening.

The shadow wavers.

'Hello?'

Anna raises her torch, and sees the velvet curtain that has come loose from its tie-back and fallen across the doorway. She wants to scream with laughter; she wants to tear it from its hanging. Anna crosses over and fumbles to set it right, with the torch clenched between her teeth. Then she goes back to the shelves, running her shaking fingers under each one. She reaches the delft-tiled fireplace, and on impulse, opens the lid of a cloisonné pot. The key is there.

With her torch in her mouth again, she unlocks the cabinet and opens the door inch by inch until she is sure it is noiseless. She swallows her saliva back down and shines the torch inside. There is a broken vase and a pack of AA batteries. And there is paper, in two large, untidy stacks. Anna pulls them out and dust pollutes the night air.

Then she gets to her knees and begins to turn the pages.

Typewritten. Some handwritten. The paper is rough and yellow, unfamiliar to the touch now that manufacturing techniques have changed. There is a flyer announcing the opening of Fallow Hall to the public for the first time, which Anna remembers was in 1980. Some invoices for furniture lacquer. Plans for a medieval fayre dated June 1985.

She flicks to the bottom of the pile. These papers are nothing. There are no names or photographs.

Anna feels more grief than she knows what to do with.

Where then? Where will she find this woman?

The Hall refuses to give her up.

There is a chance she is lost forever, and Anna will not even be able to give her back her name.

Suddenly, she is hollowed out with failure.

A pipe clanks somewhere in the house and Anna retches and swallows the thin acid back down. She sees the skull in her hands and its empty, pleading sockets.

Anna will not let go of her.

The house is two and a half centuries old – there must be papers. At the very least, Edmund must have his birth certificate, his parents' death certificates, a handful of photographs, estate documents. Maybe he has diaries, or his parents' diaries. Catherine's, even. Letters. Anything that might hold this woman.

Edmund's papers are not in his study, nor the library. She had searched his bedroom while he slept those first few days, and found only Dickens and Wilkie Collins and an old prescription for his blood pressure.

But then, Anna thinks, Edmund was not always Lord Blackwaite. The master bedroom he now inhabits must once have been his parents'. And where does anyone keep meaning but in their childhood?

Anna returns the papers to the cabinet and makes everything as it was. She can barely feel her toes now, but she makes her way silently back through the corridor and up the grand staircase.

At the head of the stairs, a grandfather clock ticks, low and rhythmic, and in her exhaustion, Anna pauses to listen to it. It lulls her. It is a peaceful, generous sound, more like listening than speaking.

Anna begins to feel warmth in her stomach.

It is what she feels when she thinks of him. When she strived all that time to peel her face back and Hitesh did not revolt from this, nor from what was underneath.

He did not take, he had been careful not to take.

Anna waits there, resting.

*Tick – tick – tick –*

'I think that was Lord Blackwaite's room when he was a boy, and that one perhaps Catherine's, and those two were guest rooms,' Pauline had answered on the first morning, when Anna had asked what the other doors were on the landing corridor.

Anna goes to the door Pauline pointed out and turns the knob a millimetre at a time, then slides through the gap and closes it again. In the next room, Edmund still sleeps.

Anna sweeps the room with the torch. A four-poster bed and a bedside table, a bookshelf and a chest of drawers.

She opens the top drawer with the hiss of wood on wood. It is all here.

Here is a photograph of Edmund as a young man, arm round another teenage boy, standing outside a school building. Here is a portrait, when he is in shorts and Catherine not yet ten. Here is his mother again, pin-curled hair, forearms that have lifted heavy mattresses to make the beds. There is a snapshot, perhaps taken by Edmund himself, of a man in a day suit. The picture is grainy, and the man is turning away, but Anna thinks his skin is damaged somehow. She recognises the library in the background. This, then, must be Edmund and Catherine's father.

There is Edmund's birth certificate, along with his mother's and father's birth and death certificates. Like Hitesh told her, Lady Blackwaite's records her death not as from self-inflicted wounds but from heart failure, in 1968. Lord Blackwaite the elder died in 1976, aged sixty-eight, of a stroke. Beneath are his documents from the Ministry of War – his service record and discharge papers. There is a photograph stapled to the file, of the same man from the snapshot, but with a face that has not yet been to war.

There are no records for Catherine, but why would there be; she will have them now, in Canada.

In the dark, progress is slow, and yet Anna feels certainty in the details of these lives. They promise something of themselves, of the Fallow sister.

At the bottom of the drawer is a stack of letters from the only period Edmund ever lived away from Fallow Hall, during his three years at Oxford. He writes to his mother to tell her he is happy and studying hard and to ask her to send socks and other items he has forgotten. He writes fondly of his family and asks after them all. He asks whether she has seen Elizabeth Millhaven, how the dog is keeping, whether his periodicals are still being sent to the Hall instead of college. Occasionally there is a letter from his father, who responds to Edmund's questions regarding financial and administrative concerns, praises his good essay results and reminds him that he is a young man who ought to enjoy himself, within bounds.

Finally, there is a letter marked May 1968.

*Dear Edmund,*

*I cannot imagine that this term has been easy. Loss does not weaken so quickly, if at all. As your father, it is my duty to assure you that it will get easier, and that the best thing you can do now is to continue your studies before returning to your home at Fallow, where I hope we might soon find a measure of peace.*

*Remember, what your mother chose to do is not something to be spoken about widely. It is not something others will understand. It is a matter for this family. But remember also – it is not something that ought to bring you shame, because it was neither of your doing or of your choosing. I hope your mother has found her own peace now.*

*Yours,*

*Father*

Anna imagines Edmund, twenty years old and all alone at college. His mother dead, and his father stern, loving, binding. She imagines the silence that Edmund has imposed upon his own tongue all these years. Beyond the wall, he is sleeping. She wonders if he is dreaming, and what of. She wonders if he has ever told a soul about his mother. She exhales and puts the papers back in the drawer. She checks the others.

'No comment.'

The duty solicitor leans over to whisper something in Michael Okeke's ear. He nods and slouches back. Over his shoulder, a middle-aged woman watches closely. The overhead lighting is harsh.

'Can you confirm who the other people in this photograph are?' Barnard asks, pushing forward a surveillance picture.

'No comment.'

The interview room is too small for the five of them and Hitesh tries to balance his file on the edge of a table cluttered with Styrofoam cups and water bottles and a tape recorder.

Barnard tries again: 'Mark Wilfield claims Patrick Tolley forced him to let the three of you stay at his address for the purpose of dealing drugs – that you cuckooed him. Is this true?'

'No comment,' Michael replies wearily. Hitesh wonders if he had a chance to sleep in his cell.

'Are you just going to say, "No comment"? There's a chance to defend yourself here,' Barnard presses.

'He's entitled not to comment, if that is what he chooses after legal advice.' The Appropriate Adult speaks softly and firmly from her corner.

Hitesh leans forward. 'We're aware that you're only one cell in a larger county lines operation. Did you have contact with any of the other players?'

Michael rolls his eyes.

Barnard sighs with frustration. 'We're trying to help. If you cooperate with us, you're going to get an easier ride in court. Drugs harm people, destroy communities. Don't you feel bad about that?'

'No one's forcing anyone to take it. It's none of your business what people do,' Michael snaps. The duty solicitor places a warning hand on his arm.

'Can we stick to the specifics of the case, please, gentlemen?' he asks.

Hitesh closes the file in front of him. 'You're a child,' he offers, 'you're a minor. Tell us how you were recruited. By whom, when? Can you at least tell us how you got dragged into this?'

'No comment.'

'At school, through an acquaintance, how?'

'No comment.'

'Your file says you saw a friend get killed a few years ago,' Hitesh says. Michael's eyes flick up, then straight back to his lap. 'That sounds hard. Were you offered counselling?'

'No comment.' Michael shifts in his seat.

'I'm not asking about the drugs now. This isn't about the case. Did you ever get seen by someone?'

Michael glances at his Appropriate Adult who opens her hands to suggest he may answer if he chooses. He looks back at his own hands. 'Had an assessment.'

'And?'

'The guy said PTSD.'

'Are you still experiencing symptoms?'

The teenager shrugs and fidgets in his seat.

'Let me guess, there was no follow-up treatment?' Hitesh asks.

Michael lets out a laugh, a surprisingly musical sound. 'I'm still on the borough waiting list.'

'What do you want to do, instead of this? Retail, hospitality? Go back to college and get some qualifications?'

'What does it matter? I'm going to get locked up anyway.'

'I can push for something else. Training, rehabilitation.'

'Were you born yesterday? *They don't care.*' Michael shoots a look at Barnard. 'I'm gonna get locked up. Just – try and get a lesser charge, yeah? Shorter sentence.'

'Will you give me something to work with? You were in care, you were vulnerable. Were you threatened if you refused to do something?'

Michael gives Hitesh a look of infinite pity. 'Push CPS for a lesser charge. Don't fucking say I was cooperative or I'll get holes before I make it to trial.'

'That's it? That's the limit of your hope?'

'That's it, man.' Michael retreats into his jacket. He tucks his chin in. 'I'm sorry if anyone got hurt because of me, yeah.'

'Anna, can I have a moment?'

She puts the tea down on Edmund's desk. 'Of course.'

He looks fresher than he has since Anna came to stay at the Hall. He has lost the pallor of his illness, and his cheeks are no longer sunken but filling out again.

'My eyes are sore from staring at these accounts. Will you have a look for me?' He pushes himself out of his office chair with a sharp exhale, and gestures to Anna to sit. The seat is warm.

'What am I looking for?'

'This column here is for total outgoings related to maintaining the fabric of the house. This one is total outgoings on visitor facilities and staff. This section is our various income strands.'

Anna scans the numbers, similar to her garden accounts, but at a scale of tens and hundreds of thousands.

'I see.'

'The donations we've secured following the gala will take care of the fabric of the Hall for a while. The question is what we do with the small amount of capital left over, how we maximise it. What do you think?' There is a strange note in his voice.

Anna is cautious. 'I'm not an accountant – what does the Trust think?'

Edmund sighs. 'They want a gift shop.'

'You're unusual in not having one. Visitors love them – it would make a lot of money.' She watches Edmund's face. 'But it's something you've been resisting?'

'I don't want a gift shop at Fallow.' Edmund rests against the side of the desk. 'I opened the Hall up to the public long ago – I understand that it's not just a private home any longer. I'm not struggling with that. Certain provisions have to be made for visitors – the van for tea and ice cream on the lawn, bathrooms opened up and so on. But there's a difference between sharing the beauty of Fallow and all its history – keeping it alive and financially viable – and letting it become just another thing for people to consume.'

Anna does not say anything.

Edmund lets his thoughts drip out. 'I don't want to rip out the drawing room to put a shop in. A spot for day trippers to buy a knickknack, then to leave and forget that this place ever existed.' He stops abruptly and looks away. 'But perhaps the line I've drawn is arbitrary. Perhaps we crossed the bridge to postcards and jam a long time ago.'

'No,' Anna replies, 'no, that bridge hasn't been crossed. It doesn't have to be.'

Edmund waits this time.

'You want the income of the shop but without structural – or moral – changes to the fabric of the Hall. Nothing commercial, nothing out of character.'

'Precisely,' Edmund encourages.

'How far is the drive to Magna village from here?'

'Four minutes, on a clear run. Almost all visitors come by car.'

'Then use what already exists; there are two cafes, a card shop, two antiques shops – look to partner with them. You'll signpost visitors to these... affiliates. In return for a small percentage of any sales. It won't make as much money as a shop here, but the ties between Magna and Fallow Hall will be strengthened, and the character of the Hall won't be eroded.'

Edmund nods slowly. 'There would be objections. Plenty of wealthy people who don't want more tourists ruining their pretty village.'

'Yes. But others own businesses in Magna, and there are others again who need jobs.'

'It's not the perfect solution,' Edmund ruminates, 'but it's what the Hall has always done for the area, acting as an employer, a part of the local economy. I'll think about it.'

Anna gets up from the desk and Edmund returns to his seat, smiling. Anna feels she has passed some sort of test.

Edmund drinks his tea, silent for a moment, then, 'I'd like you to stay, Anna. Not just until I'm recovered, but after that too. I'd like you to work here at the Hall.'

'Oh.' Anna hesitates. 'What about the garden?'

'By all means, live in the cottage, keep the gardens. Scale back a little if you need to – you would have a salary here. But help me run the Hall. Learn the ropes, see what happens.'

Anna does not know what to say, and Edmund smiles fondly and patiently. She feels her way forward. 'You aren't on your deathbed. It was an infection, and you've nearly recovered already.'

'But not forever, Anna, don't be childlike. You watch the plants growing and dying in the garden. Consider this a wake-up call to the both of us. Sooner or later, I'll die, or at least be too old to work.' He frowns. 'And then what happens to Fallow if I haven't nominated a successor? The Trust is good but they simply oversee things. Someone else will take on the day-to-day running of the house, and they will change it into something it isn't. They'll put in a gift shop.'

'There are qualified business managers, curators…'

Edmund speaks softly. 'I have watched you work from dawn 'til dusk on the garden. One in ten thousand people might understand what this place needs, and I won't find another before my time is out, and I won't take a refusal. Would you refuse? This?' He gestures to the room around him, to the house, to the weight of the bricks and the glint of the glass.

Anna pauses.

The cottage is empty, and the garden fallow. She has dug so far that she can half see what is underneath, and has found bones.

The Cirencester DCI looks disconcertingly like Paul Wolsey. He has a smart suit and a good haircut, and has learned the value of speaking smoothly. The Chief Constable thinks highly of him, and his walls are lined with qualifications and commendations.

Hitesh has to stop himself shouting. He changes tack with his boss. 'Refer them to a Youth Offending Team if you have to, but don't push CPS for a prosecution. Tell them it's not in the public interest. They're kids. They're victims of grooming.'

'A YOT referral – for class A? What are you on, Mistry? They're not puppies.'

'I know that, sir.'

'Jameson was arrested last year for threatening someone with a knife. Okeke has been stopped twice carrying a weapon.'

When Hitesh had arrived from London, DCI Harries had regarded him as something of a coup – a Brown murder cop from the capital, an asset to the modern constabulary Harries wishes to put his stamp on. Now Hitesh can see Harries' rapid re-evaluation. Perhaps Hitesh is a mistake, a gift horse he ought to have looked in the mouth.

'They're not saints, sir, I'm not saying that, but gangs pick up vulnerable lads all the time. Treat them like family, start getting them to carry product. By the time they try to leave, they're stuck. They know they'll get killed if they jump ship. And they know we'll charge them.'

'Why don't they come to us as soon as they're approached? Don't make them the victims. It's Cirencester that's the victim. Normal, honest folk don't need criminals going unpunished.'

'It's not that simple. There's multiple victims here. Charge Patrick Tolley, sir, he's twenty-eight, he's been coercing Okeke and Jameson. The boys are scared of him. We saw it during surveillance.'

Harries' tone skips the line from firm to harsh. 'I don't know where this bleeding-heart shit comes from, but it's no use here. They've broken the law, they face consequences. These are rotten, nasty kids.'

Hitesh matches Harries' harshness: 'Sir, what happens when they get out after a few months? It all starts again. These kids are traumatised and they don't have any options. *We* should be giving them options.'

'If that's your attitude, why are you a copper? Go be a social worker. There's no such thing as nice, or innocent, and there's no such thing as a perfect solution.'

Hitesh can see Jameson and Okeke's whole lives being balled up and thrown away like wads of paper. 'Thank you, sir,' he manages.

\*

The feathers have stuck to the coop. The blood is a sticky glue that pastes them onto the gatepost, the ramp up to the coop, the sliding door that the fox scrabbled open. In the torchlight, the blood is black and the feathers bright. By itself, it might look almost pretty, like an abstract painting. But under the coop is the flesh, and the gizzards, and the heads separate from the bodies.

The fox has had all six of them. Five are still here, but Nureyev has been chosen as the prize to slink away with.

Anna says sorry to the chickens, or at least to their bodies. She has failed to keep them safe. She lays a hand on Margot's wing. Margot who had liked to perch in her lap. She strokes her in silence for a while.

Then she unlocks the gouged front door of the cottage and leaves red prints on the frame. She fetches a bin bag and washing-up gloves, and goes back outside and kneels down to pick up the bodies of the animals she had named and fed and cared for. Then she walks past the woman's grave in her garden, out through the orchard and the arbour and the meadow. In the woods, she empties the bin bag out and leaves the remains for the foxes and other creatures to finish as they please, and the insects to begin work. The bin would be a waste.

Anna does not cry. She leaves what she feels in the leaf litter. Still smelling of blood, she walks back to Fallow Hall to wash and begin the day.

Reverend Watts returns from the care home carol service to find Hitesh and David sat on the rectory doorstep, boots and fur caked in mud.

'You two look like you've had an adventure.'

'I came by at three and your housekeeper said you wouldn't be back for a while, so I took David for a walk. Hope that's all right.'

'Of course it is. I'm so busy during December, David only forgives me the short walks because of all the scraps he gets.'

Hitesh gets up slowly and smiles, but Watts can smell distress a mile off. 'Come on in, then. It's bitter this week. I thought it would be better than the damp, but I'm starting to have my doubts.'

The rectory heating is on full blast, and they strip off hats and boots and David flops heavily into his basket by the radiator, too tired even to fuss for treats. Hitesh puts the kettle on while Watts unpacks a bag of Christmas cards from the care home residents, and shakes out his folded vestments to dangle from the back of the kitchen door.

'I don't know if I can do the police any more, James.'

Watts begins opening cards. 'I see. From a moral or an emotional perspective?'

'Both, maybe.' Hitesh sits at the kitchen table that has become more familiar even than Anna's. 'The kids I wanted to refer for educational programmes have been charged. CPS will have no problem getting convictions.'

Watts raises his eyebrows. 'You don't think they did it or you don't think they deserve to be punished?'

Hitesh traces the grain of the table with his fingers. 'They did it. Maybe they deserve some form of punishment, I don't know... But not this. Shit childhood, exploitation, conviction. Out of prison to start it all again. But the coppers don't see them as kids.'

'You're a copper, and have been for a long time – justice isn't something you've come to a position on before?' Watts prompts.

'I was Murder for a long time. Maybe that feels more straight-forward.'

'Perhaps. And you've got older.'

Hitesh laughs at this. 'I've definitely got older.'

'The greys suit you.' Watts opens a biscuit tin of homemade mince pies and offers them to him. 'From Maureen this time.'

Hitesh takes one but leaves it untouched next to his mug. 'And I still haven't solved Fallow. I found Elizabeth Millhaven today, Jones as she became – the thirty-fifth Elizabeth Jones I checked. Like Blackwaite said, she married, moved counties, lived a normal life, died a normal death. I'm still no closer to finding out who was buried there.'

'It isn't all on you, Hitesh. One man can't save everyone.'

Hitesh smiles wryly. 'I hope you don't tell people that on Sundays.'

'Very droll. And Anna?'

'What about Anna?'

'Are we doing this again? Have you talked to her yet?' Watts presses.

'I've caused Anna enough grief.'

Watts' temper suddenly flares and he puts down the Christmas cards. 'So *do something*, Hitesh. What is it you're waiting for? If you can't be a policeman any more, quit. Pursue something that doesn't make you miserable. Do something that might help those kids.' The priest relents a little. 'At least do something that doesn't leave you lonely.'

Hitesh looks at Watts without any resentment. 'If I'm not a policeman, what am I? I'm not a father or a husband, I'm barely a son. Being a copper was meant to be a simple way to do good, and now I can't even do that.'

'You're a friend, and you ought to be Anna's lover. More than that, if you weren't a policeman, you'd still be a human being. A good one.'

Hitesh rests his head against the kitchen wall.

'I'm not saying it isn't difficult, Hitesh. Especially not after losing your mother. No one breaks out of their personal and professional identities with any ease, but if what you want is to be *good*, to *do good*, pursue that. If you want to be happy, pursue it. Better yet, pursue both. It's not meant to be easy; a human life isn't meant to pass without trials.'

'*I cannot praise a fugitive and cloistered virtue, unexercised and unbreathed.*'

'Milton?'

'Milton.'

'Very good. Now eat your mince pie,' Watts chides.

Hitesh is grateful to his friend. He misses Anna. It is his own fault.

What should Anna do with Edmund's offer? It has burned in her since the moment he asked her to stay. She climbs the hill to the west of the Hall, and the one after that, so that the formal gardens have disappeared from view, and the cottage and her own garden are two miles away, with the Hall set between her and them.

The cold is hard and unforgiving. It is two days before Christmas and the hills are empty, apart from Anna. In her boots and waterproof trousers and fleece-lined coat and hat and gloves, she is hot and chafing, and around her eyes the exposed skin is frozen and red. She turns back to look at the land tumbling away from her, then sits below the dry-stone wall that once marked a field boundary. The wind blows swathes through the grass, then whips back on itself so that the blades turn silver blue, rippling and churning the land.

The stones of the wall are solid behind her back, and the lichen creeps over them. She is tempted to think they have seen many things, but that would be to impose on these stones the same human-centricity that people impose on everything else. Always thinking it is about them, and expecting the rest of creation to do the same. Anna has been at Upper Magna nearly two years now, and she has spent that time looking inward at herself; she does not deny the irony. But it has not been under the illusion that the earth watches a thing she does, or that she matters to it. The land is far better than a human because it is not one mind but a host of lives that propagate, synthesise, develop, die, outlast centuries. If she has been a god in her own garden, it is because she has made fealty to these systems, the infinite complexity of the soil, the microbes, the fungi, the fauna. Because she has not destroyed it with her humanness. She is a god who will not leave footprints.

She knows this, and the land has not asked of Anna, because it cannot and will not. It does not care about her, and that is freedom.

What to do with her freedom, then? With her face peeled back, and the unbeholden life. Hitesh will not have her.

Should she continue to live alone at Fallow Cottage, Anna wonders, to take what comfort she can from what freedom she has? Without Hitesh, but without, too, anyone who might receive without taking.

A pair of crows bicker their way across the pink sky. Anna twitches her legs to stop them going numb.

She knows that the hollow, heavy, bitter feeling in her stomach is loss.

She forms questions in her mind, one, then another, until they are clogged and feverish. But Anna knows, somewhere at the core of herself, that these questions do not matter.

She has lost Hitesh already. There is another she cannot lose.

She stands up and shakes herself out. There is an oak tree to her left, and on it is a bright orange bracket of fungus, wet-looking, like it will not freeze. As well as the Hall, the land is what Edmund offers her.

Anna makes her way down the hill, into the valley, following a footpath of gravel and compacted grass. The next hill is steep and she reaches the top nearly on her hands and knees. Then down again, through a clump of woodland, into the formal gardens that Keith McCarthy tends with a little care and a preference for geraniums.

She approaches from the east of the house and can see Edmund in the library, where he likes to rest after a morning in the study. She had left him there with tea and a slice of madeira cake. He gazes out of the bay window, twisting the cup in its saucer, deep in thought. When she is close enough, Anna waves, and he smiles and brings his hand up in return.

She steps in through the open mouth of the portico and opens the door she already has a key for, and feels the rush of warmth that has built up despite the emptiness of the house. She strips off her coat and waterproof trousers in the cloakroom, places her boots in the rack. Her jumper and jeans are enough to stay warm now.

She goes down the back stairs to the vast kitchen and boils the kettle on the range, and puts the fresh pot on the tray, and looks out of the sink window onto the copse, and already it is becoming the backdrop to her thoughts.

Anna brings the tray up to the library and Edmund rises from the armchair, well enough again now, to stand for a lady's entrance.

'I've been thinking about your proposal. Yes, I would like to stay here.'

Edmund leans forward, like he will crumple with relief. He straightens again. 'I am so very glad to hear that, Anna. Desperately glad. Quite the Christmas present.'

She pours tea for them, and Edmund begins on the particulars without hesitation.

'Will you continue to live at the cottage, or would you prefer to move into the Hall permanently?'

'I'd prefer to remain at the cottage, for the time being, once Pauline is back after Christmas. I want to continue with the garden as well – perhaps scaled down, as you suggested.'

'Perfectly understandable. There is a strong degree of flexibility – that's the advantage of not leaving a transition until I'm incapacitated.'

Edmund delineates his plans, and the pay he suggests, which Anna agrees to without consideration. He has been making projections and working on two- and five-year plans for the estate, which he is keen to share. He wants Anna to think about the role she envisages for herself. He wants her to think about how to capture Fallow's history and present it to the guests afresh; he fears his age is making him sentimental, and sentimentality can never be the same as effectiveness. Anna swims forward, eyes fixed on the horizon.

They talk for two hours, until Edmund is exhausted and sits back in his armchair with his eyes closed, old again.

Finally, Anna asks whether he is upset to think that the Hall will be out of the hands of the Blackwaite family once he is gone.

'I used to be. I used to think of the Hall and the family as an inseparable entity. One home and one line.'

'And now?'

'I still believe in the Hall and the family as one being, historical and yet something I hope stretches into the future. I don't wish to sound mawkish, but what has changed over time is the certainty that family need be about blood. Fallow has had a line of custodians, and they have all been male Blackwaites. But what matters about the next custodian is that they know Fallow in their bones. If I had had a son, he might have been feckless. He might have gambled Fallow away. No guarantees in blood, I'm afraid. So, instead of choosing by blood – not that I had that choice – I have chosen someone who is in the family, spiritually, if you like.' He looks Anna in the eyes. 'I have chosen someone who understands.'

In her garden, the land had eaten the Fallow sister's body with the same indiscriminate efficiency, love, disdain, as it will the chickens' bodies. Eyes gobbled up by insects, skin and hair by microbes, arms that clutched and feet that walked, taken for what they were worth.

One day, maybe Anna will be picked clean by the same earth.

'I understand.'

'Mr Mistry?'

'Yes, speaking.'

'I'm calling from the Royal Free Hospital in north London – nothing to panic about, but your father has had a fall.'

'Is he all right? What happened?'

'He was brought in by some friends from his temple. He fell on the stairs there. He has some bruised ribs, and he's a bit shaken, but he'll be absolutely fine. Are you able to come in and collect him?'

'Dad, what happened?' Hitesh starts asking before the nurse escorting his father has settled him in a chair.

'Nothing, it's nothing,' Darshan snaps back in Gujarati. He has a deep blue bruise on his cheek.

'It's obviously not nothing. What happened?'

'I slipped. Why is everyone overreacting? Drama, drama all around. It's just a bruise.'

'The registrar said you fell on the stairs – it could have been really serious. Did you lose your balance? Were you dizzy?'

Darshan waves a hand irritably.

'Dad, this is serious.'

The nurse looks uncomfortable to be caught between the father and son, arguing back and forth in angry voices. She does not know what they are saying, but she gently intervenes. 'I think everyone has had a bit of a shock. Why don't I get you both a cup of tea and you can work out the best course of action? We need to be able to discharge Mr Mistry safely.'

Hitesh feels guilty. He had forgotten she was even there. 'Thank you. If you give us the discharge papers, I'll settle Dad back at home and make sure he has people coming round to check on him.'

Darshan shoots his son a dirty look but does not disagree.

They wait on the rigid plastic seats without talking, and after a while, Hitesh watches the other patients, trying to work out what the acute outpatient care ward does. Hospitals are as opaque in their functions as the police, he thinks. Manju had affirmed as much when he had asked her. 'It's an ecosystem, dika. No one is watching all of it at once. It seems to work well enough, even if we never have staples.'

Hitesh glances across at his father, who glares into space. His hands are on his knees instead of crossed over his chest like usual.

'Are your ribs tender to rest your arms on, Dad?'

Darshan ignores him.

'Dad, does it hurt? Let me ask for some more painkillers for you.' Hitesh speaks as softly as he is able.

'Doctor gave me some already. I'll be fine,' Darshan mumbles.

The nurse comes back over with the final papers and a box of medication. She talks Hitesh through the aftercare and warns Darshan with mock sternness that he must come back for the further tests they have agreed on, and earns a rare smile from him.

Hitesh takes Darshan out to the car park in the hospital wheelchair, but when they get to the car, Darshan will not accept his help to stand up. Hitesh watches his father wince

227

and struggle to pull himself up and slide across into the passenger seat. Hitesh feels a pain in his chest, like he had when Manju had begun to struggle. It is love and helplessness. Then the progress back through London rush hour is glacial, and the men sit in silence again. By the time they arrive back at the pebbledash semi in Kingsbury, it is dark, and once Darshan has hobbled through to the lounge, Hitesh goes into the kitchen to put the kettle on, and rings for a takeaway for them both.

The kitchen is scruffier than when Manju ran things – the laminate has blotches on it and curls at the corners, a tap needs tightening – but Hitesh realises it has not deteriorated as much as he had feared. His father is managing to wipe surfaces between the cleaner's visits, and the stainless-steel tumblers sit washed up on the draining board. Hitesh checks the fridge; there is bread and the milk is in date. He relaxes a fraction.

Darshan doesn't complain when Hitesh asks for his phone to contact cousins and family friends, and by the time the food arrives, Hitesh has arranged for two people to visit each day during the week. Then they sit watching Sky News and eating from their laps.

'This is too salty, not like your mother used to make,' Darshan grumbles.

'Mm. Her dal was better too.'

'But not her dhokla.' Darshan wears the ghost of a smile.

'God, not her dhokla.'

'You didn't like them either, hmm?'

'I didn't have the heart to tell her. She thought I liked them,' Hitesh confesses.

'They were very bad.'

They chuckle, then Hitesh says, '*You* didn't tell her, did you?'

'No, you think I'm a monster? No, I wouldn't tell your

mother that.' Darshan shakes his head. 'Your mother was a gift. Dhokla or no.'

Hitesh slouches back against the sofa cushions.

'We have that in common,' his father adds. 'We thought your mother was an angel.'

'Did it hurt that I fell so far from the tree, Dad?' Hitesh asks suddenly. 'The cooking, the English degree, the police.'

'Not marrying either. We would have found a good match for you.'

'I can find a match myself.'

'Where is she then, eh?' Darshan waves his hand again. 'Your mother let you do what you wanted. That was her role: look after her son, make him happy. That is not the father's role. Father's role is to make the right choices for you, protect you.'

'Protect me from what? All we did was argue.'

Darshan shrugs. 'I stopped you doing some of the stupider things you wanted to do when you were young. I stopped you getting hurt many times.'

'When?'

'Many times. I defended you to my friends, and now you are police sergeant—'

'DI.'

'Now you are police sergeant and you have a good wage, pension, own a flat. You are not too old to marry, if you change your bloody mind.'

Hitesh rolls his eyes. 'So all the years of shouting have really been love?'

Darshan nods. 'Yes.'

Hitesh struggles to formulate what he wants to say, the memories too full of bitterness. 'You aren't disappointed in me, then?'

'Occasionally, yes. Overall, no.'

'Then why the hell have you spent all this time making me feel like I let you down? Why did you make Mum think you felt that?'

'She understood.'

'She didn't, Dad. *I* didn't.'

'I don't need to put on my emotions in a big show – hugs, tears, *natak*. I did what a father should do. No fuss.'

'But you made me feel like you didn't love me, Darshan.'

His father looks stung, and turns back to his food. 'That is not true. I did these things because I love you.'

It is Christmas Eve.

Hitesh stares at the ceiling of his childhood bedroom, the one he stayed in while Manju was dying. The Artex ceiling is greying like the curtains. He closes his eyes again. He needs to get up and drive back to Upper Magna so he can work Christmas Day. But he allows himself a few minutes more and feels himself begin to drowse. He thinks he can feel Anna's skin, warm against his.

The offering he ought not to have taken.

He opens his eyes again.

How is anything gained but by taking, he wonders? If he will never take, can he be good, can he be happy, as Watts counsels? Love, sex, jobs, feelings, property. Land, colonies. They are reached for, then taken.

It is after lunch, which Hitesh cooked, and Darshan is dozing in a chair downstairs. Hitesh turns over and looks at the painting of a peacock and horses that Manju brought with her from Surat when she moved to England.

The empire had been taken by trade, by force, by brutality. God-given right, the good of the local population, the spread of Christianity; whatever the reasons by which it had been rationalised. Right back to the beginning of time, the first land staked out, the first enclosure for goats. Nothing has ever been innate, but has been gained by the taking.

What becomes of him, if he will not take?

He closes his eyes.

It is Christmas Eve, and Anna is in the kitchen at Fallow Hall. She has told Edmund she will prepare a sort of Christmas dinner for tomorrow, and has fetched what she needs from her own kitchen at the cottage. No meat, but potatoes for roasting, carrots and onions and squash, bread to make stuffing. She has brought her bundt tin to make cherry cake too.

'Christmas dinner from Fallow's own land – I can't remember the last time I had that. Not since I was a child.' Edmund had been delighted.

She is at the sink, her sleeves rolled up as she washes the vegetables before setting them aside on the old draining board where the fruit is defrosting. The grass outside the window is a needle frost, and refuses to soften or bow to the afternoon.

She ought to call Mum and Dad, Anna thinks. They will like it. She will ask Edmund if she can use the phone in the entrance hall later.

She cuts slices from a stale loaf and begins to grate them into crumbs for the stuffing.

Anna wonders what Hitesh would do if she called him now. Would he come? Would his resolve have weakened? She knows it will not have. She had tried to give. She had wanted to give. He had thought he was taking something he should not. She understands. She wants to give again.

Anna crushes the apricots in her hands, still full of ice crystals. She squeezes again, pulping them, savouring the hot-cold burning on her skin. She is cooking, she is cleaning, she is caring. Soon she will put the kettle on again.

She remembers the details from the coroner that Hitesh

had shared with her. The Fallow sister was in her twenties or thirties. She had never given birth. She died in the vicinity of the cottage. The apricot mulch runs down Anna's arms. She discards the stone and drops the fruit into the stuffing bowl, then starts to crush another. She was killed with a rifle – ubiquitous, especially back then, in the rural community. She is not Edmund's sister. She is not Elizabeth Millhaven. There is little reason to believe she is Annette Waring.

Anna gazes through the window above the sink and the sun is already declining in the sky. The landscape shifts and forms the backdrop to her thoughts. The sun flecks the counter with gold, and lays a band across Anna's thin forearm.

The Fallow sister had broken her left arm as a child.

Anna sees the skull in her hands again. And she knows, then, who it is. It has always been simple. It has always been true.

In Kingsbury, Hitesh turns over in bed and looks at the painting again, and he knows too.

*December 1967*

'I have never made you happy, have I, Father?'

'I don't see how it's relevant to the matter, Catherine. Are parents and children meant to make one another happy?' He passes me my holdall and looks into the treetops.

I almost want to laugh with my father, and the pain he must have carried all these years, in his face, in his heart. I glance over to the cottage I had used to meet Timothy. There are winter roses growing wild over the garden fence.

'You could grow this place, Father. Not just the cottage, but Fallow Hall. It could be alive again, for us and for the village. I know – I know you were hurt by the war. I can't imagine. But I'd like you to be happy here, I'd like you to feel – whatever it is I can't give you. Wholeness.'

And I smile, because finally I feel free to do so. I love my father and I am leaving. I am free.

His face creases up with something unfamiliar. The edges of his eyes are wet, and he looks away. I can hear the ragged edges of his breathing.

'A quarter to four, your train then?' He clears his throat.

'That's right. I'll write to you. Goodbye. I love you.'

And I am free.


'Edmund?'

'Yes, Anna?' He looks up from *A Christmas Carol*. He reads it every year, delighted by the supernatural, and the way that human decency wins out. It is an indulgence he allows himself.

The library is brightened by the afternoon's winter sun and the fire he has lit to drive away the draughts. Anna has her sleeves rolled up, like she has come straight from the kitchen. 'How is it all going?' He stands.

She crosses over in her light, graceful manner, sits and crosses her ankles. He sits again. Anna looks Edmund in the eye. 'Why was Catherine buried in the garden?'

And everything drops away from Edmund, like the gallows in a puppet theatre.

'Anna, what on earth are—'

But he catches her eyes, and in them there is certainty, and Edmund knows there is no point in lying to her any further.

'How did you know it was Catherine?'

'I've always known. The *how* got in the way for a while. In the end it didn't matter – I started with her and the rest could be explained.'

Edmund shuts his eyes. Through his eyelids, the sun turns the world pink and gold.

*December 1967, three days earlier*

'Father, I need to tell you something.'

'What is it, Edmund?'

'It's about Catherine.'

Father furrows his brow. Perhaps Catherine is right, Edmund thinks. She receives none of the leniency that he does. He hesitates. 'She has a boyfriend. She's been meeting him secretly. A Canadian at the Agricultural College. I've told her to put an end to it.'

Father says nothing. He rubs his brow, rearranges the pens on his desk. 'Who knows?'

'Timothy, the Canadian, of course. Matthew Harwood, a mutual friend of ours. Perhaps one or two others.'

'Mm. You did well to tell me.'

Edmund wonders what his father is thinking. There are so few people he cannot read, but his father is one.

'Don't punish her, please, Father. I just thought you ought to know.'

Suddenly his father stands and embraces his son. Edmund is being held tight. The older man seems to cling to something he has found there.

They do not speak of it again.

A few days later, Edmund is reading in the library, ignoring the work he has been set for the holidays, when his father rushes in.

'Edmund, get the hunting rifle and meet me at the old gardener's cottage. Now.'

'What? Why? What's happened?'

'Catherine is running off with that boy. She needs some sense scaring into her. Run ahead.'

'What, Father... why—?' But his father has already gone.

Edmund reels. Father has a violent temper, but he has never

been a violent man. What can he mean by scaring Catherine so badly? What is Catherine doing, trying to leave home?

Edmund goes to fetch the gun from the case. He will ask questions later.

He cuts across the lawn at the back of the house, and as he glances across towards the front, he can see his father and sister making their way slowly down the drive. He ducks out of sight and weaves along the treeline until he can cut further into the woods and down towards the cottage. He is young, he is fit. He reaches the cottage with ample time.

Then he waits at the side of the building, tucked into a doorway. Father and Catherine have stopped and are talking. Then his father turns and catches Edmund's eye in his hiding place. He steps out.

'Edmund, what are you doing down here?' Catherine jumps as he approaches. She looks at the rifle in his arms. 'There's nothing to shoot down here.'

'There is — look, a partridge.' Father points to a hedgerow, and Catherine turns, sandy hair moving over her shoulders in a motion that will make Edmund sick in his dreams.

Father reaches across with one fluid movement and takes the rifle, brings it to his shoulder and squeezes the trigger.

Catherine falls forward, and Edmund's legs drop him to the ground. He lets out a keening noise, then scrabbles towards his sister.

'What have you done? Catherine… Father, what have you done?'

'She was leaving, Edmund.' His father stares up at the sky.

Land is claimed. It is taken by the first to claim it. Sometimes it is taken in turn by the next man.

As Hitesh drives, he lines up the queries he will have Barnard make, arranges and rearranges dates and timelines in his mind, looks for what will corroborate them. He will pin down the proof. That she is Catherine Blackwaite. And that Edmund is no Blackwaite at all.

Anna's face is pale and tight. 'But why are you and Catherine not related?'

'The DNA test that your detective friend insisted on? Strangely, it worked in my favour. Nothing that I had planned – none of what happened was something I planned.' Edmund inclines his head.

'Was it the war?'

'It was.' Edmund tips his chin back. 'You know my mother was originally the housekeeper here, to the previous Lord Blackwaite. Perhaps you will find something in this – my father was the last gardener at Fallow Cottage.'

Edmund watches Anna Deerin struggle with it for a few seconds, then she asks, 'So how?'

'It was surprisingly simple, I believe. As was typical, when the Second World War broke out, the previous Lord Blackwaite and my father, the gardener, signed up and were placed in the same regiment. The French village they were stationed in was bombed; almost everyone died.'

'Including the real Lord Blackwaite.'

'Yes. My father survived but was badly scarred. Including, conveniently, his face.'

'He came back claiming to be Lord Blackwaite.' Anna's voice is even.

Edmund turns away. He thought he had eliminated the shame he felt after all these years, but then, it has never been tested in human company. His voice cracks. 'My father came back, married my mother, who had been his sweetheart before the war, swore her to secrecy. Catherine was only a year old, mother dead and couldn't really remember her father. If my mother and father kept to themselves, as so many did after the war, who would know? The two men were a similar height, similar build, brown hair. And Father... he already knew all there was to know about the Hall. He loved it.'

'But why did Catherine have to die?'

'She didn't – she didn't need to.'

The ground had been appalling to dig. Hard and full of clay. Edmund had to keep stopping to be sick, and Father could not look at Catherine's body as they lifted it in. Then they had reached the Hall and his mother had been descending the stairs, Catherine's farewell letter in hand, already dishevelled with tears. She had seen her husband and son covered in blood and soil, and it had taken half the night before she'd stopped screaming.

Now, his father has come to find Edmund in his room.

Father is ashen and trembling, and he sits on the chair opposite Edmund's bed.

'Why?' his son asks.

His father tells him. He is John Blyte, formerly gardener at the cottage. Edmund is not the Blackwaite he has been raised to believe he is. Their bloodline is a lie. There are no Blackwaites now. Catherine was the last.

'Catherine isn't my half-sister? I'm not heir to Fallow Hall?' Edmund does not know if he is shocked any more. Today, life has been exposed as light on the surface of a mirror.

His father grabs his hand, fierce. 'You *are* a Blackwaite. You have dedicated your life to this place. Blood doesn't matter. Blood is weak.'

John Blyte had seen the flesh-and-blood Lord Blackwaite, not a care in the world and not a clue what he was doing. Fallow Hall had been declining even before the war, its finances a mess, the building crumbling. Time and again, John Blyte had urged his master to act. To preserve something so beautiful, so precious.

'I have told you so many times, Edmund. These houses do not survive by chance, they survive through care. When that man died, no one was left but Catherine, an infant.'

The Hall would be managed by strangers, sold perhaps. The bright beauty of its rooms, the great lives and the stories it told, all would be forgotten – or worse, opened up to peer around for a cheap day trip. Fallow Hall would be stripped naked and exposed to popular appetite, public regulations, and the market. The true Lord Blackwaite had made no provision before he left to fight. Through neglect, one man had risked accomplishing what time and plague and fire could not.

'And it worked well enough, didn't it, Edmund? You are here now. There's an heir again. The Hall has stood for two centuries, and the land it sits upon, for a thousand years. Great men built it, good men must maintain it.'

Edmund slumps sideways against the wall, staring.

'Catherine's death is for nothing, if you don't use it on Fallow. Edmund, listen.' His father takes his hand again. 'She was leaving. That boy, Timothy, the second they got married, he would have wanted to know about Fallow, what it was worth, its history, our ancestry. He would have scrabbled away to see what he could get, and he would have exposed us. It was too dangerous. Catherine was never supposed to leave.'

'You were going to keep her here forever?' Edmund's voice is bleary.

'Is it such a bad place to be kept?'

Edmund hands his father Catherine's farewell letter.

*Mother, I know my leaving is a shock. Father will fill you in on the details.*

*But I wanted you to know I am not leaving for love or marriage or a boy, although I had one of those until recently. I am leaving so I can choose, truly choose, what my life will be. Who I will be. Call me spoiled, if you must. Just know that I love you. I'll be back to visit; perhaps you'll even visit me in my new life. I'd like that. I left new vacuum bags under the sink, by the way. And I love you, Mother, by the way.*

'But it was done, then.' Edmund wipes his eyes, he appeals to Anna: 'She never had to die, but once she had – what, to turn in my own father? To ruin my mother? And most of all – dear God, most of all, my father had been right. He was right. I loved Catherine as my own sister, I still do. But hers was one life. If she had left, the whole edifice would have come crashing down. And the same fate would await Fallow as if my father had never stepped in as its custodian. The sale, the loss of dignity and history – the gift shop. I wish I had been the wrong child, not Catherine. I have wished for so many years. But once it was done, how could I waste her death and betray my mother and father?'

By chance, Timothy McArthur flies back home two weeks later. Edmund tells villagers that Catherine has married 'a Canadian boy' and gone to North America to start married life. Catherine has no friends of her own to tell. He burns her papers and whispers to them how sorry he is, and the heat vaporises the tears from his cheeks. Elizabeth Millhaven asks if he is all right, he seems distant, so he breaks it off with her.

His father becomes remote. Sometimes he talks to himself. Edmund finds bills unpaid and paperwork beginning to slide. Father's handwriting becomes shaky. Edmund takes on more of the work himself.

Father had said the gunshot was an accident, but his mother

drifts from room to room wailing, and Edmund knows she knows it is not true. She had loved Catherine as her own daughter.

It is the wedding cards, in the end.

*We heard of dear Catherine's whirlwind romance and wanted to send our heartfelt congratulations. Congratulations to the bride and groom! Congratulations – when will you be going out to Canada to see them? I am sure Catherine made a beautiful bride, you must be so proud. Congratulations!*

It is Father who finds Mother.

A week later, Edmund goes back up to Oxford.

Slowly, what is frozen begins to unfreeze. Edmund sees the logic in his father's words, even while he remains horrified by his actions. Edmund renews his childhood vow to protect the Hall. Knights are not without trials; duty is not without sacrifice.

Edmund graduates and returns to the Hall. He encourages his father to rest, to step back, and his father does not resist him.

Money is tight. Edmund does as much of the work himself as he can, mending fences and whitewashing the old servants' corridors in the early hours of the morning, once the paperwork is done.

The last tenant farmers get old and retire, and even that little stream of revenue dries up. He sells a parcel of land, as much as he can bear, and as little as they can manage on. After that, the property developers come knocking, asking whether he would be willing to sell the fields men perished on during the Civil War. Families are looking for modern homes, they say; we will build bungalows. He sends them packing.

In the end, the only thing left to do is to open the Hall to paying visitors. Edmund waits until his father dies, so that he does not have to see it. The Hall opens a year to the day after his name replaces his father's in the College of Arms, *Edmund, Lord Blackwaite of Upper Magna*. Edmund superintends tours, edits a sharp script so that visitors may be accurately informed of the history of the Hall.

Each night, Edmund lies alone in his bed, the last adherent of an old religion. Over the decades, he searches for others. There are a handful of men who help to manage Fallow, to increase the revenues, put it on a better footing. Once, there is a woman who looks like she might understand, and Edmund courts her and goes to bed with her. But in the end, he is wrong about all of them. Ignorance, selfishness, the desire for an easy life always overcomes duty. No one else is prepared to give in service to something greater than themselves. Each thinks themselves more important than history.

Edmund will not sacrifice Fallow for his own quietude.

'And neither will you – will you, Anna?'

Anna watches him from the chair. She has not moved, she has not cried or admonished him. 'I saw you working in the garden, Anna. And I knew that you were a Blackwaite, like I am a Blackwaite.'

She does not answer. She keeps watching Lord Blackwaite, searching him. Finally, she asks, 'And why did you attack my cottage? Why did you try to frighten me after I found Catherine? It only drew attention.'

Edmund is momentarily taken aback, then something clicks into place. 'I didn't. Keith McCarthy did.'

'I don't understand.'

Edmund shakes his head. 'When did you last see our groundskeeper?'

Anna thinks. 'Not since I came here to care for you. I thought he had gone away for Christmas.'

'No, I dismissed him a few days before you arrived. He came to me and told me he'd attacked the cottage. He said he

241

had gone to confession, his conscience was suffering, although clearly not enough to come and apologise to you. I told him if I ever saw him again, I'd have him arrested.'

'I don't— Why did he do it?'

'Because I asked *you* to provide the flowers for the gala. He's been here fifteen years. Perhaps it's no great surprise to you that a middle-aged man thought it was he who should be asked, rather than a new gardener, a woman, at the cottage.'

'And he knew I'd assume it was to do with Catherine?'

'Maybe.' Edmund inclines his head. 'I don't think he's that intelligent. He was simply angry at being passed over for a girl. I'm very sorry. I would never do something like that.' He cringes. 'My sins have been of omission.'

He sits down in the chair opposite Anna. His head is light. He has opened the chest of his life and it has all flown out, like sins from Pandora's jar.

Edmund marshals himself, since only one thing remains.

'It's in your hands, Anna. There is nothing to be done for Catherine, God rest her. If you go to the police, Fallow will close for investigation, I will go to prison. Pauline and others will lose their jobs. You will lose the cottage. The Trust would be duty bound to do best by Fallow, which they will interpret as making a profit – you have met Paul Wolsey. But it is a choice that I give to you. You are the heir now, and you know everything. You understand.'

Anna nods. 'I understand.'

The green of the hills and the bite of the air bring Hitesh's mind into focus as he steps out of his car into the car park. Peacocks and horses. What if Fallow had simply been claimed by the next man? All through the drive, he has been threading together the chain that will give weight to his suspicions. The timelines, DNA from distant family, military records.

Now it is time for Hitesh to begin, and not to stop until it is done.

The lights are on inside the police station, and through the window he can see the twisting foil decorations hanging above the desks. Hitesh wants no delay, but he ought to check that Darshan has not called during the long drive through Christmas Eve traffic. He gets out his phone, and there is a voicemail. Hitesh puts the phone to his ear, expecting to hear Darshan asking where he has moved the back-door keys.

'Hitesh.' Her voice is a shock. Crystalline, quietly urgent in his ear. 'Did Catherine Blackwaite ever break her arm as a child? I don't know if you can find out, if hospitals keep records long enough – can you ask the local hospital if Catherine Blackwaite broke her arm when she was young?'

Hitesh draws his breath in. Anna knows. Anna fucking knows as well as he does. He had not accounted for this. He rubs his eyes. Anna has always known, somehow, and now she has got to it – whatever proof or evidence or explanation.

Hitesh gets back into the car. Where did she call from? She has no phone; she cannot be at the cottage.

Anna is smarter than the rest of them, but so dangerous because she will see the risk and hurtle forwards anyway, because that is how she weighs the truth.

He puts the car into gear and drives half a mile back into the village, to St Mary's. The church glows brightly in the face of the setting sun and Hitesh has to squint past the moss-lit gravestones to where Reverend Watts is receiving parishioners from the Christmas Eve service.

'James!' he yells from the car.

The parishioners turn towards him, startled. Some of them glare. Watts raises his hand to shield his eyes from the light, then spots his friend and zigzags past his flock, robe flapping wildly.

'Hitesh, what's happened?'

'Where's Anna?'

'What? Is she in trouble?' The priest scratches his forehead, trying to quell the panic that Hitesh's tone inspires. 'Um, not at the cottage. I saw Eloise Fitzhugh yesterday, she said Lord Blackwaite had been taken ill. Anna was caring for him up at the Hall.'

Anna has listened to Edmund with a calm that she had not expected. He has brought into order the universe that has been disordered since Hitesh visited and told her it was not Catherine.

He watches her now, wondering what she will say and what she will do. Edmund has asked only feigned ignorance, another act of omission. And in return she will always have her cottage and her garden, and the Hall. She will walk the hills that are the horizon, and go to bed knowing they are hers. Edmund offers her the world.

'I called Hitesh from the entrance-hall phone. He knows.'

Edmund is uncomprehending. 'I don't— You told the policeman it was Catherine?'

'Yes. I told him where to look for proof.'

Now what comes will be beyond her control. But Anna has done it. She has done it for Catherine.

'I thought you understood.' Edmund begins to quake.

'I understand.'

'It's not too late, Anna. What did you tell Mistry? We can fix it. We can save Fallow together. Believe me when I say I mourned Catherine. It has never been about the title or the money. It has been *for Fallow*. All the lives, great or small, who lived in this house, on this land. The wars, the plagues, the births and deaths. *For Fallow.*'

Anna has the truth now. She can feel it shuddering inside her.

'I thought you understood,' Edmund wails, 'I thought you loved this place.'

Anna can see the panic in him, she can feel it in herself. She stands up, steps away. 'It wasn't worth her life.'

Edmund rises.

'Anna, stand back now.' Hitesh is in the doorway of the library. He is sweating. 'Please. Come away.'

Anna looks at him in surprise. 'How did—'

'Anna, come away.'

She motions. Her sleeves fall back down over the apricot juice that has dried into her skin. 'There are birth certificates, other things like that in a first-floor bedroom.'

Hitesh keeps his eyes on Lord Blackwaite. 'Will you fetch them?' He pulls his phone from his coat pocket and hands it to Anna. 'Call the station, ask them to send two units on blue.' Edmund has rested his head against the fireplace and his eyes are unfocused. 'Tell them to send an ambulance too.'

Anna slips away.

The dusk is at its brilliant conclusion, and the sun blazes over the ridge of the hills, trying to defy the inevitable. The air has been sucked clean of sound by all the words that have been spoken. Edmund picks up the poker and stirs the ashes in the grate. His shoulders are shaking, and Hitesh thinks he might be sobbing.

'Lord Blackwaite, step away from the fire now. Come and sit down. You don't look well.'

Edmund mumbles something which Hitesh cannot hear.

'Come and sit down,' he repeats softly.

A damp patch has appeared on Lord Blackwaite's shirt. He is sweating profusely. Hitesh crosses the room to help him to the armchair.

Edmund twists round and brings the poker up, striking Hitesh's chin and piercing the jaw. Hitesh tips backwards and Edmund brings it back down again, striking him on the crown, through the eye and the cheek. His face splits open, and he falls to the ground and is still.

Edmund reels around.

He has given everything to Fallow and still it has not been enough. He can feel himself dying, cell by cell, and the world threatens to crack.

It is not too late. He will not give up now. He has not strived and sweated and forsaken his sister to lose Fallow now. He can still save it. Only Anna and the policeman know. He will remove their poison and make Fallow whole again. He will tear down the cottage and plant a new garden for Catherine. In the spring, he will turn away the visitors. He will give Fallow back its dignity. *He* understands.

It is nearly dark now, and the sun has been dragged back down into the earth. Edmund staggers out into the corridor, his hand tight around the poker. Anna's betrayal has been the worst of all – the others had not known Fallow's value, but she does, and still she chooses this. How could she?

He moves through the entrance hall, eyes roving. The bedroom, she had said, his childhood room. He mounts the stairs as she is coming down, papers in hand.

Put those back.

He thinks he says it aloud, but maybe he does not.

Everything passes across her young face.

He drags his tired body forward, and every treasured inch of the Hall denigrates him, and his failure.

'*Put those back.*'

He lunges forward, up the stairs, but she is faster and he cannot reach her before she is back on the landing. He follows in the space she has been and thrashes with the poker, close enough to graze her wrist. She yelps, and he screams back. He lunges again, and she twists her body to the side. Edmund is falling through empty space, and it is enough for Anna to push his shoulder, and his head lands against the bannister, and his skull cracks at the forehead.

*December 1967*

I don't know what is waiting. But somehow I feel like I have been born without a face, with an identity that was embryonic, and kept that way by the circumstances of my life so far. I'm ready now. I'm ready for my face to emerge, to become human. Soon I'll know. I hope that I am someone beneath the empty years. I hope that I am happy. I hope that I am good.

Everything is pain and noise. He thinks his face is wet, but he can't move to touch it. Somewhere, a voice that sounds like Barnard's is echoing.

Everything is pain and noise. Until he feels something in his hand; another hand.

'How bad is it?' Hitesh's speech is low and distorted from the grafts to the left of his face.

Anna touches the right side, which is unaltered. 'It's very damaged.'

'Can you see that the eye is missing?'

Anna examines the side that is marbled with bruises and burns and stitches. 'It's too swollen to tell yet.'

He laughs. 'A blessing, then.' But laughing hurts. He winces, and that hurts too.

'Do you want to see?' she asks him.

'Not really.' Anna lies on the hospital pillow next to him. He breathes in the smell of grass. 'Does it bother you?'

Anna rests her head on his shoulder and he can feel her raise her eyebrows.

'All right then,' he says.

\*

The nights are heavy. Alone in the hospital bed, Hitesh can hear the individual footsteps of each nurse, each doctor as they pass in the corridor. The hours are slow, and he can think about what Edmund and his father did, how much sense they made and how little. He listens to the clanking and humming of the building and all its machines, and can feel the gnawing guilt because he did not realise what they had done until he and Anna had nearly been killed. Until Anna had had to kill for him. It takes a long time for dawn to come each day.

When it does, Hitesh can see his face in the mirror by his bed. He finds he is unmoved by it. It is monstrous, and the doctors have confirmed it will never heal properly. He won't be able to drive any more, with the one eye. And he will need further surgeries to make the damaged tissue more comfortable. Apparently, there are chips of bone they could not get out during the first night he was brought in.

Hitesh sits up to read during the mornings, continually shifting to get comfortable, trying to ignore the throbbing in the left side of his face. In the afternoons, it is visiting time.

'Hitesh, what did he do to you?' Watts covers his mouth with his hand.

'James, it's okay – I never set any stock by my looks anyway.'

'I'm so sorry I couldn't tell you about Keith McCarthy and the cottage – I told him to come to you. I begged him. It might have removed some confusion, solved the case faster—'

'It's not your fault, James. It's not. None of this is.'

Watts sits down heavily on the end of the bed.

'Are you praying for me?'

'Maybe. You can't stop me.'

Watts tries to smile, but he looks so wretched that Hitesh

wants to comfort him. 'Look, Mother, it hasn't stopped me getting a girlfriend.'

Watts looks uncomprehending, then gleeful.

Hitesh waves him away with the hand of his unbruised arm. 'Can you bring David next time?'

'Will anyone ever love me as much as they do the dog?' Watts raises his eyes to heaven.

'There's enough for you both,' Hitesh tells him.

Ifeoma watches Anna curiously, sympathetically, until she is ready to start speaking. Anna begins to unfurl. To walk forward and step back, sideways, over and returning.

'This is trauma therapy, and it will take time,' Ifeoma says. Which it does, which Anna does not grudge. Hitesh has been sent to see her too, by the police. Both will have the balm of her patience and expertise laid upon them.

Anna does not doubt that she saved her own life and Hitesh's. And the pathologist said Lord Blackwaite was already having a heart attack when she pushed him. In effect, she had killed a dead man. But it bothers her a little, as it is bound to. She tells Ifeoma about it. It does not upset her as much as the idea that Hitesh nearly died. That she could have lost him. When she tells the therapist about this, the tears come quickly, unbothered by her audience. They spend their time on this instead.

'And this cleaning girl who went missing, Annette Waring, she still haunts you?'

'Yes. The unfairness of never having a chance at life. A life that didn't leave enough of a mark for us to find her. To hear her.'

'It feels unjust.' Ifeoma nods.

'Do you think – is there a world, a future, where her fresh start happened?'

'What do you think?'

'I hope so. But...' Anna shrugs. Whatever they wish, they both know what her chances were. Anna ventures forward. 'The ghost story – the one Thomas Fitzhugh told – the star-crossed lovers, and the woman killed by the man who loved her. It was a garbled version of something. Catherine Blackwaite and Timothy and her murderer. Or a devastated Lady Blackwaite. Or Elizabeth Millhaven left by Edmund. Upper Magna knew, in a way, all this time. People knew *something* had happened at Fallow. But they didn't want to know, really. They buried their understanding in a story. They chose not to know about Catherine.'

'And Catherine Blackwaite, what does she mean to you?'

'I felt like—' Anna searches for it. Ifeoma waits, an island of hope in her tailored dress. Anna swims forward. 'I think—'


Hitesh is discharged to Anna. She has found a camp bed and pushed it up next to the single bed in the cottage.

'You're sure?'

'I'll throw you out if you don't stop asking that.'

For a while, they lie there without talking. Then he reaches a hand out, and Anna takes it, works around his injuries, tastes him, knows him.

Afterwards, Hitesh strokes her hair with his good arm. She still smells of grass and fresh air.

'I got given my police pension. Turns out I'm worth more than I thought.'

'Are we leaving for Vegas?'

He frowns. 'Do you want to stay here? Did Lord Blackwaite destroy this place for you?'

Anna keeps looking at the ceiling. 'Catherine gave it back. Besides...' She pauses. 'Besides, Eloise Fitzhugh and Watts came by yesterday.'

'What did they want?'

'Us. The Trust have talked it over and they want to provisionally offer us guardianship of Fallow Hall.'

Hitesh pushes up onto his elbow. 'What? Watts is a sly fucker. They want us to – what, live at the Hall?'

'If we want to. And if we can present a plan for what we would do with it.'

'Jesus.'

Anna laughs. 'Someone has to run it. The Trust members are all too old. I know the cottage gardens, and I know a lot about the Hall now, thanks to Edmund.'

'What would you do with it?'

'What do you want to do?' She grins.

He thinks for a minute. 'I want to – not like a philanthropist – I don't know, give back. Not taking. Giving.'

Anna rests a hand on his chest. He smiles to feel its weight resting there.

'You'll be wearing a mask in your own home, when there are visitors,' he tells her.

Anna looks at him with her depthless gaze. 'I'll take it off again when they're gone.'

Hitesh holds her for a while.

'I still miss Mum. And sometimes I dream Blackwaite has hurt you, and I've done nothing. But—' He searches for it. 'There's also something light in my chest.'

'I've heard that's allowed.'

Anna kisses him. He is sure she can taste scar tissue, but it strikes him that it has never bothered her.


'What will you do about money? Can you still work?' This is as close as Darshan can get to asking how Hitesh is.

'I'll be fine, Dad.'

Darshan nods. He cannot bring himself to look at one side

251

of his son's face. 'That's good then.' The news burbles on in the background.

'Is Anil-bhai okay to take you to your scan on Tuesday?'

'Yes, yes. Don't fuss. I'm in better shape than you now.'

An hour later, Darshan is dozing, and Hitesh feels bad for Barnard, waiting in the car on his day off. He shakes his father's shoulder.

'I'm going now, Dad. I'll come back on the train next week.'

Darshan half opens his eyes. 'The girl I met in hospital – is she your girlfriend?'

'Yes.'

'She's not Gujarati.'

'No.'

'She's stubborn, I can tell. Like your mother.'

From: Anna Deerin
Subject: Visit?
Hi Dad,
Things are changing quite a lot here. I might have somewhere you can stay, if you want to come and visit? It would be nice to see you and Mum.
I love you x

The lawn outside Fallow Hall has gone unmown. It is only the first year, but already there is ragwort and herb Robert and love-in-a-mist. Next year there will be more wildflowers. As it is, the air is thick with the droning of insects, pollinators drunk on plenty. The long grasses issue their susurrus, and near the door, their tips brush the plaque below which Anna has buried Catherine's bones.

The day is hot already, and the scent of the lavenders threatens to undo them all. Anna looks across to the library in the east wing, preserved as part of the historic home, then turns to the lawn outside the west wing, where Hitesh and Watts and a few others are working. David has crashed out in the heat and lies on the cool stone of the terrace.

In September, a forest school will move into the classroom. In October, there will be a food bank and cookery classes in the old kitchen. Anna had expected coldness and suspicion from Magna. But she had been wrong. There had been kindness, an openness of heart. The wealthy and the lean had supported what they proposed.

'Okeke, can you get the timber for the coop?' she hears Hitesh say.

'Yeah, yeah. Over here?'

And the community farm. That, she cherishes most of all.

Hitesh straightens up. He looks over to where Anna is standing in the meadow-lawn and waves. She waves back at Hitesh, and a cabbage white launches itself into the air.

Return, *remeo, revenir.*

He is the other meaning of return. The returning of a feeling or a gesture, a look, or a kiss, a smile. Of complicity, of giving.

Anna is returning, un-alone.

# ACKNOWLEDGEMENTS

Thank you to my lovely agent Jane Finigan, for all her help and belief. Susannah Godman, for giving me that first chance. To Carolyn Mays for her editorial advice and for knowing what I wanted as much as I did. Laura Fletcher for her brilliant marketing.

To my early readers Swapna Gavaskar-Mistry and Vandana Patel. To Julia Roscoe for the wonderful ballet insight. Noi, for her support. Melissa Chapman for being my oldest friend and sweetest cheerleader. Jacob Lister, a friend and an honest man. To the Colour Squares, for the intensely competitive distraction. To Anita, for everything.

Mum, Dad, Verity, Connor, Tadg – ad finem.

To all the Patels – Think Bike.

Boopy, faithful editorial assistant and stander-on-keyboard.

To Kawan and Som, I love you. You're the best.

# ABOUT THE AUTHOR

Photo courtesy of Bonnie Burke-Patel

Born and raised in South Gloucestershire, Bonnie studied
History at Oxford. After working for half a decade in politics
and policy, she changed careers and became a preschool
teacher, before beginning to write full time. She lives with
her husband, son, and needy cat in south east London, and is
working on her next crime novel about fairy tales, desire, and
the seaside.

## Bedford Square
### Publishers

Bedford Square Publishers is an independent publisher
of fiction and non-fiction, founded in 2022 in the historic
streets of Bedford Square London and the sea mist
shrouded green of Bedford Square Brighton.

Our goal is to discover irresistible stories and voices that
illuminate our world.

We are passionate about connecting our authors to readers
across the globe and our independence allows us to do this
in original and nimble ways.

The team at Bedford Square Publishers has years of
experience and we aim to use that knowledge and creative
insight, alongside evolving technology, to reach the right
readers for our books. From the ones who read a lot, to
the ones who don't consider themselves readers, we aim to
find those who will love our books and talk about them as
much as we do.

We are hunting for vital new voices from all backgrounds
– with books that take the reader to new places and
transform perceptions of the world we live in.

**Follow us on social media for the latest Bedford
Square Publishers news.**

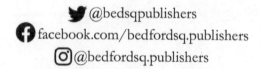

🐦 @bedsqpublishers
facebook.com/bedfordsq.publishers
@bedfordsq.publishers

**bedfordsquarepublishers.co.uk**